WHO THE HELL IS GOING TO BELIEVE
YOU'RE AN ALIEN?

He chuckled, but his laughter stopped when his gaze met hers. He lowered his mouth, his lips brushing hers. She accepted his kiss, knowing this might be her last, savoring his taste, inhaling the musky scent that clung to his body and hoping it would be enough to last a lifetime, but knowing just one minute away from him would seem like forever.

He ended the kiss and went to his room where he changed clothes. She followed, not wanting to be away from him for even a second.

As soon as he left, she would find her craft.

Then she would leave . . . forever.

Close Encounters
of the
Sexy Kind

KAREN KELLEY

BRAVA

KENSINGTON PUBLISHING CORP.
http://www.kensingtonbooks.com

BRAVA BOOKS are published by

Kensington Publishing Corp.
119 West 40th Street
New York, NY 10018

All Kensington Titles, Imprints, and Distributed Lines are available at special quantity discounts for bulk purchases for sales promotions, premiums, fund-raising, and educational or institutional use. Special book excerpts or customized printings can also be created to fit specific needs. For details, write or phone the office of the Kensington special sales manager: Kensington Publishing Corp., 119 West 40th Street, New York, NY 10018, attn: Special Sales Department, Phone: 1-800-221-2647.

Brava Books and the B logo Reg. U.S. Pat. & TM Off.

ISBN-13: 978-0-7582-1175-0
ISBN-10: 0-7582-1175-9

First trade paperback printing: April 2007
First mass market printing: June 2009

10 9 8 7 6 5 4 3 2 1

Printed in the United States of America

Here's to a fun weekend at a cabin on Nocona Lake. A little wine, good food and Shelley Bradley, Sheila Curlin, Mary Beth Lee, Melissa Schroeder, Darese Cotton and a little more wine. This book is the result of a fabulously fun time, so if anyone has a problem I'll just blame it on the wine.

To Mike and Shelly Clark: The fabulous Clay County Computer Guru and the wife who tolerates him. Thanks bunches for helping me out of my numerous computer jams!

And to my fantastic friend, future published author and website designer, Leslie King! Check it out at www.author karenkelley.com

Chapter 1

"I'm going crazy," Mala murmured. Jumping to her feet, she strode to the plate glass window overlooking the pristine city surrounding her town house.

The planet Nerak, where the light never faded and everything was white. So horribly white—colorless, stark and cold. Just like everything on her planet.

"Would you like a hormone smoothie?" Barton asked over the monitoring system.

She stuck her tongue out. "No, I wouldn't like a smoothie."

A small aero unit whizzed past, rattling her window. Everything moved too fast. Instant gratification. Sad? Drink a happy smoothie. Tired? Drink an energy smoothie. Horny? Drink a hormone smoothie. Everything was a quick fix.

"You get this way every year. I'm only suggesting a smoothie because it usually calms you."

She cocked an eyebrow. "Maybe because it has a sedative in it?"

"We could copulate." A door that blended with the wall whisked silently open.

She turned as Barton stepped inside the room. He was like no other. Six feet, three inches of rugged, sexy male. Blond hair, blue eyes . . . she should be happy. She should. Shouldn't she?

Then why was she so frustrated?

"It's been three years, twenty-one days, fourteen hours, twenty-two minutes and nine seconds since you've had an orgasm," he informed her.

And he was driving her crazy. She didn't want perfection, but Barton was exactly the way she'd ordered him. A gift from her cousin on Mala's twenty-first birthday. Together they had chosen everything about him. He was their creation.

At the time, her older cousin, Kia, had been going through a rebellious period and had smuggled a catalog of male specimens into Mala's apartment. Barton was born from a sketch they'd compiled.

But they had taken their creation a step further. They'd practically breathed life into him. At least, as much life as could be breathed into a companion unit. Barton had all the emotions of any Nerakian.

He was the perfect male.

He was still perfect five years later.

Everything about her life was perfect.

She hated it.

"You're grinding your teeth again. I take it sex is not an option."

"No, sex is not an option." She turned back to the window.

"Ahh."

"Ahh, what?" she asked without turning around.

"You've been looking at that book again."

She stiffened, then quickly relaxed her shoulders. "What book?" That was the most un-innocent sounding question she'd ever asked.

"You're being evasive, aren't you? You know perfectly well what book I mean. The one from your grandmother's travels. The one about that other place . . . Earth."

Why had she even thought she could fool him? He'd been around her too long. There was nothing she could hide. So why did she even try? She might as well confess. But first things first.

Her eyes narrowed as she faced him. "You swear on the promise stones that you won't say a word? Even if they threaten to remove your microchip?"

His chin jutted forward. "Have I ever betrayed you?"

"Sorry." Damn, she had to remember that Barton was special. Although very analytical, he still had feelings. She'd made sure of that even though her cousin had warned against adding the sensitivity chip . . . among others. But she didn't want just a companion unit. She had to have more than a machine. Well, she'd certainly gotten more than she bargained for with Barton.

She went to the bookcase and pulled three reference books from the shelf and reached to the back of the case, pushing a hidden button. Her fingers tingled when they brushed over the book—her grandmother's diary, and even more precious . . . the film.

She glanced behind her before bringing them out. "Hide the window."

Barton waved a hand and the window disappeared, soft lights automatically came on, and only then did she bring the materials out.

"Do you realize how much trouble you can get into by just having these documents?"

"Of course I do," she told him as she carried everything to the lounging sofa. "They barred distant travel after my grandmother's last voyage—the year I was born. They said our society was being tarnished by the ideas that were brought back.

"You do realize the Coalition is looking out for your best interests. From the small amount of information on space travel that I have programmed into my system, Earth is by far the most untamable."

"But don't you see, that's what makes it so exciting. People can actually think for themselves. They don't have a Coalition of Elders telling them what's in their best interest. They're allowed to make their own mistakes. They can grow and learn from them."

She placed the film in the change port. A hologram filled the room with sound and color. She could almost reach out and touch the trees, could almost feel the spray from the waterfall as it cascaded over the mountain and splashed down into the pond.

She inhaled. "I wonder what it smells like on Earth?"

"Earthy?"

She frowned at Barton before letting the unfolding scenes capture her attention once more.

The hologram wasn't much different than the ones she inserted into the port when she wanted to go to a park or just get away from the noise inside the town bubble. This hologram really existed. That was the difference.

Her grandmother had labeled the documentary an XXX-rated Western movie. Whatever that meant. Not that it mattered that much. This was her proof there was more in the universe than Nerak.

There was even a title on the box: *Callie Does The Sheriff.* She wished her grandmother had explained more instead of leaving so many unanswered questions.

She returned her attention to the waterfall. The woman washed herself beneath the spray of water. her thin pink dress transparent as she slid a small white brick over her body. From the expression on the woman's face, the sensation must have been enjoyable.

Her grandmother's journal had described something similar and called it bathing. She said it was a barbaric custom Earth people did to cleanse their bodies.

How odd they had to run a white brick over their body. Every morning, Mala went to the chamber, waved her hand and beams of light rid her body of bacteria.

But the woman did seem excited. For a moment, she wished she had a white brick to rub over her body. It looked much more enjoyable than beams of light she never felt.

Sighing, she watched what happened next, even though she'd secretly watched the film before.

The woman hadn't seen the man yet. When she turned from the waterfall, her pupils dilated.

The man sat atop a four-legged beast, gazing upon her, but there was something in his eyes that made Mala's thighs tremble. It was as if no one else existed for him.

He climbed off the animal, the shiny metal star he wore on his shirt sparkled in the sunlight. She held her breath, watching his face and the lazy look he gave her before he sat on a rock and pulled off his boots.

"Sheriff, what are you doing?" The woman's voice trembled.

"What I should've done a long time ago, Callie May."

He removed his clothes before stepping into the water, every inch of his backside displayed for Mala's enjoyment. Muscles rippled as he waded farther out, then dove beneath the murky green water.

When Sheriff emerged, he was beside Callie May, taking her into his arms, lowering his mouth to hers. He moved his hand to her breast, massaging.

Mala could barely swallow, let alone breathe, her gaze riveted on the couple.

Sheriff tugged the front of Callie's dress and it opened. "I want to see you, darlin'. You've been teasin' me for a long time."

"But we're out in the open." She glanced furtively around, her eyes wide, but Mala didn't think she looked that upset. "What if someone sees?" she said in a breathless voice.

"I don't care." He cupped her breast before lowering his head and covering it with his mouth. He suckled for a moment, then raised his head. "I'm going to make love to you, baby. The hot, dirty kind. You ain't never had an orgasm like you're gonna have with me."

"Isn't he magnificent?" Mala breathed.

"This was what I was designed from? He seems rather savage if you ask me." Barton sniffed.

Sometimes she wanted to remove Barton's sensitivity chip. She turned off the hologram. "It's a primitive planet. I've read my grandmother's journal. The beast the man sat upon is a horse." She frowned. "Or maybe a cow. I'm not quite sure. Her journals are a little difficult to translate. She was only there to gather the minimum amount of information. Her time on the planet was very brief."

"And the couple in the hologram? They were about to copulate?"

"I'm not sure. I think so." She bit her bottom lip. "Yes, I'm almost certain of it. Some of the film was damaged so I'm not positive how their encounter ended. I think they joined, but it was more intense than just copulating, more going on than relieving stress."

"Would you like me to do what Sheriff did? I can, you know."

How did she tell him something would be lost in the process? She didn't want to join for the sake of release. She wanted someone who would . . . who would make love to her. Was that asking too much?

"Why are you so fascinated with Earth?" He changed the subject. "It's not like you'll ever go there."

A half smile played around her lips.

"Mala?"

"I have her journal. It contains all the information I would need to survive." She took a deep breath. "I know where they store the space travel crafts."

"Those old scraps of metal? I doubt you'd be able to get one of them out of its port." His beautiful blue eyes grew round. "You don't actually plan . . ."

"Yes!" She flung her arms wide and twirled around the room. "Barton, I don't belong here. I want to experience life, not watch it on a hologram. I want to know what dirt feels like. I want to walk barefoot through a meadow. I want to stand beneath a waterfall."

"But you can do that now."

"No, a hologram isn't the same. I don't want to find myself transported to a make-believe park. I want the real thing."

"But with reality comes other things—like pain. There are no thorns to step upon in the Coalition's Safety Travels. You can have the pleasure without being hurt. It's perfect."

She plopped down on the lounging sofa and drew her knees up. "Don't you see? I don't want perfection. I want to experience everything."

"I . . . see."

Now she'd hurt his feelings. Barton had been programmed to see to her every need. There were no men left on her planet. He was the perfect male specimen.

"You're my friend," she told him. "But I need more. Please try to understand that it's not you. It's me."

He raised his chin. "When are we making the journey?"

She flinched. This was the hard part, but she couldn't risk putting him in danger. "Just me. I won't take a chance with you." When he opened his mouth, she hurried on. "Besides, the Coalition won't even realize I'm gone if you're here. I just want to see what this planet is like. I'll be gone no longer than a few rotations."

He hesitated. "You'll swear on the promise stones?"

"I'll swear."

"I still don't like it. They may be closer to us in language and atmosphere, but their culture is so far behind ours. How will you manage?"

"Grandmother's book." She raised the journal. "I've studied it very carefully. I know their favorite saying is, *well, hell,* and that it's early summer on the planet. I have everything I need right here." She tapped her finger on the book.

What she was about to embark on finally sunk into her brain. She was going to Earth. A slow smile curved her lips. Maybe she'd even meet the man in the hologram. The one called Sheriff.

Earth! It was beautiful. A big round . . . ball. Much bigger than she'd expected. A lot bigger than Nerak. Her planet wasn't much more than a dot in the sky.

But Earth sparkled.

Mala sighed with utter joy and tried to focus, but it wasn't that easy. She was here—at least, almost. Her palms began to sweat. Her heart beat faster. This was it, and the most important part so she had to stay calm.

The craft began to shake as she entered the atmospheric pull. Her grandmother hadn't mentioned such violent movement, but then, the craft hadn't been nearly as old, either.

"Please don't fall apart," she breathed, grasping the guidance bar and manually steering the craft. She would be fine. She was almost positive. Her coordinates were exactly with her grandmother's—sort of.

She pointed the craft toward Earth. It plunged downward.

Here I go!

The blue sky filled her glass shield. She was moving faster than she could maneuver the small ship. Mountains whizzed past with her barely having time to get out of the way.

"Tree!"

She dodged it; limbs slapped the side of her craft.

"Bushes!"

She steered to the right, then the left.

Oh, no, this wasn't good. Things were moving way too fast!

Bam!

Her head rammed against the craft's guidance panel as the craft jerked and bumped to a grinding stop.

Dry, powdery dust swirled behind Mason McKinley's Jeep like a small tornado in the fading light of day. If they didn't get some rain soon, his small ranch would dry up and blow away. He glanced upward. Not a dark cloud in the sky. He wished he could say the same about his life.

Too many complications.

He stopped in front of his modest log home and killed the engine, slipping the keys into his jeans pocket as he climbed out and started toward the house.

His dog, Blue, jumped out of the open back and took off at a run chasing an imaginary jackrabbit.

Good old Blue. He shook his head. The dog wouldn't know what to do if he ever caught a rabbit.

The radio on his hip crackled.

He stopped, one foot on the bottom step, knowing the dispatcher at the office was about to speak.

"Sheriff, we have a situation."

Francine's new word this week—situation. Everything was a situation.

He removed his Stetson and ran a weary hand through his hair before taking the radio out of the leather holster and keying the mike. "What kind of situation?"

"Harlan says he saw a flying saucer."

He gritted his teeth and counted to ten. If Harlan didn't stop this nonsense, he was going to lock him up for disturbing the peace—namely his.

Mason's gaze shot toward the town he'd just left. The reporters from *The National Gossip* were still at the motel. Somehow, Harlan had convinced them Bigfoot roamed the surrounding woods. Bigfoot, of all things! How could anyone actually believe that kind of nonsense?

Now there were about three reporters wandering around their small Texas town in search of anything they could claim was the mythical beast. They weren't even looking at it from a scientific point. They were only in it to make a buck, but all they'd accomplished was pissing off a lot of people who in turn kept the phone lines to his office lit up.

Jimmy Wilson said some idiot was snapping pictures of his Braham Bull. Mason shook his head. Old Red was the meanest bull in the county. The reporter was lucky to get back across the fence before the angry animal trampled him.

His radio crackled again.

"Sheriff, he said it was on the north side of your property. Close to the highway. Said there was a bright light—like maybe it crashed."

He keyed the radio again. "It was probably one of the big rigs going around Devil's Bend. You know when it gets close to dusk the lights flicker about. People have been reporting spaceships for years now."

"You want me to tell him that?"

Harlan wouldn't give him any peace until he checked it out. Damn, how the hell had his life become so problematic?

His gaze moved to the barn. He hadn't ridden Dancer in a couple of days. The ride would do them both good and he still had a couple of hours before it got good and dark.

"Tell him I'll check it out."

"Ow!" Mala's head pounded horribly. Was this what physical pain felt like? She wasn't sure she liked it. In fact, she was positive she didn't like it.

Tentatively, she reached up and lightly touched her forehead. Her finger came away wet . . . and tinged red. Oh, no, she was starting the deep sleep cycle, her lifeblood draining from her body.

Her bottom lip trembled. Not before she set foot on Earth. She'd at least have that much before the air left her body.

Except the door didn't open when she stood in front of it and waved her arm. She manually pushed on the button.

Nothing. Not even a little squeak. It didn't budge.

Now what? She didn't want to fade away without at least stepping on Earth's surface. That wouldn't be fair at all.

She pushed the manual button again.

And again . . . nothing.

She glared at the door. Not that she could move it with the force of her thoughts. One of her cousins had that kind of power, but not her.

But what she did have was a temper that could flare up. As it was doing now. "I am going to get out! A mechanical object will not beat me!"

Grunting, she planted her back against the metal door and shoved as hard as she could.

It swished open.

She toppled through and landed with a hard thud on her bottom. "Ow!" She rubbed the tender spot.

So far, all she'd discovered about Earth was that it hurt. There had to be more than this. She took a deep breath, blew her hair out of her eyes, and glanced around.

Oh, no.

Her bottom lip trembled.

The light was going out. Her final minutes were upon her. In the book of death, it stated that when the dimness came upon you, then you would begin the final hours of life.

She sniffed.

It wasn't a bit fair. Her end shouldn't come for at least another one hundred and twenty years.

She raised her chin. Better to die having lived her dream than to have lived without experiencing Earth at all. Poor Barton, he would miss her. Her cousin Kia would be distraught. She and Kia were closer than any of her other cousins.

But she was here . . . on Earth. That had to count for something.

She planted her palms on the ground to push up and realized she was actually touching dirt. Tingles traveled over her. Dirt! Real dirt. She scooped up a handful and rubbed her hands together, laughing when it sifted through her fingers.

And leaves! She grabbed a handful of green leaves. Magnificent. She brought them to her face and inhaled, but couldn't detect a scent. It didn't matter, she liked the texture.

Before her light faded, she wanted to walk on this Earth. She would have that much before her life slipped away. She pushed again with her hands and stood.

A wave of dizziness swept over her, but she clamped her lips together and forced it to go away. She refused to let her life extinguish before she had time to see some of the planet.

Her gaze swept the area.

Trees. She bit her bottom lip and touched the bark, feeling the bumpy outer core she'd seen only in a hologram. Rough wood and . . . and . . .

She jerked her hand away. It was alive! Her grandmother hadn't mentioned trees as living beings. Leaning forward, she looked closer.

No, it wasn't alive. There were tiny black creatures crawling up the bark. Maybe these were the insects her grandmother mentioned. She reached out and let one crawl on her hand.

"How cute," she murmured. "Little insect . . . ow!"

She slapped the insect, smashing it, and furiously rubbed where she'd been bitten. Her grandmother hadn't mentioned things that bite. Now, not only her head hurt, but so did her hand. So far, Earth wasn't all her grandmother claimed.

There had to be more to this planet. Grandmother had written about so many things. Maybe if she could leave the dense forest, then she might find something on the other side.

She struggled through the brush, thorns scraping

her legs, letting more of her blood flow. Where was the weakness that came with the end of cycle? If this was what it felt like to extinguish, then it wasn't so bad. She might yet see a bit more of this planet.

If she hurried.

A burst of energy bolted through her as she pushed forward, clamoring into the clearing, landing on her knees when her legs tangled with bushes.

Exhilaration, and yes, regret swept over her. She'd made it out and was still alive, even though the light around her was fading fast.

"Ma'am, you okay?" a deep voice spoke from high above her.

She jumped, her gaze jerking upward. He sat upon a black shiny animal that pranced beneath him, the fading light washing over man and beast.

His hat was pulled low on his forehead, practically obscuring his rugged features. What little breath she had left, he was stealing away from her as her gaze traveled over the handsome stranger. Her inspection of the human came to an abrupt halt when her gaze landed on the star pinned to his shirt.

"Sheriff," she whispered. Tears formed in her eyes. How appropriate that she should see the man in the movie. Not that this one looked exactly like the other one, but he was the same breed.

"Ma'am, you okay?" he repeated.

"No," her voice hitched. "I'm . . ." She sought words he would understand. "Well, hell, I'm dying."

All the strength drained from her body and she collapsed on the ground.

Chapter 2

Mason jumped off Dancer and rushed to the girl, questions running around in his head. Had there been a wreck on the highway and she'd stumbled through the woods looking for help?

Or maybe a snake had bitten her.

He did a quick survey of the area. Nothing out of the ordinary except where she'd plowed through the underbrush, but it was getting dark and harder to see. Any number of things could've happened.

Kneeling beside her, he checked for a pulse. It was steady and strong. He breathed a sigh of relief even though he knew CPR. Knowing and doing were two different things.

He didn't rule out internal injuries, either. He moved his hands slowly over her shoulders, but didn't feel anything out of place. The thin dress she wore clung to her curves, which would make it easy to detect if something wasn't right.

His hesitation was brief before he slid his hands over her rib cage, brushing the contour of her full breasts. He swallowed past the lump in his throat.

Damn, he needed to get out more often if an unconscious woman could turn him on.

Taking a deep breath, he continued with his exploration, rocking his palms against her hips before moving his hands lower, over her bare thighs and down to her ankles.

At least she didn't have any exposed bones, but she did have a small gash on her forehead. He brushed her long golden-brown hair away from her face. Her skin was pale—delicate features, almost like fine porcelain.

He drew in a deep breath, reining in his thoughts. He wouldn't know how bad her head injury was until he had the doc check her out.

The cut had stopped bleeding. It wasn't so deep it needed stitches, but she did have a knot the size of a bird's egg and it was already turning purple.

He had two choices. Wait on an ambulance, and he wasn't sure how far one would get across the rough terrain. He could almost picture the medics stumbling around in the dark with only flashlights and the full moon to light their way. It would take hours. Or he could get her to the emergency room himself.

He didn't really have much of a choice at all.

Gathering her in his arms, he stood. She didn't weigh much more than a good-sized bale of hay, but Dancer wasn't going to like the added weight.

He hefted her over his shoulder, soothed Dancer with a few soft words, and managed to climb on without dropping the girl. As soon as he was in the saddle he eased her across his lap. She moaned, her bottom shifting against him.

He sucked in a deep breath. "Lady, you'd better quit moving or you'll have us both hurting," he mumbled. Damn, like he wasn't already in pain. The sweet kind, though. The kind right before he had sex—except he wouldn't be having sex, so maybe it wasn't so sweet after all.

Maybe he should just concentrate on getting back to the ranch.

It would take him a little longer than it had coming out. He didn't want to move too fast and jar something loose inside her. Besides, it was dark and it would be too easy for Dancer to step into a hole and get them all bungled up.

But it damn sure didn't help, feeling the warmth of her body pressed close to his. He drew in a deep breath and caught an unusual fragrance. Bewitching. For a moment, he let her scent swirl around him. It defied description, but he liked it.

Suddenly the moon slid from behind the clouds, lighting their way, and he could at least breathe a little easier. It might not take as long to get home as he'd first thought.

He glanced down into her face. Damn, she was sweet to look at. Long dark lashes hid the color of her eyes, as they rested on the paleness of her skin. She hadn't been close enough for him to see what shade they were before she'd fainted, but it didn't stop him from looking at the rest of her. Her features were delicate, like a perfectly carved statue, except she didn't feel cold and hard.

His gaze moved lower. She wore a gold-colored dress—the material soft to the touch. He couldn't remember ever feeling fabric quite like this. She must be from a city. New York, maybe? They seemed to be on top of the latest fashions up North. They'd had New Yorkers come down occasionally. Nice people, but they had some odd notions sometimes.

He glanced up. The ranch was in sight. He breathed a whole lot easier.

When Dancer started for the barn, he nudged the horse toward the front porch instead. He shifted the woman's weight as gently as he could, but she still moaned when he climbed off the horse.

"Barton, what happened?" She opened her eyes.

The light from the front porch cast shadows over her face, but he could see the color of her eyes now. They were a clear shade of turquoise that captured his attention and wouldn't let him look away.

"You're not Barton." Her forehead bunched. "Ow." She tenderly touched her head before her eyes widened. "Oh, I made it, and there's light once again. You saved my life."

He smiled, glad to see she looked a little better than when he'd first seen her. There was even some color in her face. "I wouldn't say I saved your life. Do you think you can stand?"

She nodded, then frowned. "My head."

"You took a pretty hard hit. Want to tell me about it?"

Her hesitation was brief, but he caught it.

"I don't remember?"

He set her on her feet, keeping his arm around her shoulders to steady her. "Do you have a name?"

"Mala."

"Last name?"

She paused. "I don't remember?"

"You can't remember your last name?"

Again, she paused.

"No, I can't remember."

"Who's Barton?"

"Barton who?"

She might have a concussion. That could bring on a case of temporary amnesia. Or she might be a criminal. Great, another complication in his life to add to the growing list. At least this was a sexy one. Now that he could see her in better light, damned sexy.

The pale gold dress clung to every soft curve. He'd already discovered just how soft those curves were, too. He cleared his throat. "Do you think you'll be okay long enough for me to put my horse in the barn?"

"Horse." Her eyes widened. "Oh, I see."

"See what?"

"Nothing."

He felt like he'd been cast in a bad movie and only one of them had a script. Maybe he was just more tired than he thought. He took off his hat and ran a hand through his hair before readjusting it to a more comfortable position. "You can wait in the Jeep."

"Jeep."

"Yeah, the Jeep." He pointed to it. She seemed steady enough, just not quite cognizant of her surroundings. He took her hand and led her to his vehicle. When she stood silently beside the passenger door, he opened it.

"Well, hell." She slid into the seat.

A simple thank you might've been more polite. His vehicle was a little rough around the edges, but it got him where he wanted to go. She was injured though, so he'd cut her a little slack.

"It won't take me that long. Just try to relax." He shut the door behind her. "I'll hurry and put Dancer in the barn, then I'll take you in so Doc can check you out." He tightened his hand on the reins and led Dancer away.

Mala watched as Sheriff hurried toward the wooden structure.

"Barn," she repeated. The word sounded strange when she said it aloud. No, she didn't think her grandmother had mentioned the structure. Mala had an excellent memory and she would've remembered "barn."

Her gaze stayed on Sheriff as he walked away. He had a very nice structure, too. When he'd removed his hat, she'd seen his dark thick hair. It was the color of night. And his eyes were a deep, mesmerizing shade of green.

She couldn't have done better if she'd designed

him herself. He was a human, too. She had known it as soon as she'd awakened in his arms. There was something different about him.

For one thing, his manhood had risen to very nice proportions when she wiggled against it. She hadn't pushed any buttons, either. She would enjoy discovering all there was to know about this man.

But first she had to wait for his return. Her gaze drifted around the interior of the Jeep. Apparently his automatic opener was broken, too.

She tentatively poked her finger against the door. Metal, not as strong as her craft. Strangely built. She moved the handle up, then down, pushing on it to open, then pulling it closed.

It had a clear shield, just like her craft. Except his had dead insects stuck to it. Bleh!

There was something shiny attached to the shield. She wiggled it around, jumping when she saw a face inside it. Did they capture people and somehow get them inside the shiny object? She eased closer and peered inside.

When she bumped her head she must've loosened her brain, she thought when she realized it was her reflection staring back at her. A looking glass, nothing more.

Her gaze fell on what appeared to be some sort of circular steering mechanism. That at least looked a little familiar.

She shifted in the seat. Not as comfortable as her hover air seat, but it would do. This was after all a primitive planet. There would be discomforts. That was all right. She wanted to try new things. Sort of.

As she waited for him to return, she looked around at the darkness. How foolish she'd been—again. Her life force had not been draining away. Barton would laugh when she told him she'd forgotten this planet experienced darkness—after one rotation the sun would rise again so the people understood a new day had begun.

Her planet had two suns, each rotating opposite the other. One always shone brightly, keeping her planet in the light. How lucky humans were to be covered in a blanket of stars. It seemed rather magical.

Sheriff returned to the Jeep and opened the door opposite hers. "I'll take you to the ER so Doc can check you out. He'll probably want to run a few tests."

"Well, hell."

"Don't worry. It won't be that bad."

She loved the sound of his voice: husky, the words lazily rolling off his tongue. It sent little bumps over her arms. Barton could be too formal at times, but Sheriff's voice was deep and soothing. She liked the way it sounded.

He adjusted his looking glass, then turned a metal object and his craft roared to life. She grasped the edge of the seat, hoping he knew how to guide it properly.

They bumped down the road, her teeth rattling inside her head. Soon he would take off and they'd be airborne, then the horrible bouncing would stop.

Apparently he wasn't well trained in maneuvering his aero craft because the voyage did not get any better. Once she was even raised up several inches out of her seat and had to grasp the side so she wouldn't fly through the shield.

She sighed with relief when they pulled under a concrete canopy.

"You'll like the doc," he told her again.

It made her wonder what this man called Doc would do to her if Sheriff had to keep reminding her he was good. She was thoughtful for a moment. Doc. Ah, now she remembered. Doc was a shortened version of doctor. A healer. She remembered her grandmother mentioning a healer.

She hadn't mentioned this conveyance, though. But then her grandmother hadn't actually spent a lot of time on Earth.

Sheriff came around to her side and opened the door, holding her arm as she stepped out of his Jeep.

There was more concrete beneath her feet. Her grandmother had spoken of the structures and how they were made of different materials. She found it odd, yet was pleasantly surprised by the multifaceted characteristics of humans and how they constructed their buildings.

As they approached the glass doors whished open. Ah, this door worked. They approached a desk and the plump woman sitting behind it.

"Hey, Emma, I need Doc to check this young woman out. She was in an accident."

The woman stood, coming around her desk, staring at Mala as if she'd grown two heads. Her species hadn't done that in eons. They'd evolved and become what they were now, which was much like the human species. She resented that this woman treated her like she was an oddity.

"Oh, my goodness, that's a bad bump you have there. I bet that hurt a lot, you poor dear."

She'd been so wrong! Mala's bottom lip trembled. Compassion was nice. She had a strong urge to lay her head on the woman's shoulder and tell her all about the rotten experience she'd had entering the Earth's atmosphere. How she'd bumped her head, then was bitten by an insect. But rather than explain what exactly her day had been like, she only nodded.

"Why don't you go into that room right there and I'll send the doc in and he can examine you? The sheriff will help me fill out the paperwork."

She nodded again, not trusting herself to speak. Earth people were so kind. She walked to the door, slamming into the wood.

"Ow." She held her head. "Ow."

"Here, let me help you," Sheriff said, rushing forward. He turned the knob and pushed on the door.

"It didn't open." She sniffed.

"Sorry, this isn't New York or some other big city. We're not as high-tech. I should've opened the door for you. I'm afraid we do a lot of things differently in our small town."

She sniffed again and went inside. He helped her onto a paper-lined table that crunched when she sat upon it. A very hard paper-lined table. Didn't people on Earth believe in comfort?

"You going to be okay now?"

His eyes looked worried. She sniffed again and lowered her head. This was a big mistake. She should've been happy living in her perfect little world, but no, she had to look for something more. She'd found more, all right.

Suddenly there were two very warm fingers lifting her chin. She met Sheriff's tender gaze.

"I always say things can't be as bad as they first seem. I know you're feeling sort of lost and all alone right now, but just know that I'm here and I won't let anything happen to you. Okay?"

She nodded, unable to trust herself to speak. What were all these emotions running through her? She didn't much care for the sad feeling, but she liked the reaction she got from Sheriff. It made her want to lean forward and absorb his warmth, but before she could, he left, closing the door behind him.

For a moment she stared at the space where he'd been. His body heat lingered a moment before slowly fading.

She exhaled a deep breath.

What had he said? That she was from New York? She wondered about the place that was apparently different from this one. She would file the information away in case she needed it in the future. "New York." She said the words aloud, testing them on her tongue. It sounded strange to her ears, but not much different than when Sheriff had said it.

The door opened and another stranger appeared, a man with lined and wrinkled skin. He must be more ancient than one of the Elders.

She wondered what their custom was. Should she bow before him in deference to his years? She settled for slipping off the table and lowering her eyes.

"It is a great privilege to be in your presence, sir," she murmured.

"Now that's the kind of respect I deserve, but I don't get a blasted ounce of it around here." He looked over the top of his glasses at Emma, who'd followed him into the room carrying a thin board with papers on it. "Maybe I should move to New York where they apparently know how to treat doctors." His eyes narrowed on her. "You are from New York, aren't you?"

She smiled. "Yes, New York."

"That would explain a lot of things."

She had no idea what that meant, but she had a feeling it would be wise if she kept it to herself that she was from another planet. They might not understand.

"I'm Dr. Lambert, and I'll be making sure you're okay."

He glanced down at the chart Emma had brought with her. His eyes narrowed and a frown marred his features before he looked up at her again.

"So, young lady, what exactly happened?"

"Well, hell, I don't remember."

He patted her on the hand. "Quite all right. I'm sure it'll all come back to you so don't you worry one little bit."

He stepped closer, and helped her back onto the table. Taking an instrument from the wall, he shined a light in first one eye, then the other. When he moved it away, she had to blink rapidly so she could see again.

"I don't think I've ever seen eyes the color of yours before. Quite remarkable. Not blue, not green, but a beautiful turquoise."

She smiled, liking this gentle healer.

"Are you hurting anywhere?"

"My head."

He nodded. "Let's draw some blood and get an X-ray."

"Draw blood?" She gripped the sides of the table. He was going to take her lifeblood. Oh, this was a barbaric planet. No doubt why the Elders had discontinued interplanetary travel. They tortured people.

He patted her hand. "Only a little. Don't worry."

Some of her tension eased. She trusted him. She wasn't sure why, but she did.

He walked out of the room but Emma stayed, gathering up supplies.

"I take it you haven't been to many hospitals." The woman moved a tray closer to Mala.

"I've never been to a hospital," she answered truthfully.

"Well, this may sting a bit. You might want to turn your head."

Like the insect in the woods?

She didn't think she was going to like this, but if it had to be done, then she would be brave. She gritted her teeth and closed her eyes.

Chapter 3

Mason jumped when the scream echoed down the hall. The lights began to wildly flicker on and off. A housekeeper looked up before quickly moving farther down the hall, pulling his mop and bucket behind him.

He frowned as he came to his feet and strode toward the closed door of the examination room. What the hell were they doing? Electrocuting her? He remembered an old movie where they shocked people in an attempt to restore their memory or something. Surely that wasn't what was happening.

Doc said all they were going to do was draw a little blood. From the sounds coming from the other side of the door, he'd say they were doing more than drawing her blood.

He turned the knob and shoved the door open . . . and met chaos.

"I'm sorry, honey. I didn't know you've never had blood drawn before or I would've warned you." Emma turned as Mason pushed inside, her face stricken with worry. "All I did was draw a little blood." She held up the tube for him to see.

"That's my blood," Mala gasped, her face draining of all color.

Mason had seen enough women faint in his time

that he was able to get to Mala before she passed out and fell off the table. He caught her slight form in his arms and laid her carefully back on the paper-covered exam table.

"This is just awful. I feel so bad, but I swear that I was really gentle with her, Mason."

"I know you weren't rough, Emma. Hell, I've known you all my life and you hate causing anyone pain. I suppose she's just not used to needles."

"She did tell me she'd never been in a hospital. That alone would be enough to scare anyone."

"What's all the ruckus?" Doc came running into the room. "I heard her scream all the way down the hall. Then the lights were going on and off. Damned squirrel in another transformer again."

"She's never been in a hospital before," Emma explained. "I think her accident and not remembering, then me drawing her blood, might have been too much for her. Poor little thing." She reached over and patted Mala's hand, even though she still hadn't come around.

"I think we'd better keep her overnight," he said.

Mason took one look at Mala, then his gaze moved around the white sterile room before returning to the small form lying on the cold table. Something pulled at his gut. He didn't want to think of her here, lonely and scared.

He made a quick decision. "Why don't I take her to my ranch? She seems more comfortable around me. I can check on her during the night. Don't you think her memory will have a better chance of returning if she's under less stress?"

Doc reached into a drawer and pulled out an ammonia capsule, looking thoughtful. He broke it open and waved it under Mala's nose.

The sting of ammonia bit Mason's nostrils, causing his nose to twitch and his eyes to tear. He took a step back.

"Other than a bump on her head and not remembering what happened, she seems okay," the doctor said.

Mala coughed and pushed the doc's hand away.

"Just to be on the safe side, let's get a CT scan and if it's clear I'll let her go home with you. That is, if she's agreeable. First sign of any problems I want her back in the ER.

"You got it, Doc."

It was another couple of hours before Mala was released. While they'd waited on the preliminary results of the CT scan, Mason called the office to have one of the deputies check to see if a car had gone off the road near Devil's Bend.

Nothing. No skid marks, no abandoned cars.

He didn't want to think she'd gotten into a fight with a boyfriend—or worse, a husband—and maybe he'd kicked her out of the car. Could be that Barton guy she'd mentioned. It wouldn't be the first time something like that had happened, though. Damn, he'd lock the bastard up and throw away the key if that were the case.

He drew in a deep breath to clear his mind. He'd put out an APB on her. Something would probably turn up and he'd have his answers soon enough.

Mala shifted in her seat with a deep sigh.

"Tired?" he asked as he pulled to a stop in front of his house.

"I hurt."

"Doc gave me some samples of pain tablets. That should help. By morning you'll probably have your memory back and be feeling a lot better."

There was something guilty in the way she looked out the window rather than meet his gaze.

Now he was reaching. What did someone as sweet-looking as Mala have to feel guilty about? His imagination was kicking into overdrive.

"Come on, let's get you into the house and tucked into bed." An image of actually tucking her into bed filled his thoughts. He jerked the keys out of the ignition, pocketing them as he climbed out of the Jeep. That's not why he'd brought her home. He'd felt sorry for her. Nothing more than that.

Blue barked and wagged his tail as he ran to greet him. Absently, he patted the dog's head and scratched him behind the ears. "Now, you be good, we have a guest."

He opened the passenger-side door, but rather than get out, Mala warily eyed Blue.

"Don't worry. This is just my dog, Blue. I've had him since he was a pup and he wouldn't bite a biscuit."

She nodded, slowly exiting the vehicle.

He took her hand, intending to show her how gentle Blue was, but the moment he touched her something passed through him. Almost like an electrical current, but a pleasurable one.

When she looked up at him and smiled, he remembered what he was going to do. "Blue is about as gentle a dog as there is." He brought her hand forward so she could touch Blue's head.

"He's so soft," she said on a whisper, but jumped back when Blue licked her hand. A bubble of laughter spilled from her.

Mason grinned, liking the sound. He studied her as she reached toward Blue again. There was something unusual about her but he just couldn't quite put his finger on it. Even the way she interacted with Blue was . . . strange. It was almost as if she'd never seen a dog before, but that was crazy. Everyone had seen at least one dog.

"Come on." He tugged on her arm. Blue whined. "You can come, too." What was wrong with Blue? He acted like a love-struck pup.

They went up the steps but Mala stopped at the door, eyeing it with apprehension.

Was she scared of being alone in his home—just the two of them? He was a stranger, even though he was the sheriff.

"You'll be safe here," he said and opened the door.

Mala immediately relaxed and walked inside. She would have to remember that some doors opened and some did not, or her head was going to be really banged up when she returned to Nerak.

Barton would certainly tell her that he'd tried to warn her about pain. She could hear his "I told you so" now. For a companion unit, he could really make her want to scream sometimes. She was sure the human male would be much less aggravating.

She stepped into the room and glanced around. How odd-looking. Similar to her apartment, yet different.

"Would you like something to eat?"

Eat? She'd had two food capsules prior to leaving her planet, which was enough nutrition for one rotation, but she was curious about the food on Earth. Her grandmother had mentioned it was almost as good as sex. She just couldn't imagine that.

"Yes, food would be nice."

"Why don't you sit on the sofa and rest while I throw us something together." He picked up a black object. "Here's the remote. I have a satellite dish so you should be able to find something to entertain yourself while I rustle us up some food."

She nodded and took the remote, then watched

him leave the room and go into another. The remote felt warm in her hand. A transferal of body heat? Tingles spread up and down her arm. The light above her head flickered.

She glanced up. Now that was odd. But then, she *was* on Earth.

Her attention returned to the remote.

Very primitive. The history books on her planet had spoken about remote controls in the old days. You pointed it at the object it was programmed to work with so you wouldn't have to leave your seat.

She pointed it toward the door and pushed the power button. The door didn't open. She tried different objects around the room without success. Finally she pointed it toward a black box.

The screen immediately became a picture. Of course—television. She made herself comfortable on the lounging sofa and began clicking different channels. Everything interested her, but what she found most fascinating was a channel called Sensual Heat.

She tossed the remote to a small table and curled her feet under her, hugging the sofa pillow, her gaze glued to the screen. A naked man walked across the set, his tanned butt clenching and unclenching with every step he took. When he faced her, the man's erection stood tall, hypnotizing her. It was so large she couldn't take her gaze off it.

A naked woman appeared behind him. She slipped her arms around him, her hands splayed over his chest. Slowly, she began to move her hands over his body, inching them downward, ever closer.

Mala held her breath.

"I want you," the woman whispered. "I want to take you into my mouth, my tongue swirling around your hard cock."

The man groaned.

Mala leaned forward, biting her bottom lip as the man's hands snaked behind him and grabbed the woman's butt. In one swift movement, he turned around. "Damn, you make me hard with just your words."

"And I love when you talk dirty to me."

"So, you want me to tell you what I want to do to your body?"

The woman nodded.

He grinned, then began talking again. "I want to squeeze your breasts and rub my thumbs over your hard nipples." His actions followed his words. "You like that?"

"Yes!" She flung her head back, arching toward the man.

Mala leaned forward, her mouth dry, her body tingling with excitement. Yes! She wanted this, too!

"Do you like French bread, or white bread?" Mason asked, walking into the room.

She dragged her gaze from the television. Bred. That was what humans called copulating. Getting bred. Her nipples ached. "Yes, can we breed now?" She stood and began slipping her clothes off.

Chapter 4

"No! That's not what I meant." He hurried forward and grabbed her dress as it slipped off one shoulder, quickly putting it back in place. Damn, what did Doc give her? This was one hell of a side effect.

"You don't want to copulate?" Her forehead wrinkled, causing her to wince and raise her hand to the bump on her head. "Do you find that I'm not to your liking?"

"Yes, I like you."

"But you do not wish to . . ." She bit her bottom lip as if searching for the right words. "To have sex?"

His hand rested lightly on her shoulder as he met her gaze. "Of course I'd like to . . . uh . . ." He marveled at how soft the fabric felt. His fingers brushed her skin, thinking it felt just as soft. What would she taste like? His gaze moved to her lips. Soft . . . full lips. Kissable.

He jerked his hand away from her shoulder. Anyone watching would think he'd been burned . . . and maybe he had, because he certainly felt hot.

He cleared his throat, his gaze not able to meet those innocent, sensuous turquoise eyes. He felt like such a heel. He'd invited her to his home and all he could think about was having hot sex.

He looked anywhere but at her until his gaze slammed to a stop when it landed on the television. A naked couple was going at it on a kitchen table.

"Well, hell," he breathed, grabbing for the remote and turning off the television. Damned satellite dish. No wonder she was having sexual thoughts. The porn movie, combined with what the doctor had apparently given her—no wonder her thinking wasn't clear.

"Why don't we eat, then I'll show you the guest-room."

When she nodded and smiled, he let out his breath. He'd at least averted that problem, but when he glanced down into her eyes, he was lost. For a moment, he couldn't look away from her beauty. He was tempted to make love with her. Damn was he tempted, but he'd never taken advantage of a woman in his life and he wasn't about to start now.

He turned on his heel and strode back to the kitchen, her soft footfalls following.

This wasn't the best idea he'd ever had, and right now he needed to think about something besides how she would feel in his arms. All soft and snuggly . . . and naked as . . . He cleared his mind, turning his thoughts toward food.

"I hope you like leftover spaghetti. I'll just pop the bread into the toaster oven and it'll be ready in less than five. Why don't you take a seat at the table?"

He didn't look around to see if she took his suggestion. In fact, he forced himself not to look at her, but he heard the scrape of the chair as it was pulled away from the table.

He stirred the spaghetti, knowing it wasn't the heat from the gas burner that made him sweat, but images of the two of them getting it on. Having her around wasn't going to be easy.

Why in the hell *had* he said she could stay at the ranch? He'd met vulnerable women before and never offered them a place to stay.

He frowned.

There were other reasons, though. When he thought about it, it wasn't such a bad idea. He was the sheriff and there was something odd about her situation . . . something a little odd about Mala. He should probably keep a close eye on her.

Yeah, right. If he repeated that another thousand times, he might actually start to believe it.

He busied himself setting the table and throwing together a salad until the toaster oven's bell sounded. But when it was all on the table, she looked at her plate as if she'd never seen food before.

"Don't worry, I've been told I'm a pretty good cook. At least I haven't poisoned anyone yet." He stuck his fork in the spaghetti, twirled the noodles around and ate the first bite.

She repeated his action, closing her eyes as she chewed. "This is . . . soooo . . . good. I've never tasted . . . anything . . . oh, it's wonderful."

The lights flickered, drawing his attention for a moment off her reaction to his cooking, but a sexy little moan from her drew it right back.

He knew he was a fairly decent cook, but Mala acted as if he were a world-class chef, and when she opened her eyes and looked at him he could almost swear she'd like to taste more than the food in her mouth.

His workload had been a little heavy the last couple of weeks, but damn it, he was almost losing it as he watched her chew. How could eating look so damned sensual? He swallowed past the lump in his throat.

It wasn't even homemade. It was bottled spaghetti sauce for cryin' out loud!

"This is . . . fabulous."

The way she spoke the words, like they'd just had sex, made his heart skip a beat.

He mentally shook his head, pulling his gaze away and staring down at the food he'd barely touched. It didn't look all that tempting to him. Could there be something else going on here? How long had it been since she'd eaten? Had she been starved? When he'd lifted her up she hadn't seemed to weigh all that much.

Damn, here he was with his thoughts in the gutter and she might be half starved. He didn't even want to think that someone could be so inhumane that they would deny her food. The woman was . . . was . . . perfect.

He glanced up, letting his gaze linger. Her brown hair fell past her shoulders in soft curls. Golden highlights shimmered when the light caught it just right. But the color of her eyes captured his attention. They were such a clear turquoise. He'd never seen anything quite like them.

"You're not eating?" she said.

"Yeah, I just got lost in thought for a moment." He nudged the breadbasket toward her. "Try some bread."

A smile curved her lips, making him think she might be thinking about something else. He looked away, taking a slice of French bread and biting into it. She did the same.

"You like it?" he asked.

She nodded and took another bite, her eyes closing again in rapture.

He'd never seen anyone enjoy food quite so much.

Maybe she was from another country and had landed in New York. That could explain why she looked a little different from Americans. Swedish, maybe? He had a feeling she'd have an interesting story to tell once her memory returned.

When she'd completely cleaned her plate, he stood and carried the dishes to the sink.

"I'm sure you're tired. I'll get you something to wear to bed." He hurried from the room, going straight to his bedroom, and opened a drawer. They'd be way too big, but she could manage for one night. When he turned around, he almost ran over her. He shoved the pj's into her hands. Damn, he'd never had a woman unnerve him quite as much as Mala did.

"Follow me and I'll show you where you'll be sleeping."

Mala followed him, enjoying the way he moved. She liked the blue material that covered his lower half. It fit nice and snug against his backside.

"This is where you'll be sleeping," he told her, opening a door. "The bathroom is down the hall. I'll get you those pain pills." He turned and hurried away.

Bathroom, bathing . . . oh, she liked that idea, then her attention returned to what he'd called the bedroom. She was familiar with this room. They called it the same thing on Nerak. But when she stepped farther inside, she saw that it looked quite different.

Her gaze swept the room. The walls were painted a happy yellow and lace dripped from the top of the four-poster bed. She dropped the things he had given her to wear, and ran over.

Oh, this was nice.

She had a bed on Nerak, but nothing like this. Not so pretty. She liked this one much better. She pushed on it. The mattress was soft, and had substance. She crawled onto the middle part and sat cross-legged, looking at the fine workmanship of the canopy.

Not even the holograms on Nerak were this nice. Just to be sure, she stretched her hand out and brushed her fingers through the lace. This was real.

Something tapped on her door, drawing her attention. She stared at the wooden rectangular door with the shiny knob. Were there insects on the other side? They had enjoyed crawling up the wooden tree. A shiver ran up and down her spine. They must be really big insects to tap so loudly.

"Is it okay if I come in?"

Sheriff. She sighed with relief. "Yes." Had he forgotten he had to turn the shiny thing?

He opened the door, but paused when his gaze found her in the middle of the bed.

"I like your guestroom very much. The bed is pretty," she told him.

"My grandmother made the bedspread and canopy." His smile was soft, as if he had a good memory of his grandmother.

Something puzzled her, though. "It did not go with her . . . passing?"

"Beg your pardon?"

"Where I'm from, when someone passes, everything that was theirs goes with them."

"That would stop a lot of family arguments," he said. "No, it all stays behind. He handed her the tablets and water. "Pain pills."

They weren't quite as backward as she'd thought if they had medications to reduce one's pain. She swallowed the tablets and drank the water. She grimaced. The pills were bitter. Not good at all. Smoothies were much more pleasant to swallow.

"Uh, better get in bed before those take effect. 'Night."

She glanced out the window. It was still dark outside, distinguishing it from day. Sheriff was very observant. "Yes, it is."

She watched him leave before scooting off the bed and going after the clothes she'd dropped on the floor. She slipped her dress off, then pulled on the bottoms, stifling her laughter when they fell off.

Obviously they were Sheriff's. She kicked off the bottoms and tried the top, marveling at the row of buttons. She knew about buttons.

The top came to just above her knees. This would do. Now to find the bathroom.

She traipsed down the hall and opened the door. She was getting very good at remembering to turn the shiny knob.

A green patterned room greeted her. Leaves, like on the trees, were scattered on the wall. She touched them. They didn't feel the same, though. She closed the door and went to the cabinet with a bowl that was sunk in it. Nothing happened when she moved her hands beneath the spout. No beams of light to cleanse away the bacteria.

Well, the door opened when she'd turned the knob so maybe this would work in a similar fashion. She turned one of the shiny things and water came out.

Oh! Just like the waterfall. She dipped her hands into it and splashed it on her face. Wonderful, magical.

She turned the shiny thing and it stopped flowing. What a marvelous creation, capturing the water. Maybe if her people could capture water it wouldn't be in such short supply. A soft square of cloth was near so she dried her face. She started to turn away, but at the last minute, let the water flow again.

What fun. Off, then on, then off again.

A pretty green cloth curtained off an area. She dried her hands and wandered over, hesitant, then bolder, and pushed the curtain open.

"Oh, my," she breathed as her gaze slowly traveled up to the shiny metal poking out from the wall, then back down. Hmmm, if water came out of the top it would almost be like the waterfall. Would Sheriff join her beneath a cascade of water? Would he put his hands upon her? His mouth sucking at her breast? Her hands trembled as she turned each one.

Disappointment was swift.

It only came out the bottom. Unless . . . She pushed the button on the bottom spout, laughing when water doused her head. She pulled the curtain back and stepped under it.

Just like in the hologram. There was even a white brick. She rubbed it over her body. Her nipples immediately pushed on the material of the nightshirt Mason had given her.

Her gaze went to the door. No Sheriff.

She closed her eyes and bit her bottom lip. Even so, this was . . . very nice, but how much better would it be if she shed the shirt?

She didn't wait to find out, but quickly unbuttoned the top and let it fall at her feet. She rubbed the brick over her breasts, then her other hand over the bubbles left behind.

Beams of light didn't even come close to the white brick. She moved the brick over her abdomen. When she slid it down to the juncture between her legs and rubbed against her pleasure center, she almost crumpled.

"Ohhh, yesss, this is good."

The light began to flicker. She vaguely heard a popping noise in the hall, but the sound didn't regis-

ter as her body throbbed . . . as it strained toward fulfillment. She rubbed harder . . . faster.

"Ohhhh . . ." She leaned her head against the tiled
wall, dropping the brick as her body quivered.

If it was that good with the brick, how much better
would it be with Sheriff? Her body trembled just
thinking about it.

She raised her head toward the waterfall, eyes closed
as the water sprayed over her.

Earth was going to be a wonderful experience.

She sighed as she stepped from the waterfall, remembering to stop it from flowing, but she didn't
want to put the wet shirt back on. Instead, she found
more squares, bigger ones, behind another door and
wrapped one around her.

What other delights would she find in this little
room?

Above the bowl on the counter there was a small
cabinet. She slid the door open. Oh, an assortment
of products. How interesting, she thought, reaching
for one.

"Shaving cream," she read, laughing when it squirted
out white foam.

Ugh, but it tasted horrible.

She picked up a pretty tube and read the side.
"Toothpaste. It whitens and brightens teeth." She
dabbed a bit on her tongue. Much better than shaving cream, if she remembered not to swallow.

Sudden languidness swept over her so that she
could barely stand. She stifled a yawn. The pills were
making her feel funny . . . drowsy. She'd have the next
few days to explore, but she'd better seek out her bed.

She made it to her room and let the square drop
to the floor before crawling beneath the blankets. This
was nice. She sank into softness. Her eyes drifted

closed. It would be much nicer if Sheriff were curled next to her. She wondered if he was asleep in his bed.

She stifled a yawn.

Did he sleep with clothes on or naked with only a sheet to cover his body? And what dreams visited him? She hoped he thought about her.

Mason wondered if Mala was asleep. He hoped someone was resting—he damn sure wasn't getting any . . . sleep *or* sex. It was his own fault. She'd offered her body.

Crap! He might as well get those thoughts out of his mind right now.

Like that was going to happen. He'd heard the guestroom door close about an hour ago. Since then, he hadn't been able to sleep. Usually work kept him awake, ongoing cases, but not tonight. No, Mala kept him awake tonight. All he could think about was that she'd asked him to make love to her.

A beautiful, vibrant, sexy woman had asked him to make love to her and he'd said no. God, he was losing his freakin' mind.

He drew in a ragged breath and flung the covers away as he swung his feet over the side of the bed and sat up.

Hell, she was probably in shock after her accident. He'd seen people act really out of character when something major happened to them. She probably wouldn't remember a thing in the morning. If she did, she'd more than likely be embarrassed.

He stood and walked to the hall, flipping on the light. Nothing. He flipped the switch rapidly up and down. Still nothing. The bulb must've burned out. He'd change it in the morning.

Right now all he wanted to do was take a warm shower and see if that wouldn't relax him enough so he could fall asleep. He went inside the bathroom, but stumbled to a stop when he flipped on the light switch.

What the hell had happened? It looked like a war zone. His gaze slowly moved around the room. His shaving cream was on the cabinet . . . literally. White foamy clouds. The tube of toothpaste looked like an hourglass and the lid was off the mouthwash.

He walked farther inside, his feet splashing through little puddles of water. What had she done, taken a shower with the curtain open?

Shaking his head, he began cleaning up the mess. At least it gave him something to do. When he saw his pajama top in a soggy heap in the tub, along with the bar of soap, he swallowed past the sudden lump in his throat. If she wasn't wearing the pajamas, what was she wearing?

He shook his head, refusing to even go there.

When the bathroom was clean he started back to his room, deciding against the shower, but paused outside Mala's door. He'd better check on her. Doc said he should keep an eye on her through the night.

He slowly turned the knob and nudged the door open. The curtains were fluttering in the breeze from the half-open window. The full moon made the room brighter than normal. He walked closer to the bed, skidding to a halt when his eyes adjusted well enough that he could see her. His heart began to pound in his chest.

Mala lay curled on her side, the covers pushed to the foot of the bed . . . and she was completely naked. Nothing short of an atomic bomb going off could have stopped him from looking his fill.

Her raised arm shielded her face, leaving her perfectly rounded breasts bare to his view. The areolas were a dusky rose, her nipples puckered. He dragged his gaze downward, skimming over her hips and wishing she'd open herself.

As if his thoughts had miraculously made their way inside her mind, Mala rolled to her back. He drew in a sharp breath, unable to look away. The thatch of dark curls captivated him. If there was just a little more light in the room or if her legs would open just a little . . .

Damn, she was under the influence of pain medication and all he could think about was jumping her bones.

She was hard to resist, though. Her skin was like fine porcelain, so fine that if he were to reach out and caress it she might shatter, but damned if he wasn't tempted.

Instead of carrying through with his fantasies, he walked over and pulled the sheet up to her shoulders and closed the window. She moaned, or maybe it was a purr, as she snuggled down. A slight smile curved her lips. At least one of them was having sweet dreams. He damn sure wasn't, and had a feeling he'd be lucky if he slept long enough to even dream.

He turned on his heel and left, but rather than go to his room he went to the kitchen and grabbed a beer, then wandered outside to the patio.

The night air was brisk, the wind stirring through the trees. The mournful cry of a coyote echoed through the hills, breaking the silence.

Mason ran the cold bottle over his face before twisting off the cap, then emptied half of it before taking a deep breath. The beer quenched his thirst, but it did nothing to dispel the memory of Mala lying naked on the bed.

He closed his eyes for a moment. When he opened them, he looked around as if seeing everything for the first time.

This land had been his father's and his grand-father's before him. The name McKinley meant something in this little part of the world. His gaze turned to the guestroom window.

Damned if he didn't feel as if something was missing in his life. Why now? What was it about this stranger that made him feel like this?

He downed the rest of his beer and went to bed before temptation proved to be too much. Why the hell was his life starting to have more complications than he'd ever wanted to encounter? He was afraid it was going to get a hell of a lot worse before it got better.

Chapter 5

Mala yawned and stretched, groaning when she snuggled her head against the pillow.

"Ow."

She sat up, the sheet falling to her waist, as she gingerly touched her forehead, sucking in a mouthful of air. It was still tender.

And her head pounded.

She closed her eyes for a moment. When she next opened them, it took a couple of seconds for the room to come into focus. The pounding stopped, replaced by giddiness. She'd made it. She was on Earth.

And she'd met Sheriff.

"Well, hell," she whispered, then grinned.

Her smile lasted as long as it took another memory to intrude. Sheriff hadn't wanted to copulate. Maybe she wasn't as worthy as the women who lived on his planet. Odd, but that hurt almost as much as her bruised forehead.

A sound on her door drew her attention. Just like last night. Maybe it was Sheriff again.

"Are you decent?" he called out.

Decent? Was he asking her if she was suitable to copulate with? She wasn't sure about all their customs. Maybe it was best to ask if your partner would be a worthy mate.

She thought she might be a decent partner. Yes, she was almost sure of it.

"Yes, I'm decent." She sat tall in the bed, her nipples tight, her body tingling with anticipation.

His gaze was fixed on the tray he carried as he balanced it and the cups while pushing on the door at the same time. When he looked up, his eyes rounded. The tray dropped from his hands, splashing brown liquid on the floor and breaking the white cups.

"I thought you said you were decent," he croaked.

"Wouldn't I make a decent partner to cop . . . have sex with?"

"No!"

"No?" Her bottom lip puckered.

"I mean yes . . . but no. Damn it, I thought you meant you had your clothes on." He bent and picked up the cups and tray. "I have to get a mop." Grabbing her dress off the back of the chair, he tossed it to her. "Would you please put that on before . . . before . . ."

"Before what, Sheriff?"

"Before you find yourself with more trouble than you bargained for. I'm only human." He turned but, before he left, called over his shoulder, "And my name is Mason, not Sheriff."

"You're not Sheriff?"

He expelled an exasperated breath. The broken cups on his tray rattled. "Yes, I'm the sheriff of this county but my name is Mason."

"Mason," she said, testing this new name. "It has a nice sound."

"I'm glad you like it," he grumbled before he left the room.

Humans were very odd. She smiled. But she'd seen the way Sheriff . . . Mason had looked at her. It was the same look that Sheriff from the documentary had had in his eyes. She frowned. Then why did he deny the inevitable? If you wanted sex on her planet, you had sex. Humans apparently did not feel the same way.

Definitely odd.

She tugged her dress over her head and scooted off the bed. She had other things to attend to. Humans and Nerakians shared the same bodily functions, and hers was about to bust. She stepped over the spilled liquid and went to the bathroom.

Though primitive, she did understand the workings of one of the fixtures. When she finished, she pushed on the shiny thing and closed the lid. Definitely primitive.

Her gaze strayed. But then again, there was the bowl on the counter. Primitive, yes, but oh so wonderful.

Anticipation skittered down her spine. She turned the shiny handle. Yes, it still had water. She splashed it on her face. Laughter bubbled out of her. Sometimes advanced technology wasn't a good thing.

When she returned to her room, Mason had cleaned the spill and left again. Had he gone back to the food room? She sniffed.

Oh, wonderful smells drifted to her olfactory system. Closing her eyes, she let the delicious scent seep into every pore. Then she followed her nose.

Food. This was a good thing. On Nerak, scientists had discovered a way to convert food to a pill, and medication to a smoothie. It was perfect. No preparation. Over the centuries, the animal population had died out because there was no need for them.

It was the same with the men. They fought wars until the women rebelled at their sons and husbands dying in battle. That's when women began to experiment until they came up with a way so that only female children were created from eggs and developed in tubes. Eventually there were no more wars, but there were no more men, either. Only companion units. She didn't think it was such a good solution.

When she walked into the preparation room, Mason was cooking. For a moment she just stared, watching the way he moved. His arm muscles flexed in a very nice way. Her gaze lowered. She liked watching his butt as he shifted from one foot to the other. He had very sexy moves.

No, it wasn't a good thing having pills for food. She liked watching a man cook. Mason looked as if he was very good at it, too. Last night's food had been delicious. It was a shame they had no men on her planet to cook for them.

He glanced up, noticed she stood in the doorway and looked relieved she was dressed, although she noticed the way his gaze lingered.

"I'll have breakfast ready in a second—have a seat." He quickly turned back to his task.

Mala had a feeling he didn't want to look at her. It might be more difficult than she first thought to have sex with a man. She had to be doing something wrong.

She strolled to the table and sat in one of the chairs. In a few minutes he set a plate in front of her.

"Bacon, eggs and toast. Nothing fancy."

She poked the yellow things that looked like eyes staring at her. The yellow burst and ran to the side of her plate. It might taste great, but it looked really awful.

"Jelly?" He opened a container and handed it to her. "Strawberry."

She took it, and tentatively poked her spoon inside. The first bite almost sent her into orbit. This was good. This was so good. Even better than the food last night. She stuck her spoon inside and took another bite.

The lights flickered.

"Here, it goes on the toast." Mason took the jar and scooped out enough to spread on the crusty square.

"Why can't I eat it the other way?"

"You still don't remember what happened to you last night, do you?" he countered.

She shook her head, feeling a little remorseful that she wasn't speaking the truth. It was for the best, though.

"I didn't think so. I have a feeling you're not from New York. Do you remember being up North?"

"Up North."

He nodded. "They have people come into port from all over. Maybe you're from Sweden."

"Sweden." She smiled.

"Sound familiar?"

"No."

"They're a little more . . . uh . . . open-minded about some things than what we're used to in Texas."

"Texas?"

"Texas. That's the state you're in." He shook his head. "You *must* be from another country."

"Yes, another country." That should serve her well. She wouldn't be expected to know everything if she wasn't from this part of Earth.

He pointed toward the jar. "Well, this is jelly, and it goes on your toast because that's the way it's done."

"I liked it better my way," she mumbled. Mason was becoming rather bossy. Now she knew why there'd been wars in the first place.

"I have to go to work this morning. You think you'll be okay here by yourself?"

By herself? She nodded. This was great. She would have time to explore. He finished eating, gave her the number of the sheriff's office and showed her where the phone was before he left.

She stood at the door and watched while he climbed inside his Jeep and drove away. An odd feeling washed over her. She almost wanted to call him back. But if she did that, she wouldn't be able to look around. Sex with him would've been nice though.

As soon as his Jeep was out of sight, she went to the black object he'd called a phone and picked it up. There was a buzzing noise coming from it, as if she might have made it angry, so she put it back.

There were other things that interested her more. She began going into rooms and opening drawers. She was tempted to watch more of the coupling channel, but she wanted to see what else of interest Mason had.

In his room she found pictures of people. Not like a hologram. These were framed. She liked the hologram better. If she was lonely she could open the port and actually listen to her grandmother tell stories. It was like being with her, except she hadn't really known her that well. The hologram, and her journal, linked Mala to the past.

She wandered into another room and found a computer. Very primitive, but she discovered it worked. It took her a few minutes to figure it out, but she was fairly good with electronics. Even as antiquated as it was, the machine was familiar.

She found the information center with little trouble. Now, what to ask? What was her main goal?

An ache began to grow inside her. She wanted to copulate with Mason: feel his arms around her, caressing, bringing her to fulfillment.

She drew in a shaky breath, returning her attention to the screen. First she had to convince him it would be a good thing. She typed *copulate* into the dictionary search engine. A few seconds passed. She tapped her fingers impatiently on the desk. Very slow.

Definitely primitive. The screen changed and the definition came up.

> *Copulate: have sex, intercourse, penis, to join, mate, seduce into having sex . . .*

Seduce?

One eyebrow rose. She quickly typed her new word and again waited.

> *Seduce: to entice one into having a sexual relationship.*
> *Entice?*

Ah, now she understood. She needed only to seduce Mason. She began clicking on sites, absorbing everything written on the subject.

Techniques for seduction and keeping a man satisfied. Hmm . . . . *How to become a sex goddess.*

She read very fast.

Creating the mood. That was interesting. With a companion unit you didn't have to know about the techniques of seduction. She had a feeling women on her planet had been missing out on a lot. She continued to read.

Sex toys? Interesting. Her thighs quivered as she ran through the very long list. But how did one get these fun instruments?

She scanned the page. Ah, there it was at the bottom. All you needed was an account with PayPlan and it would transfer funds to this store.

It wouldn't be hard for her to find out if Mason had one of these accounts that stored a card number. It would only take a few clicks—yes, there it was. And he had plenty of numbers on his Visa to spend on the fun-looking toys. She could buy lots of stuff.

She read further. One-day delivery. They would be here tomorrow. Today she would seduce, tomorrow they would play with these fun toys.

Exhausted after a couple of hours of reading, she leaned back in her chair. By tonight she was sure she would be able to seduce Mason. Her gaze skimmed over the last bit of information. Her body began to tingle as ideas exploded across her mind.

The first thing he would see would be her wearing very few clothes, but she would act as if she were covered from head to toe. She would move her hands in a way that would draw his eyes to her body.

For a moment she closed her eyes and could almost see what would transpire. She sighed deeply, then opened her eyes as the seductive scene vanished. If that didn't work, she had more options, and she planned to try all of them until she met with success.

She only hoped he had some of the items she'd read about. Like chocolate. It was supposed to aid in setting the mood. She had no idea what it was, but she'd try anything.

She jumped from the chair and hurried to the food room and began opening cabinets. Her eyes lit on a black can.

Cocoa. Chocolate.

Ah, yes, tonight would be very good indeed. She pulled off the lid and stuck her tongue inside.

"Ugh!" She blew out a breath and a black powder cloud poofed into her face. Not good! The article had lied. This chocolate was not good. Not good at all!

She wiped her tongue with her hand as she tried to remove the horrible bitter taste. This couldn't be the stuff. She hurried to the water and washed her mouth out. A shiver of revulsion ran up and down her spine.

She spat and rinsed until the awful taste was gone. This couldn't be the right stuff.

But she wasn't about to give up. Surely Mason had one or two of the items that would help her seduce him. She continued her search, more determined than ever.

The next cabinet yielded a bag of chocolate bars. She grimaced as she warily opened one of them, tearing off the foil covering. First she sniffed. It smelled a lot better than the powdery chocolate. She took a tiny bite off one corner.

Closing her eyes, she let the taste swirl through her senses. Oh, yes. This is what they'd meant. She took a bigger bite. A blast of wonderful sensations hit her taste buds. She slid down the side of the cabinet and plopped to the hardwood floor, letting the bag rest between her legs.

This was definitely worth the trip to Earth even if she never had an orgasm with a human. She unwrapped another candy bar and shoved it into her mouth. Chocolate was good. Very good. She closed her eyes and leaned her head against the back of the cabinet.

The light flickered around and above her head, but she hardly even noticed.

Chocolate.

A surge of pleasure rushed through her like nothing she'd ever experienced. Earth was very, very good.

Chapter 6

Mason wondered how Mala was faring. He'd meant to leave early, but something kept coming up and now it was late afternoon. She hadn't answered the phone when he'd called, but she could've gone for a walk . . . or something.

Guilt washed over him. What if . . . No, he wouldn't go there. It could be nothing. She'd looked fine when he'd left this morning.

Then why did he feel such a sense of dread?

He drove across the cattle guard and down the road toward the house. Everything looked okay. At least the house and barn were still standing. He cut the engine and got out.

She didn't meet him at the door. Not that he'd expected her to, but what if she didn't have amnesia at all? She was a stranger. Hell, she could've robbed him blind . . . but not likely unless she wanted a lot of mismatched junk, and he kept less than fifty dollars in cash at the house.

No, he didn't really think she was a criminal. Still, he was more than a little cautious when he opened the front door and stepped inside. He hadn't ruled out the possibility she might have escaped from the state hospital.

It took a few seconds for his eyes to adjust to the dim interior after being in the sun.

"Hello, Mason."

Her soft, sultry voice reached out to caress him, like fire licking in all the right spots. His eyes adjusted and as they did, an ache began to build inside him.

She stood in the doorway of the kitchen wearing one of his sleeveless white undershirts. It was loose on her, reaching mid-thigh.

Slowly his gaze moved over her. Even in the loose shirt her nipples poked against the thin fabric, her areolas clearly outlined. But he knew what they looked liked without the covering of material.

That made it even worse.

He tried to swallow and couldn't so he just concentrated on breathing, which right now wasn't that easy.

"Are you hungry?" she asked.

"Yeah," he croaked. But he wasn't thinking about his stomach.

"Good, I fixed us something to eat."

She looped her hands behind her like a mischievous child, and turned to her side. Ah, damn, the shirt's armholes just barely skimmed over her breasts. Definitely all woman. He stumbled forward, blindly following wherever the hell she wanted to lead. He didn't care. Since she was dressed like that, he'd follow her to the moon if she asked. Damn, he didn't think she had on any panties, either.

Okay, maybe she'd just needed something else to wear. She looked innocent—sort of. Damn, but she was killing him. He had to think of something else real quick or he might do something he'd regret.

If he were honest, he'd even admit he probably wouldn't be that regretful. Even more reason to get his mind on something else. Fast!

He glanced around the kitchen. There were two plates set at the table with a chocolate bar on each and a glass of chocolate milk in front. More chocolate syrup was puddled on the plates.

Who the hell cared if she fed him dessert first? Maybe it was a custom in Sweden to eat the sweets before the main course. Damn, he'd love to eat her sweets.

Ah, man, don't even go there.

"Looks good," he managed to get out.

Stay focused!

She didn't know who she was. She could be married. He glanced at her hand. She wasn't wearing a ring. That didn't mean she wasn't married, but it was a good sign. He still couldn't have sex with her, though. He was the sheriff. Sworn to protect. Not sworn to go to bed with.

She sat down, her eyes immediately rounding. "Oh!" She smiled. "The chair is cold on my bare bottom."

He'd never make it through the meal. Oh, God, she was killing him. Would he be legally bound if he took his badge off?

She unwrapped her chocolate and laid the paper to the side of her plate. "I *love* chocolate." She licked the bar, slowly running her tongue over it. "I've never tasted anything like it."

He drew in a deep breath. He had to remember to breathe. It could be detrimental to his health if he forgot, but right now it felt as if he were dying tiny little deaths. But damned if it wasn't the sweetest death he'd ever experienced.

"Oh, it's really good." She closed her eyes, swirling her tongue over and around the chocolate. It smeared across her lips. She didn't get in any hurry as she licked them clean.

"I'm only human, Mala." His words were raspy as his throat constricted.

"And I want you," she told him. "Don't you want me?" She stood, coming around to his side of the table, looking much like a shy little girl asking if she could have a cookie before dinner.

She gripped the undershirt's hem. Whether she meant to tug it down or not, he didn't know, but that's what happened. Her breasts were crushed against the tight cotton material, the shirt lowered enough to show her dusky areolas, but didn't quite reveal her nipples.

Air whooshed from his lungs as she straddled his legs. Her breasts were right there in front of him, covered only by the thin material.

Nope, this was no little girl. Mala was a full-grown woman and she wanted him.

He should gently explain to her that he didn't want to take advantage of her predicament. He should tell her that she would probably regret throwing herself at him when all was said and done. He should do a lot of stuff. For Pete's sake, he was the sheriff, but damn it, he was also a man, she was a beautiful sexy woman, and he was no fool.

He snaked a hand behind her neck and brought her mouth down to his. Chocolate smeared across his face, his lips, but he didn't care. He'd always had a sweet tooth, and she was very sweet. He licked the chocolate off her mouth before slipping his tongue inside.

Damn, she was so hot. Her tongue met his thrusts, sparring with him as her fingers curled in his hair, pulling him closer.

He stroked her velvety softness, keeping a tight control on the situation. When she slowed to his rhythm, he moved his hands over her back, beneath the shirt, cupping her bottom, moving her closer to his erection.

Could she feel how much he wanted her? Her sudden gasp of pleasure told him yes, she did.

His mouth moved to her neck, lightly kissing the tender skin. "I've never met a more sensual, sexy creature." He slid his hands beneath her shirt, caressing her breasts, brushing over her sensitive nipples.

It barely registered that the lights had begun to flicker. Squirrels in a transformer? They were bad this year. He didn't really care. Not right now. Not at this moment.

He tugged her shirt higher. She pulled it over her head and tossed it to the floor.

"Beautiful," he whispered, his gaze taking in her full breasts, slender waist and thatch of dark curls before he surrendered to temptation.

His mouth closed over one sweet nipple. He sucked, gently pulling with his teeth before taking her full into his mouth. He swirled his tongue over the little bud. She cried out and arched closer. He massaged and caressed with his other hand, tweaking her other nipple.

When she pushed against his chest, he thought he might have hurt her in some way. He immediately released her and sat back, but she didn't look like a woman suffering. Passion glazed her eyes.

"I want to see all of you." She scooted off his lap and tugged on his shirt. "Take off your clothes." Her words were husky, sensuously cascading over him.

He stood and quickly unbuttoned his shirt. She danced behind him, a naked nymph, pulling on the material and sliding it down his arms until it slipped to the floor. She scraped her fingernails lightly down his bare back, sending tremors over him.

"Do you like that?" she asked.

"You know I do."

"You're right, I do." She moved to stand in front of him, tugging at his belt. "It's easy to see I pleasure you."

His belt dropped to the floor. She hooked her fingers into his waistband and unbuttoned his pants. He watched her face as she undressed him, saw the excitement and let her have her way. Hell, just watching her gave him pleasure.

"Oh, nice," she said, encircling his penis with her hand and sliding the foreskin down, then slowly back up. Her forehead wrinkled. "I think we got this part slightly wrong. Do you vibrate?"

"Huh?" Did she want to use a vibrator? "I don't have a vibrator." He'd never really tested the boundaries with toys when making love, but he didn't mind trying something new. If his partner was willing, that is.

"It doesn't matter," she said. "We'll make do with what we have . . . this time."

Before he could kick the rest of the way out of his pants, she grabbed the chocolate syrup out of the refrigerator and uncapped it, then dumped it over him, starting at his chest.

"Son-of-a-bitch! That's cold!"

"Well, hell, Mason, don't you know I'll make you warm again." She plastered her body against his, smearing the chocolate between them. Her laughter bubbled out and filled the room.

When she turned and began rubbing her backside against him, he grabbed her breasts. There was something to be said in favor of chocolate-dipped sex.

"Isn't this fun, Mason?"

He laughed. "Yeah, it's fun." She was right, too. He'd never had quite this much enjoyment when making love. Sure, he'd had plenty of orgasms, plenty of sex, but he had a feeling none had been like what he would experience with Mala.

She turned around and kissed his chest, moving to his nipples, sucking on first one and then the other.

"Umm, you taste good."

He caressed her back, his hands sliding through the chocolate syrup. It was kinky and sexy the way her slick skin felt beneath his calloused hand.

She pushed with the palms of her hands, and he sat in the chair. Their eyes met.

There was a streak of chocolate smeared across her face and still she looked wanton rather than comical. Slowly, she smiled. Her grin spoke of better things to come.

"Who are you? Where are you from? How did I get this lucky?" He didn't even realize he'd spoken the words aloud until she answered.

"I'm Mala, from the planet Nerak, and I'm the lucky one." There, now he knew the truth.

"And you have a great sense of humor." He chuckled. "Okay my little alien, do your worst, or best. I already feel as if I might disintegrate from the heat building inside me."

She shook her head. "I promise not to turn you into a pile of ashes, but I do promise we'll have many orgasms. This is what making love should be—exploring and testing what each one likes or dislikes. Are you ready to walk on the path of discovery?"

"Oh, yeah, I'm more than ready." He pulled her down onto his lap so that she straddled his legs, and he began licking the chocolate off her body. "Umm, you taste pretty good yourself." He'd never liked chocolate as much as he did right now.

Mala leaned her head back, enjoying the way his mouth closed over first one breast and then the other.

He tugged on her nipples, causing an ache to stir low in her belly. So lost in her haze of pleasurable sensations, she wasn't aware he was standing until he set her on her feet. Disappointment flooded her. Not fair. She wasn't ready to end the fun. She wanted an orgasm!

"We're not stopping, are we?" Surely humans finished the act and didn't change their minds in the middle.

"Oh, no, my little alien, I'm just getting started." He scooped her up and carried her to his room, jerking the covers back with one hand before laying her gently on the sheets.

Mala was glad she'd told him she was from another planet. He'd taken the news very well. He'd even said she had a great sense of humor, too. Not that she thought anything she'd said had been humorous, but apparently Mason had thought so.

And she'd been worried. Her worries seemed silly now.

He scraped his fingers through the curls between her legs and all thoughts of where she was from were swept away on a tide of ecstasy.

"You like that?"

She nodded.

"Then you'll probably like this even more." His mouth covered her sex.

Barton had never done this. "Ohhh . . . ohhhh." She clasped his head closer. "Please don't stop. Oh . . . my . . . yes!"

From a distance she heard noises from the kitchen. It sounded as if all the little appliances she'd played with this afternoon were going off at once, and there were popping and hissing noises. Had she left the television on? Who cared, as she lost herself in the sensations Mason created. His tongue scraping over her sex, delving inside the very heart of her being.

"You taste sweet," he murmured against her sex, his breath fanning against her sensitive flesh.

"Please, don't stop tasting."

He nibbled, sucking her flesh.

"Yes . . . yessssss!"

Her back arched as fire swept through her body. There was an explosion of colors, a roaring in her ears as she came. Before she had a chance to take a breath, he slipped something on and entered her. He filled her, but for a moment he did nothing except stare into her eyes.

"You okay?"

The room came into focus. "Better than okay."

He began to move . . . slowly at first. His eyes closed, but she continued to watch his expression as their bodies moved to the rhythm. She loved watching the intensity on his face.

Her body began to heat once again as the friction from their movements stirred the embers inside her.

"Do you feel it?" His words were raspy. "Electrically charged impulses of pleasure. Damn . . . so . . . fucking . . . fantastic. It's never been like this before. It feels . . . so . . . Ahhhh . . . ahhhh."

His words didn't register, as another orgasm washed over her. She grasped his buttocks and pulled him closer, her legs wrapping around his waist, her inner muscles clenching against him.

Yes! This was what she'd been searching for. Her body trembled as the ache inside her eased and a feeling of languidness washed over her.

As she floated back to earth, his words sank into her muddled brain.

Electrical charges?

The noises from the other room she'd heard?

Oops.

Chapter 7

Mason must've dozed off for a moment, because when he awakened Mala was gone from the bed. He heard someone moving about in the kitchen and smiled. She hadn't gone far.

Damn, now that was mind-blowing, body-jarring, down-and-dirty, explosive sex. Just the way it should be. He knew he was grinning like a fool as he turned onto his back. Maybe she *was* from another planet. She'd definitely sent him into a galaxy beyond any he'd ever been in. For a moment, he'd actually thought he'd heard the siren on his Jeep going off and the television blaring. Ridiculous.

Oh, yeah, Miss Mala was definitely hot.

Almost as quickly as the grin on his face formed, it was gone.

What the hell was he thinking? He rolled to a sitting position, planting both feet on the floor. How stupid could one person be?

This was another complication in his life that he didn't need right now. He had more than enough to deal with already. Harlan and the reporters were driving him crazy with all their notions of Bigfoot running loose in the area.

Now he had a woman living with him that he knew nothing about.

Something banged in the kitchen. Mala. She'd told him that she was an alien. He'd known she was joking, but still, it could cause a stink if she said the same thing to someone else.

This was just great. He raked a hand through his hair. Wouldn't all hell break loose if she jokingly told one of the reporters she was from another planet? He laughed without mirth, and for a moment visualized reporters running all over his property with their cameras, ready to snap pictures.

What the hell was he going to do?

Okay, that was an easy fix. He'd just warn her not to say anything, even in fun. His shoulders relaxed. He was making more out of the situation than was there.

Ahh, Mala. What had she done to him?

He should feel guilty for making love with her, but he didn't. It might've been a dumb move, but no, he didn't feel guilty.

Standing, he headed toward the shower to get some of this mess off him. Chocolate had been fun, but now it was drying and didn't feel quite as sensual. More like he'd rolled around in the mud, then lain in the sun so it could dry. He was starting to crack. He only hoped it didn't become literal.

He frowned when he opened the bathroom door. Apparently they didn't have showers where she was from because she hadn't closed the curtain . . . again, and there was water in puddles all over the floor.

Ten minutes later, and much cleaner, he went in search of Mala. He found her in the kitchen. Damn, she looked good wearing one of his shirts. This one covered her a little more than the last one but left her long legs bare. Long slender legs that went all the way up to form the cutest ass he'd ever seen.

She had her back to him and it was all he could do

not to scoop her up and carry her back to bed. Instead of acting on impulse, his gaze slowly moved around the room. It looked like a disaster area. There was chocolate syrup everywhere.

But that wasn't all. The dishwasher door was broken down on one side. It must've been loose. Hell, the thing was at least ten years old.

But what he couldn't quite understand was why the refrigerator door was open and everything had iced over, as if the thermostat had been turned down. Mala must've accidentally lowered it.

"I guess we made a mess," he said as he strolled over and turned up the thermostat on the fridge and shut the door.

She jumped, turned and smiled. "With the chocolate . . . yes." She eyed the room. "The other things I'm afraid are a result of the electrically charged currents that were created when we copulated." She paused, looking thoughtful. "Much like your aurora borealis phenomenon, which I read about on your computer, except on a smaller scale, of course. I think we might have produced at least one-tenth of a gigawatt, but even that would be more than enough to blow the appliances out of kilter. It could've been less. I'm just estimating. Did you see any lights hovering above the house?"

She turned those sexy eyes on him and his insides felt as if they were turning to mush. How could he be falling for a woman so fast? There was so much to like about her, though. Like her sense of humor.

"Aurora borealis—cute, but you might want to watch the alien talk. People around here would actually start to believe you. I'd hate if someone locked you up and threw away the key. I rather like having you around."

He liked a lot of stuff about Mala. Like the way she

looked, her inquisitiveness. He *really* liked the way she looked—man, did she look great. He didn't even mind she'd left the bathroom in a mess—again.

As Mason ambled toward her, Mala suddenly felt cold. Lock her up and throw away the key? Would they treat her so harshly just because she was a curious alien who only wanted to explore Earth? And maybe have a little sex while she was here? It didn't seem fair.

He wrapped his arms around her. "Why so quiet all of a sudden?"

Warmth settled around her. This was nice . . . and safe. In Mason's arms she felt so very safe. She inhaled and caught his scent: like the trees and the earth, the wind and the air.

Her heart squeezed tight. She must have made a noise because he pulled back from her and looked into her eyes. "You okay?"

She touched the center of her chest. "I hurt, right here, at the thought of leaving you."

"Why would you leave? Unless you've remembered what happened?"

Maybe he didn't believe that she was an alien. If he did, would he be honor-bound to lock her away? Sometimes discretion was the smarter path to take when exploring another planet.

Humans had only touched the surface of space travel. The interplanetary travelers on Nerak had been careful to keep their identities a secret. Did she really want to ruin what little time they had together?

"No. I don't remember anything," she lied. "But I might have to leave someday. You won't want me to stay with you forever."

"Who knows what the future will bring?" He hugged her tighter. "Hey, why don't we run to town today and see about getting you some clothes to wear?" His grin sent tingles down her spine. "Not that I don't like what you're wearing now, but I'd hate like hell if someone came to the door. I don't want to have to fight the men off."

She grinned. "Town would be nice." She frowned. "What is town?"

"Yep, you gotta be from another country. I'll have my deputy extend the APB."

She had no idea what an APB was so she just nodded, then bent over to retrieve a cup that had rolled under the cabinet. She heard Mason cough, or it might have been a gurgle. When she straightened and looked at him he was striding toward her.

He scooped her up and into his arms. "Tomorrow will be soon enough."

The next morning Mala slipped into her dress and followed Mason to the Jeep. She wasn't especially thrilled she would be riding in it again, but she could survive knowing she was going somewhere new.

Staying in bed would've been nice, too. Mason had made sweet love to her early this morning until she felt quite satisfied, then they'd had more food. Earth was a nice place to be.

Maybe they would even have chocolate in this town.

When they passed the hospital, she sighed with relief. She liked the Elder, and the one Mason called Emma was nice, but she didn't want to lose any more of her lifeblood.

He apparently noticed she was staring. Mason nodded toward the concrete structure. "The hospital is pretty new. The board used donated land and had it built on the outskirts of town. We're trying to recruit new doctors."

"One of my cousins is a healer . . . doctor."

"You remembered something?" His eyebrows rose as he glanced her way before returning his attention to the road.

She would have to be careful. "Well, hell, I suppose I did." She focused on the scenery going by.

"Don't worry, everything will come back in time. At least you've made a little progress." He flipped a lever beside his steering mechanism, turned and stopped in front of a building.

"Carol's Boutique," she read. "What's a boutique?"

"We'll be able to find clothes for you."

He stepped out of the Jeep. She lifted the lever and opened her door, quite proud she'd managed it. Living on Earth wasn't so hard.

"Carol's is the only store in town that has women's clothes, but I've heard she has a nice collection."

The plate glass storefront showcased an array of dresses, hats with feathers, and pretty pins decorated with shiny stones.

She breathed a sigh of relief. This was more like her planet. Nerak might not have a lot of water, or men, but they had things that sparkled. Just like her promise stones.

The door jangled as Mason opened it and motioned for her to precede him. She stepped inside, her senses assaulted by wonderful smells.

Yes, she liked this store. She moved forward to a table with balls and squares—all differently colored. Picking one up, she brought it to her nose.

Nice.

She took a bite. Ugh. She spit the piece into her hand.

Mason grabbed the pretty ball from her. "You don't eat candles."

It was a good thing. The candle didn't taste nearly as good as it smelled.

"What is it for, Mason?"

"A candle. You know, you light it." He frowned. "But you don't eat it."

"And the fragrance?"

He brought it to his nose, then looked at the bottom. "Vanilla."

"At least it smells wonderful. We don't have candles in . . . in Sweden." When he looked at her rather oddly, she knew she'd blundered. "At least, not this nice or that smell so wonderful."

"I thought I heard the bell," a woman said as she came from the back carrying a box.

Mason's attention turned toward this new person, and Mala was able to breathe a little easier. She would really have to watch what she said.

Mason hadn't believed her when she'd told him that she was from another planet. She certainly didn't want him to think she'd lost her mind and lock her away. Barton would be terribly upset if she didn't return.

As the young woman came closer, Mala stared. They looked to be the same in years, almost the same height, but her hair was a bright red and her eyes a pretty green. And she had funny little dots on her nose. When she smiled, her face lit up.

"I was afraid it was one of those pesky reporters. Did you hear one of those idiots tried to get a picture of Jimmy's bull? Craziest thing I've ever heard."

Mala stepped around Mason and the woman came to an abrupt halt, her words stumbling to a stop.

"Oh, I didn't know you had someone with you or I wouldn't have been talking nonstop." She set the box on a counter, and looked at Mason with questions in her eyes. Before he could answer them, she turned to Mala. "I'm Carol Dobson. Welcome to my store." She stuck her hand out.

Now what was she supposed to do? She hesitated, then handed Mason the piece of candle she'd spit out, and clasped the woman's hand in hers.

Carol pumped it up and down. This was fun. She pumped back. What a nice way to greet someone. She wondered if everyone did this. Mason hadn't, nor the nurse nor the doctor. They were certainly missing something enjoyable.

"This is Mala," Mason explained. "She was in an accident and needs some clothes. If you can start me a bill, I'll pay it later." He looked at Mala. "Carol will take care of you and I'll be back to pick you up after I check in at the sheriff's office." He hurried out the door before she could answer.

Carol shook her head. "Men—they never stay more than five minutes in my store. I think it threatens their masculinity or something." She looked at Mala. "So, you and Mason have a thing going?"

Thing going? "I don't understand."

"Are you dating? You know, going out with each other?"

"We had sex."

Carol opened her mouth then closed it. The next time she opened her mouth, laughter spilled out. "That's what I like, someone who isn't afraid to speak her mind. You must be from up North."

"Sweden."

Carol nodded. "Ah, that explains a lot." She narrowed her eyes on Mala's forehead. "That's a nasty bump you have there. What happened?"

"I don't remember."

Carol nodded. "Amnesia." She frowned. "Mason isn't . . . uh . . . didn't take advantage of you or anything?"

Take advantage? She didn't understand what Carol was asking.

"I don't mean to be nosey or anything. It's just that I was married to a real jerk once." She shook her head. "Dumbest thing I ever did."

Mala touched the woman's arm and focused on her inner feelings. A current passed through her, and for a moment she felt the pain Carol had gone through. It ripped through her with lightning speed, leaving her trembling and weak.

"I'm so sorry this man treated you bad."

She shrugged. "Water under the bridge. But Mason, he's done okay by you?"

"Well, hell, I seduced him," she explained.

Carol laughed and Mala decided she liked the sound. In fact, she liked this Carol person. She brought a smile into the room with her. This person she'd been married to apparently hadn't appreciated her very much. A shame.

"Come on, let's go to the back before we start trying to find you something to wear. I have a pot of Cranberry Crème tea steeping."

Mala followed behind her. "Do you have chocolate?"

"No, but I have some banana bread that's out of this world."

Maybe she'd been wrong and humans were traveling to other planets. Although she had never heard of any worlds that sold this banana bread. As she stepped behind the curtain, more smells assaulted her senses. Yes, Earth was a nice experience. She wondered if the people appreciated all that they had.

An hour and a half later Mala had eaten her fill of the wonderful bread and tried on nearly everything in the store, choosing several outfits.

And she missed Mason.

What was he doing? Did he miss her? Was he

thinking about having sex again? This wasn't good. She had too much time to think about him. Especially now, since a couple of ladies had come into the store and Carol was busy with them.

She glanced out the window. More crafts of different shapes, colors and sizes traveled down the road. She'd come to the conclusion none of them could fly.

There were people strolling down the concrete walkway. All shapes and sizes there, too. Some as old as the Elders and the healer she'd met the other night. Odd, no one seemed deferential toward them. Did they not realize the wisdom these Elders could impart? What a pity.

So, was she going to tell Barton she'd looked at Earth from a window, or was she going to explore it?

She squared her shoulders. Not if she had anything to say about it. She set her packages by the counter and pushed on the door, smiling because she'd remembered, and stepped to the concrete walkway.

After all, how much trouble could she get into?

The store next door was called The Blooming Idiot, whatever that meant. But as soon as she opened the door, her senses were again assaulted with wonderful fragrances. She closed her eyes and inhaled.

"Hello, can I help you?" The woman was very thin, her smile almost too big for her tiny face.

Mala stuck her hand forward and the woman took it, pumping it up and down just as Carol had done. Yes, she liked this custom very much. "I'm Mala from Sweden."

"I'm Modine. Nasty bump you have there."

She liked the voice of this Elder. It was warm and full of laughter. "I was in an accident. I'm staying with Mason."

"Oh, you know Mason . . . the sheriff."

"Yes," she smiled. "We had sex and it was wonderful."

The older woman's mouth dropped open, then she chuckled. "Well, I'd heard he was a stud, but I've never had an actual first-hand accounting. So, are you wanting some flowers?" she asked.

"Flowers. They're beautiful." She walked toward some pretty red ones and lightly touched one. "Oh, it's so soft," she breathed.

"They don't have roses in Sweden?"

She had to remember to be careful what she said. "The weather does not permit it where I live." She held her breath, hoping her answer would suffice.

After a moment, Modine nodded. "Lots of snow there, I suppose. Well, come on to the back. I was doing an arrangement for Billy Mack. He made that fiancée of his mad again so he's trying to make it up to her with flowers. I think I might have enough left over to make a little nosegay."

Twenty minutes later, Mala left the store, her nose pressed into the little bouquet of baby pink roses and baby's breath. It smelled as wonderful as it looked.

She liked this town very much. Her gaze wandered to the next store. "Anna's Sweet Delights," Mala read. It sounded nice. So far she'd had very pleasant experiences in the stores. She pushed on the door and went inside.

She hadn't thought Earth could get any better. This was much superior to the flowers. A place where they actually created the wonderful chocolate.

"The look on your face is probably the highest compliment I've received all week," a woman behind the counter said as she poked her head above the glass and smiled.

Mala hadn't seen her. She was too entranced looking at all the sweets temptingly displayed in glass cases. "Is it . . ." she thought back over some of the words in the English language. "Edible. Is it edible?"

The woman laughed. "My customers seem to think it's pretty good. At least, I haven't killed off anyone yet. But you be the judge."

She opened a sliding door, reached inside with a thin sheet of paper, brought out a small sample of something chocolate, and handed it to her.

"That fudge is from my grandmother's recipe. I make it myself the same way she did—in an iron skillet. When it's done, I pour it onto a platter and let it cool. You can't beat the old recipes. Try it." She nodded toward Mala.

Fudge, chocolate . . . her pulse began to race. She took a small bite at first, then popped the rest in her mouth. It was so good. Closing her eyes, she let the explosion of flavor coat her taste buds.

Something popped. She opened her eyes.

"There goes a light bulb. Squirrels in another transformer again. A real pain this year." She returned her attention to Mala. "So do you like the fudge?"

"It actually might be better than sex with Mason."

"Uh, excuse me?"

She stared at the other woman. "I'm staying with Mason. We used chocolate syrup when we had sex last night but this chocolate tastes much better."

The woman grinned. "You're not from around here, are you?"

"Sweden."

"Ahh, that explains it."

"Can I have more?"

"Well, Mason does have an account." She paused, then smiled. "I'm sure it'll be all right."

Mala strolled out of the store, nosegay in one hand, a sack of candy in the other and her mouth full. She had to cross the street to get to the next store. One car honked as she stepped onto the road. She smiled and continued across. Humans were very nice people.

She waved back with one finger in the air, just like the woman had done, but she was afraid the navigator of the craft didn't see her in time.

The next store was shadowy, the windows a little dirty. She read the white lettering: ADVENTURES IN THE UNEXPLAINED. OWNER AND OPERATOR, HARLAN GENTRY. It sounded interesting. She pushed the door open and stepped inside the dingy, dusty store.

Her nose wrinkled when the musty smell attacked her nostrils. As she stepped around a corner, she came face to face with a huge beast well over eight feet tall. She almost dropped her bundles.

"You lookin' for something in particular?" A medium-built man stepped from behind the very large animal.

"Are you Harlan?"

"The one and only."

Rather than answer, she pointed toward the beast that she'd figured out wasn't real. "It's very scary."

"This is Old Grizzly." He proudly patted Old Grizzly, stirring up a cloud of dust. "I bought him at a traders' market." He chuckled. "Stole him, actually. We've been buddies for a long time now."

Yes, she could tell the animal had been around for quite some time. Not only was the dust a good indication, but the odor was quite strong.

There was so much to see that the smelly grizzly didn't matter. A lot of things captured her interest.

Her gaze landed on a jar. "Oh, what's that?"

Harlan's chest puffed out as he walked over and picked up the container. "Now this is Abigail and

Ebenezer. Bet you've never seen a pickled two-headed snake."

Mesmerized, she shook her head and looked closer. Fascinating.

"You aren't from around here, are you?"

She looked at Harlan through the glass. His face was odd-looking. Could he change his appearance? She straightened and saw that it was only the jar that had distorted his image.

"No, from Sweden."

"Who you stayin' with?" His forehead puckered. "I didn't know anyone had kin from across the water."

"Mason. I was in an accident and he's letting me stay with him."

His hands shook when he placed the jar back on the counter. "Accident?"

"Yes."

"Wasn't out by Devil's Bend, was it?"

"I don't know this place. Mason found me."

How odd that his face could turn a rosy hue, then drain of all color. Very odd.

"Talar ni . . . Swedish?"

She understood the English language because it was so similar to what was spoken on her planet, but she had no idea what Harlan had just said. She also had a feeling she might be in trouble.

Please don't let them lock me away! she silently begged.

Chapter 8

Mason's steps quickened as he hurried from store to store. When he'd left the boutique, Carol had warned him that he'd better not take advantage of Mala. Apparently Mala had left quite an impression on Carol. But Carol had known him all his life, so why would she think he would take advantage?

But then, look at what Carol's life had been like before her divorce from Scott.

Of course she would be leery of all men, and he didn't blame her. Carol's ex had been a real jerk. He'd almost wiped out the inheritance her parents had left her. After they split, she'd had enough money to buy the small boutique. She lived in the apartment above it.

So maybe Carol had reason not to trust men. Not only had Scott taken her money, but he'd played mind games. He'd told her how worthless she was as a human being. When that wasn't fun any more, he began to push her around. Mason had finally convinced her to end the marriage. She did, but by then Scott had spent most of her money. A shame.

Mason walked inside the florist shop. Modine chuckled when she saw him, but quickly covered it with a cough.

What the hell was wrong with all these people? They were looking at him as if he was from another planet or something.

"Uh . . . hi, Modine. You wouldn't happen to have seen a young woman about this high?" He held up a hand chest high. "Blondish-brown hair with beautiful turquoise eyes . . ."

"Mala was in here. Cute little thing. I fixed her a nosegay. No charge. But when you decide to make an honest woman out of her you'd better let me do the wedding arrangements."

What the hell was she talking about? Had someone spiked the water system? "Is she here or not?"

Grinning, she shook her head. "Left about twenty minutes ago."

He turned on his heel and shoved against the door. "Damn town is going crazy."

Out on the sidewalk, he bumped into one of the reporters. The glare Mason cast his way sent the man in the opposite direction.

With his hands fisted on his hips, he looked up and down the street. There were a few window shoppers. Steve and Mike, two old-timers from way back when, occupied the metal bench on the courthouse lawn as they swapped stories about the good old days.

But no Mala.

Where the hell would she have gone? He drew in a deep breath as his gaze fell on the store next door. The tempting aroma of chocolate swirled around him.

Of course. Anna's Sweet Delights. Mala seemed to have a weakness for chocolate. He stared at the storefront, momentarily lost in thought as he remembered just how much she'd liked chocolate.

A slow burn began inside him as visions of Mala rubbing her naked body against his, her breasts crushed against his chest, her . . .

"Mornin', Sheriff," Sam Jackson said as he exited the candy store, interrupting Mason's delicious mental images.

It took a few seconds for Mason to rein his thoughts in. Sam was a local farmer who liked to talk . . . and talk . . . and talk about the good old days. Maybe he would join Leroy and Bernard on the bench.

He didn't.

No, he waited patiently for Mason to return his greeting. Even though he wasn't tall, only about five feet seven inches and as skinny as a rail, there'd be no getting around him.

"Hello, Sam." But he could try. When he stepped to the side, Sam followed him.

"You look like a man on a mission."

"Yeah, you could say that." He started to push on the door to go inside the candy store, but Sam spoke again before he could escape.

"Anna tells me you've got a little gal livin' with you. Are you going to get married?"

Mason expelled a sigh of irritation. The bad thing about living in a small town was that everyone seemed to know your business and they all thought it was okay to butt their noses into it.

"She was in an accident. I'm just giving her a place to stay."

"Not what I heard." He reached in his sack and pulled out a chocolate chip cookie and took a bite. "You ever tried Anna's cookies?" He smacked his lips. "Damned tasty. I just wish my Betsy could bake cookies this good. Course, don't tell her I said that or it'd hurt her feelings."

Mason's eyes narrowed. Betsy's cooking didn't interest him. Everyone in the county knew she couldn't fix toast without burning it, but she made up for it with her sweet personality. No, he was more interested in what Sam had let slip.

"Exactly what have you heard about Mala?"

He looked thoughtful for a moment. "Well, the wife asked me to see if that dress she'd ordered from Carol's Boutique came in today, but it didn't. While I was in there I ran into Myrtle. Myrtle said . . . you know Myrtle, don't you? Married that new fella in town what come here from Wichita Falls?"

Mason took a deep breath and silently counted to ten. The man Sam spoke about had moved here ten years ago. It wouldn't do any good to rush Sam, though—but he might be able to lead him back to the original question.

"And Myrtle apparently knows something about the woman staying at my ranch?" he prodded.

"In a round-about way. You see, Carol told Myrtle you been playing more than footsies with that foreigner."

"And you believed her?"

"Not exactly, but I had to go into Modine's to order flowers for a cousin of mine that passed on." He scratched his head. "Damnedest thing I ever heard—heart attack and him a younger fella. Can't be more than seventy-four." He shook his head.

"Modine?"

For a moment he looked as if he'd forgotten where he was, then it dawned on him. "Oh, yeah, Modine. Well, she told me that young girl what's staying with you told her y'all been fooling around a bit. Mind you, I didn't really believe her."

Heat crawled up Mason's face. "And what convinced you otherwise?"

He thumbed over his shoulder. "Anna. She said that young girl bought some chocolate. Said she wanted to smear . . ."

"Okay, I get the picture." His face already felt like a furnace heating up. Did they actually talk openly about their love lives in Sweden? He'd better find Mala fast before she created any more havoc in his life. How the hell did he get himself into these fixes?

"Betsy and I ain't never gotten what you might say kinky," Sam continued. "Been married fifty-three years, but she might enjoy . . ."

"Is Mala inside?" Mason nodded toward the store.

"Nope, I didn't have the pleasure of meeting her. Sure would like to, though."

Before Sam could say anything else, Mason quickly thanked him and hurried away. At the corner, he looked around, wondering where she might have gone next. Damn, all of Washboard was going to be laughing at him if he didn't find her soon. Hell, from what Sam had said, they probably already were laughing.

He scanned the stores, sweeping past Harlan's, then jerking back to it. The blood in his veins ran icy cold. The way his luck was running today, she was in there telling him she was an alien or something else equally bizarre. He started toward the store with determined strides.

Before Mala had a chance to answer Harlan, the bell over the door jangled. She turned.

Mason.

Relief washed over her. She wouldn't have to answer Harlan, after all.

But then again, Mason didn't look especially happy. His forehead was wrinkled and he wore a very serious expression. Maybe she should offer him a piece of chocolate.

But she only had one left, besides the chocolate fudge sauce and the caramel sauce. To share or not to share? Earth was full of hard decisions. She brightened—the store was near and they could get more.

"Would you like a piece of candy?" She held the bag toward him.

"Not now. We need to get back to the ranch." He took her arm and started to pull her away.

"Me and your *new* friend have been talking," Harlan said before they could get out the door. "Said she's from Sweden, but she doesn't speak the language. I find that a little odd, don't you?" He scratched his whiskered chin, his eyes narrowing on the two of them.

Oops.

"Actually, she's from the northern part of Sweden and speaks Finnish rather than Swedish."

Harlan was right on their heels as he followed them toward the door. "Awful strange that I saw that UFO crash, then this girl shows up."

Mason abruptly turned. "No, I don't find it strange, Harlan. What I find strange is a two-headed snake, rag publications that report Elvis is alive, and a store owner that is old enough to know better than to believe in things that go bump in the night."

"She's an alien, ain't she?" he spoke with awe.

Mason muttered something under his breath that wasn't in her vocabulary. She would get Mason to explain what it meant later. Right now, she didn't think he looked as if he wanted to talk about much of anything. Especially the fact she *was* from another planet.

With his hand still clasped lightly on her arm, he jerked the door open, the bell wildly tinkling as he aimed her outside onto the sidewalk.

"Mason . . ."

"Later."

Was he angry? If only they had smoothies on this planet. But then, if they did, she wouldn't be here.

This was what she was looking for. Real emotion. Not something that could be immediately suppressed with a tonic.

Tingles swept over her.

She wanted to be sure. "Are you mad, Mason?"

"No."

Her forehead puckered. "You look mad."

He stopped in front of his Jeep. "Get in." He strode to the driver's side and opened the door as she slid onto her seat, then shut the door.

"My packages are at Carol's. I'll need to change my clothes eventually."

He muttered something under his breath that she didn't understand and got out of the Jeep. He strode inside Carol's Boutique. A few seconds later he came back, tossing her packages in the back.

She thought he might be lying about not being mad. He definitely had the look of someone who was angry. She continued to study his face on the drive back to the ranch. His jaw twitched. A little jerking motion. And his hands gripped the steering column so tightly that his knuckles turned white.

He pulled in front of his house and turned the key that shut off his craft, but he didn't say anything. Just reached in the back for her packages and got out. He didn't even speak to Blue.

She patted the dog as she stepped out, then followed behind Mason, noting the stiff set of his shoulders and the long steps he took.

This was all very interesting. She wondered how long he would stay mad. Not long, she hoped. Mala wanted to try the caramel syrup.

She followed him inside, reaching into her bag for the last piece of fudge. She was just about to take a bite when Mason turned on his heel, hands braced on his hips, and glared at her. Maybe this wasn't a good time to indulge. She slipped the chocolate back into the sack.

"Did you have something on your mind, Mason?"

"You're not from Sweden, are you?"

She shook her head.

"Then why the hell did you tell me you were?"

"I didn't, you did."

"Then where are you from? And no lies. I'm not buying your story that you don't remember, either."

She closed her mouth. Then what should she tell him? Since eating her chocolate or dousing him with yummy syrup looked to be out of the question, she might as well try to explain the truth again and hope he didn't lock her away.

"I'm from Nerak."

He raised an eyebrow. Her eyes wandered down to his mouth and her mind was suddenly filled with visions of what he could do with his mouth. She dropped her bag of goodies on the lounging sofa and sauntered toward him.

"And just where is Nerak?"

He didn't look nearly as fierce as he had when they first got here. She trailed her hand over his shirt, circling where his nipple would be. She felt it tighten beneath her touch.

He grabbed her hand. "No, I'm going to get to the bottom of this if it's the last thing I do. What country is Nerak in?"

"Make love to me and I'll explain everything." She rubbed her body against his, felt his erection.

"No . . ." He cleared his throat and stepped away from her. "First, tell me about Nerak."

She sighed, knowing there was no way around it. Crossing her arms in front of her, she leaned against the back of the lounging sofa. He'd give her no peace until she convinced him of who she was.

"Nerak is Nerak. There are no other countries where I live." She held her breath.

"It's not even close to Sweden?"

She shook her head.

His face turned a little gray. "You're defecting, aren't you?"

She straightened. "You think I'm defective?" Her bottom lip trembled.

He gathered her in his arms. "No, sweetheart. I don't think there's a thing wrong with you. I meant, defecting. As in running away from your country. Communism. Is that it?"

"Communism?"

"Do you have leaders that tell you what to do rather than a president who is elected?"

"Yes." She nodded her head. The Elders took care of them. They wanted for nothing.

He expelled a breath. "I'm so sorry. But don't worry. I'll see what I can do so you won't be deported." He kissed the top of her head. "But you have to promise me one thing."

"What is that?"

"You can't talk to strangers about what we do in the bedroom."

"Are you ashamed you made love with me?" She looked up into his face.

"No, but well, we just don't talk about sex in public. At least, not in Washboard, Texas."

"Okay, but they seemed very interested."

His chest rumbled. "Lord, I'm sure they did."

There was another rumble, but this time from outside.

"Now who could that be?" he said absently as he moved away from her. He went to the door and stared out. "UPS? I haven't ordered anything."

"Oh! One day delivery." She clapped her hands.

"Huh?"

"I ordered from your computer."

"How? You don't have any money."

"It was easy. You have a PayPlan account that let me order anything I wanted." She made a motion of punching with her finger. "One little click."

The big brown craft lumbered to a stop and a cute man in a brown top and short pants stepped out and went to the back of the craft. Very nice legs, but she didn't feel the same yearning for this man as she did for Mason. Odd.

"Exactly how much did you spend?"

"Three thousand two hundred forty-three American dollars and twenty-two cents."

He choked.

"Are you okay?"

"What the hell did you spend it on?"

She watched the man come toward them rolling a stack of boxes, and her thighs trembled when she thought about the contents.

Mala took a deep breath. "Raunchy Romps for Adults."

"Well, hell," he moaned.

Chapter 9

What was he going to do with her? Mason thought as he signed for the boxes.

The UPS guy grinned as he rolled them past the door Mason held open, set them in the living room, then wiggled his dolly out from under the bottom box. "Y'all have a . . . nice day." He tipped his cap.

Mason glanced at the boxes. RAUNCHY ROMPS FOR ADULTS was emblazoned across the top box in big bold red letters. He ran a hand through his hair, closed his eyes and counted to ten. It didn't help.

"Mason, hurry so we can see what's inside," Mala said as she practically jumped up and down.

Damn, she looked liked a kid at Christmas. When she began trying to rip the tape, he moved her to the side and slipped his knife from his pocket before she could hurt herself. He opened the first box and she plowed into it, Styrofoam peanuts going everywhere. He just shook his head and opened the other eight. From the look of excitement on her face, he didn't think he had much choice except to open them. Damn, what had he gotten himself into?

When he looked up from splitting open the last box, she was holding a candle to her nose, her eyes closed as she inhaled. He could only stare. Damn, she was sexy as hell. Her hair had a coppery sheen, her features were delicate. He wanted to take her into his arms and kiss her. Hell, if the truth be known he wanted to do a lot more than that.

"Another candle." She brought it to her nose, then looked at him. "It smells nice."

She picked up a piece of paper and read. "It says it releases a sensual aroma therapy to enhance the sexual experience. Can we light it?"

How could he resist her when she looked at him like that?

"It's pretty, too," she said.

He took the holder off the floor beside her and placed it on top of the coffee table, setting the candle inside, then lighting it. The space around him filled with the scent of fresh peaches. He had to admit, the fragrance was nice.

Would it actually enhance any sexual experience he had with her? He had a feeling every time they had sex it would be a unique experience.

That wasn't a bad thing.

When he turned back around, she was holding up a wicked-looking black cord with a metal triangle at the top. He had no idea what the hell it was, and he wasn't real sure he wanted to know.

But curiosity got the better of him. "What's that?"

She looked at the paper. "A love swing."

He couldn't help it. He began to laugh.

Her bottom lip stuck out.

"Ah, I'm sorry if I hurt your feelings . . ." He waved his arm. "But we don't need all this."

"You don't like my toys?"

Now he'd really hurt her feelings, but he couldn't quite see himself swinging from that contraption, she lying spread-eagled on the bed, and he plowing into her.

Maybe they could use a few of the things she'd ordered, though. They were paid for, he thought with more than a little derision.

"I've never used toys," he told her. "It's just a little new to me." That seemed to satisfy her—for now.

The phone rang, drawing his attention. He leaned over and picked it up.

"We have a situation, Sheriff," Francine told him almost as soon as he answered. "Sam has one of those reporters locked in his storm cellar. Caught him snooping around. Clayton can't respond to the call because he's out on a missing cattle report."

Two more days and Bill would be back from vacation, then he wouldn't be quite so busy. Damn, this wasn't how he wanted to spend his evening. He sighed.

"I'll take care of the reporter. Call Sam and tell him I'll be there in a bit."

He replaced the phone and looked at the pile of toys Mala had unboxed.

Complications. What was he? A complication magnet? He was beginning to think so.

"I have to take care of some business," he explained. "It shouldn't take me long."

She looked up and smiled. He couldn't resist. He scooped her under her arms and pulled her to her feet. His lips closed over hers as her arms wrapped around his neck. She tasted sweet . . . and oh so hot.

He didn't need toys, but if it made her happy, he'd agree to just about anything. Strange that a woman he'd just met would capture his attention, his senses, so quickly. He moved out of her arms, staring into her face. She had that sleepy, passion-filled look in her eyes. He was tempted to call Sam and tell him he wouldn't be there for a few hours.

"Hurry," she breathed.

"You can count on it." He practically ran out the

front door and jumped into his Jeep, Blue right on his heels.

By the time he got to Sam's ranch, it was late afternoon. He was hungry and he was beat. It had been a long day and all he wanted to do was get back to Mala.

Just the thought of her openness regarding sex gave him a hard-on. Playing games was starting to sound intriguing. Playing them with her—priceless.

When he thought about it, not priceless at all. Damned expensive, in fact.

He pulled to a stop in Sam's driveway and climbed out. Blue jumped out and trailed beside him until the dog spotted a jackrabbit and took off after it. The rabbit didn't know Blue only wanted to play. The dog would never hurt anything.

"I got him in the cellar," Sam said as he came out of his house, screen door slamming behind him.

"Did he do any damage?"

"Nah, just scared Betsy a might. I should make him eat one of her meals. That would fix his wagon."

Mason chuckled as they walked around the side of the house. Sam had one of Betsy's brooms stuck through the door handle of the cellar so the reporter couldn't escape. He guessed that would work for a lock as well as anything. He leaned over and removed it, then opened the door.

A short, skinny reporter came flying out, his suit covered in a thick layer of dust, cobwebs clinging to his ears, and his face pasty white.

"He's crazy!" The reporter scurried behind Mason, slapping at his clothes. "I want to file a complaint. Kidnapping! Unlawful restraint or whatever the hell you call it." His voice rose an octave with each word out of his mouth.

Mason pushed his hat higher on his forehead. "Would that be after Sam files his complaint against you for trespassing?"

"I was only looking around," he whined.

"Trespassing carries a pretty long sentence around these parts. You're looking at a few years, unless you get Judge Wilkins. He doesn't take too kindly to strangers."

"Oh, God." The reporter's face went a shade paler.

"Sam, you going to file a formal complaint? If so, I'll lock him up." He winked at Sam.

Sam rubbed his jaw. "Well, he did scare Betsy. I don't know . . ."

"Please, Mister. I swear I'll never come on your property again." The man's eyes were wide with fright.

Sam narrowed his. "I reckon not—this time, but come around again and I might just salt a few shotgun shells. Now git!" Sam stomped his foot on the ground.

The reporter didn't let any grass grow under his feet. Sam and Mason chuckled as they watched him crash through the brush and between the trees. A few minutes later they heard a vehicle start and peel away like the hounds from hell were after him.

"Thanks for coming out, Sheriff. That ought to stop them reporters from bothering me."

"No problem, Sam." He whistled for Blue and started back toward his Jeep, but before he could leave, Betsy came to the porch carrying a plate of cookies covered with plastic wrap.

She reminded him a lot of his grandmother— from the blue flowered dress to the white apron. Her gray hair was pulled back into a bun. She was plump and always wore a smile. The only thing different was that his grandmother was the best cook in the county.

"I just thought you might want something to take

home with you. Chocolate chip," she told him, her smile beaming. "I added some of the pecans Sam shelled for me."

"Now Betsy, you didn't have to do that," Mason told her. She *really* shouldn't have done that. The last time he'd eaten something she'd made he'd nearly broken a tooth.

"Try one." She shoved the plate toward him and he had no choice except to take it.

He looked at Sam, but Sam refused to meet his eyes. Coward. When he looked at Betsy, he could see she was waiting expectantly for him to sample her cooking.

Mason hoped his smile came off cheerful rather than slightly ill as he slipped his hand beneath the plastic to get a cookie. They were still a little warm. That was a good sign . . . wasn't it?

He took a bite. Oh, damn, they were awful. Had she added vinegar? At least he hoped it was vinegar and not arsenic. "You make the best cookies," he said around his chewing. The only good thing he could say about them was they weren't burnt. Burnt might actually have been better though. He could've handled charred a lot more than this godawful shake-in-your-boots bitterness.

"And I have plenty chocolate chips left." She winked at Sam. "I'm going to melt them in the microwave in a baggie."

She looked at Mason. "Sam told me what your girlfriend and you did with the chocolate. It sounds like fun." She turned and waltzed back inside the house.

Mason's brain couldn't quite make the transition from grandmother to the worst cookies he'd ever had the misfortune to eat, then to her and Sam in the bedroom. He coughed and began to choke. Sam pounded him on the back until the chunk of cookie dislodged from his throat.

"You okay?"

"Yeah, fine," he croaked.

"Are they really the best cookies you ever ate?" Sam asked with raised eyebrows.

"No."

Sam nodded. "Thought as much. She has a big heart, though."

"Good thing."

"And she's one hot babe under the sheets. I hate to cut this conversation short, but you know how it is when you've got a woman wanting you really bad. See ya later, son." He took the steps two at a time and hurried inside.

"Blue!" The sooner he left the better. "Blue!" He jogged to the Jeep and climbed inside, setting the plate of cookies in the passenger seat. Blue came at a run, jumping in the back as Mason started the engine.

Don't think about Sam and Betsy, he told himself. Just get the vision out of your mind. He drew in a deep shuddering breath, grabbed the bottle of water he kept in the Jeep, rinsed his mouth and spat out the window. "Ugh!"

Leaning across the seat, he grabbed a pack of Juicy Fruit and popped a piece of gum in his mouth. Okay, that was better. The taste was gone. All he had to do now was think about Mala. Visualize her waiting for him . . . and not . . . Yeah, just think about Mala.

He headed away from Sam's, his foot heavy on the gas pedal. Maybe Francine wouldn't bother him anymore tonight with *situations*. God help her if she did.

Glancing at his watch, he saw it was almost six. He wondered what Mala was doing right now. Just thinking about her and all her sex toys made his pulse pound in anticipation. He couldn't seem to get home quick enough. He'd never wanted a woman as badly as he wanted her right now.

But as he drove over the cattle guard and down the road, the house looked dark. Had she left? Maybe decided it was time to move on? Just the thought left an emptiness inside him that felt awfully uncomfortable.

He pulled to a stop and killed the engine. His steps were heavy as he trudged toward the house, but as he stepped on the porch he could see the soft glow from candles. A slow smile curved his lips.

She met him at the door wearing a tight-fitting, black lace and silk teddy that had cutouts for her breasts and at the juncture of her legs. Fishnet hose and black leather, thigh-high, four-inch boots completed her outfit.

"You look . . . nice tonight." Nice? Yeah. That was an understatement!

He didn't stop walking forward until he was standing right in front of her. His gaze slowly roamed over her luscious body, taking in the fact her nipples were tight little nubs. She arched toward him as if begging him to touch them, to take them in his mouth.

If she wanted to play games he was more than willing. He ran his hand through her hair, tangling in the long, golden-brown tresses.

"In fact, you look damned sexy." He began to massage the back of her neck. "One would think you wanted me to make love to you."

She moaned.

Her eyes were half-closed, her breath already coming out in tiny little puffs. He leaned down, his tongue scraping over her lips. She opened her mouth to accept his kiss, but he moved to her ear instead, pushing her hair out of his way.

"You have the sexiest little ears I've ever seen on a woman." He bit her lobe, gently tugging on the tender flesh before moving his mouth and slipping his tongue inside her ear. Damn, even her ears tasted sweet.

She grasped his shoulders, her crotch rubbing against his thigh, seeking more. He moved to her mouth, tasting her as his tongue delved inside. She squirmed against him. He'd have her doing that and a whole lot more before this night was over. He planned to fulfill every one of her desires . . . and then some. And he was going to have a hell of a good time doing it.

He lost himself in her kiss, the heat of her body nearly consuming him. She tasted sweet. A lot like chocolate. He smiled to himself as he stroked her tongue, then sucked. Her lips crushed against his.

She ended the kiss, pushing away from him, dragging his shirt off as she did. He hadn't realized she'd unbuttoned it. Maybe she had the power to affect him more than he thought.

"I like you naked," she said in a husky whisper, tossing his shirt on the back of the sofa.

Like a sexy black cat, she stepped toward him again, flicking her tongue over his nipples. He sucked in a deep breath.

He didn't know how much more of her teasing he could stand. He undid his belt and tossed his holster and gun on the couch before undoing his pants. While he took off his clothes, he watched her.

"I wasn't sure what these were for," she said, her voice husky. "They're called nipple clamps." Her gaze met his.

When his head began to swim, he realized he should breathe. He quickly inhaled a deep shuddering breath.

She fastened the clamps in place. "They hurt a little

at first, but when you roll the dial they begin to heat and vibrate." She arched forward, her teeth biting her bottom lip. "And it feels so nice. Tingles go all the way down to here." Her hands slid downward, grasping her thighs.

The lights flickered, but he paid little attention.

When she touched between her legs, he almost fell forward, then remembered to kick out of his pants and briefs. Just the sight of the clamps on her nipples nearly sent him over the edge.

Damn, she might come from a Communist country, but she didn't have any fears when it came to sex.

She raised her head, undoing the clamps and tossing them to the side. "I'm wet and oh so hot. I want you between my legs licking and kissing me." She met his gaze. "Will you give me pleasure, Mason?"

Before she could taunt him more with her sex talk, he scooped her up and carried her to the big overstuffed chair. He sat her down on the cushion and spread her legs wide, dropping down in front of her.

She moaned, arching forward. He wanted to cover her with his mouth more than anything, but instead he scooted closer, running his tongue over her hard nipples, scraping his teeth across first one, then the other. He sucked on each of her breasts while he lightly caressed the insides of her thighs. Coming close to her sex, but then moving away, teasing her, taking her a little higher with each fluttering touch of his fingers.

He straightened. For a moment he stared at her, with her legs spread. Nothing was held back from his view. "You know, you can use the nipple clamps somewhere else, too." He reached over and picked them up. "They can go here." He lightly brushed his fingers over her sensitive sex. She jumped and cried out—

letting him know she was so damn close to having an orgasm. He clamped first one then the other on her clit.

She drew in a breath that turned into a gurgle of pleasure when he turned the dial and applied heat along with a slow vibration.

"Do you like that, Mala? Is this what you want?"

"Yesssss!"

"What about this?" He lowered his head and ran his tongue over her sex. She whimpered. The vibration tickled his tongue. He inserted two fingers inside her. Damn, she was wet and so close to coming. He wasn't far off himself. He grabbed his pants and dug through the pocket until he found what he was looking for. He quickly slipped the condom on and slid her hips forward.

"Ahh, Mason, that feels so good," she cried when he entered her.

He closed his eyes and gritted his teeth, sinking deeper inside her. Hot, wet heat closed over him. Her inner muscles tightened around his erection, sucking him in farther, deeper. When he leaned forward, he could feel the vibration from the clamps.

Grabbing the box, he turned the dial higher. Her body arched forward as the vibration and heat intensified. Vaguely he heard noises coming from the kitchen, but dismissed them as he lost himself in the ecstasy her body was giving him.

He began to move inside her, slowly at first. She grabbed his buttocks and slid farther down in the chair, her heels planted on the floor.

It felt so fucking fantastic as hot tight wet heat closed in around his dick. His pace quickened. His breath came hard and fast. She cried out, her body stiffening.

The television clicked on, the noise from some sitcom filling the room.

He jerked forward, every muscle contracting as he came. His body was on fire, electrically charged, and he was flying higher than he'd ever flown. Man, this was fantastic.

He sucked in a mouthful of air and slumped forward, his head resting on the arm of the chair. This was the most incredible sex he'd ever had.

There were no words between them for a few minutes, until they'd each gotten their breathing back under control.

"Toys are good, aren't they, Mason," she said on a breathy whisper.

He chuckled. "Yes, they are, Mala."

Silence.

"I think the remote might be in the chair somewhere." He searched with his hand, couldn't find it, so reached across and punched the *off* button on the television set. When he turned back, Mala wore such a serious expression that he felt a moment of worry. Fear swept over him. He didn't think he'd like what she was about to say, but he knew she was going to say it anyway.

"I don't think it will be easy if I have to leave you." Her voice cracked. She nibbled her bottom lip as tears filled her eyes.

Cold chills washed over him in waves. "I won't let you leave me." He gathered her in his arms and held her close. "Not right now. Not until we know what there is between us."

"I might not have a choice."

"I won't let anyone take you away from me."

"There are things you don't know. Things you don't want to see."

He pulled back and looked deep into her eyes. "I know everything I need to know."

She wrapped her arms around him and held on tightly. "I don't want to leave, either," she whispered against his neck, "but I'm afraid they will come looking for me."

"It doesn't matter who comes. I won't let you go back to Nerak."

He hadn't known her long, but he knew there was something between them that no one would rip apart. Not any person or country. Whatever he had to do, he would do it, but he refused to let her go.

Chapter 10

Mala lay curled next to Mason. After they'd stood beneath the waterfall in the bathing room they'd eaten a delicious meal that Mason called store-bought pizza, then he'd carried her to bed. Slowly he'd stripped her, then snuggled her naked body next to his before pulling the cover around them and tucking them both in.

It felt so right, so perfect, to lie next to the warmth of his body, as if this was where she was meant to be. But she'd promised Barton she'd only stay a few days. Tomorrow she would go to her craft and repair any damage.

Someone would eventually discover a country called Nerak didn't exist on Earth. If she stayed and anyone found out she was from another planet, they would lock her up. Hadn't Mason said as much? What would they do to him for harboring an alien? Her heart skipped a beat. No, she wouldn't let any harm come to him. She'd leave before that ever happened, no matter how much pain it caused her.

She wrapped her arms tighter around him and closed her eyes, willing her bad thoughts away. Tonight, she would believe what they had could last forever.

Still, it was much later before she fell asleep.

The next morning she woke again to the smell of

food. She pulled Mason's pillow close and snuggled against it, listening to the sounds coming from the kitchen. The rattle of pots and pans, bacon sizzling in an iron skillet.

After a few minutes she wanted to do more than listen to Mason moving around. She needed to see him, to have him hold her close. This might be her last day with him. She stifled the urge to let her tears fall. She would be strong.

Pushing the covers to the side, she went to the bathroom. This morning she didn't savor the water as she stood beneath the spray. She was in a hurry.

She pulled on the clothes she'd gotten from the boutique: jeans and knit top. After running a brush through her hair she padded softly to the kitchen. Mason stood at the stove just like yesterday, frying bacon. The smell drifted to her nose, she inhaled, her stomach rumbled. She loved bacon. But then, she'd discovered she pretty much loved all food. Yes, food was good.

As if sensing he wasn't alone, Mason turned . . . and smiled. Tingles of pleasure ran up and down her spine. She liked when he smiled. It made her feel strange, but in a good way.

"Are you hungry?"

She nodded.

He turned back to his cooking, scooped up the crispy brown bacon and placed it on a plate. The table was already set so she took her usual seat.

"I thought I'd stay home today. Clayton, my lead deputy, can handle anything that comes up, and if he can't I'll have my radio with me. I thought you might want to see more of the ranch." He placed the plate of bacon on the table next to the eggs and pulled out the chair across from her.

Would a few more hours make that much difference? Her gaze fell on him and slowly slid down. His shirt was unbuttoned, hanging open. His jeans rode low on his hips. Her mouth watered. How much difference could a few hours make?

"I'd like that," she told him.

"Have you ever ridden a horse?"

Like the creature he'd been riding that first night? She'd never really been afraid of anything, but right at this moment she wasn't too sure about climbing onto the back of an animal she knew nothing about.

She shook her head, hoping it wouldn't be the end of their day together.

"Don't worry. I'll show you. You can ride Shasta. She's a really gentle mare that doesn't spook easily."

"If you say I won't come to harm, then I'll trust you, Mason."

But she didn't feel nearly as trusting an hour later as she followed him into the dimly lit barn.

A horse whinnied.

She jumped, then cleared her throat and gathered her courage. She *had* said she didn't want to just look through a window but preferred to experience what Earth had to offer. Still . . .

"Well, hell, it looks pretty . . . uh . . . big," she mumbled, eyeing the creature.

He chuckled as he reached for a harness of sorts. "I felt the same way the first time I climbed on a horse. It's a little scary in the beginning, but once you get used to it you'll love riding. There's nothing quite like climbing on a horse early in the morning, breathing in the fresh air."

She wasn't so sure. In fact, she thought she could breathe quite well without climbing to greater heights, but Mason hadn't seemed nervous when she'd seen him on top of his beast, so maybe it wouldn't be all that bad. Just in case, she needed a little more assurance.

"Will you swear on promise stones that the beast, I mean horse, won't throw me off?" Her gaze never left the one he'd called Shasta as she asked her question. She didn't think this was such a very good idea.

"Promise stones?"

Oops.

She took a deep breath. "In my country if we swear on promise stones then we do our best not to break that promise." She watched him closely, waiting to see what he would say.

He nodded. "Then I swear on your promise stones that you won't come to harm riding Shasta."

She exhaled, feeling a little more relieved.

"I didn't bring a carrot or any sugar, but if you want to make friends first, you can give her a little of that hay." He pointed toward some loose yellow grass.

She reached for a handful and froze as the hay rustled. Was it alive? "Mason?"

He glanced her way as he strapped the harness in place.

"Something moved." She pointed. "Over there."

"It's probably Stripes."

"Stripes?"

"Yeah, she's just a barn cat. Showed up one day and sort of adopted me and Blue. She keeps the rat population down so it's a good deal for both of us."

A few minutes later, an orange- and white-striped creature emerged. Mala's eyes grew round when the little beast curled around her leg. "Is she tame?"

"About as tame as she'll ever be." He glanced her way. "She seems taken with you. I've got a feeling she only tolerates me. But then, I've always gotten along better with dogs than I have cats."

Cat. She silently repeated the species of this small beast. Tentatively, Mala reached down and stroked the orange- and white-striped creature. A deep-throated rumble suggested the cat received pleasure from her touch. What soft fur. She squatted for a closer view.

An even smaller cat emerged from the hay, then two more, all looking just like Stripes.

"Mason, little cats."

"Kittens." He grinned and her heart fluttered inside her chest. "Looks like Stripes has a boyfriend."

The kittens crawled over and under her. What she wouldn't give to have a kitten of her own.

"You ready?"

With a sigh, she put the kittens from her, out of harm's way of the horses, and walked beside Mason as they left the barn.

"I forgot the hay for Shasta."

"I don't think you'll have anything to worry about. Animals seem to respond well to you." As if to reinforce his words, the horse nudged Mala with her nose.

She laughed, patting Shasta's sleek neck.

Mason boosted her onto the horse's back and into what he'd called a saddle, and she didn't feel quite so comfortable. She grasped the leather protrusion at the front with both hands. She was really high and she didn't care much for the feeling. Not one bit.

"Just take a slow deep breath."

If one deep breath would be good, then two or three had to be better.

"Don't hyperventilate."

She nodded and slowed her breathing. "Won't she mind having me on her back?"

"Nope. Here, pet her neck."

He took her hand and gently nudged her forward

a little. She clutched the saddle with one hand and patted the horse with the other.

"See, she's as gentle as a rabbit."

Since she didn't know what a rabbit was, she wasn't at all comforted.

She patted the horse a little more in case it really did create some kind of bonding between her and the beast. Okay, this wasn't so bad. Shasta still seemed to like her even though she was bearing Mala's weight. The horse nickered. She laughed.

"Okay?"

She nodded.

"I'm going to mount Dancer and then we'll leave."

Delicious thoughts of him mounting her instead swirled through her head, but she firmly pushed them away. Today she would explore the planet, tonight . . . she'd explore Mason and she would dwell more on leaving tomorrow . . . maybe.

"This land—it belongs to you?"

"Passed down from generation to generation. It's not a lot, around three hundred and fifty acres, but it's mine. I run a few cattle."

Three hundred and fifty acres. She knew this measurement. Land was scarce on Nerak. To own even an acre would be paradise. Her gaze roamed over the land before her. Gently rolling hills dotted the landscape along with tall, majestic trees.

"Your land is beautiful." Her eyes misted. What would it be like to live on Earth where you could have animals and space? Where you could eat chocolate and have sex whenever you liked? It was paradise.

No, she couldn't let herself think like that. There were things about her planet she enjoyed. She straightened her spine. It was just like Barton had said—on

Nerak there was no pain, no violence. It was . . . perfect.

She drew in a deep breath and concentrated on staying on top of the horse. The area looked familiar. She looked up at the sun, judging the direction they were traveling. They were going toward the place where she'd crashed.

They rode for a while in silence. Occasionally, she would steal glances at Mason. He sat on top of his horse as if he'd been born on one of the beasts.

"What does it mean to be sheriff?" she asked, suddenly curious.

He paused for a moment. "I keep the peace. At least, I try."

"People do not want to live peacefully on your . . . in your country?"

"Do they live peacefully anywhere? If you know of such a place, that's where I want to live."

For a moment hope sprang inside her. Maybe she could take him back to Nerak. Pass him off as a companion unit. As quickly as the thought formed, it fizzled away. "No, you wouldn't be happy. Sometimes perfection can become quite boring."

"It would be a nice change occasionally. Too many complications can drive a person crazy."

"But you must enjoy the challenge of not knowing what will happen as the sun rises each day."

"I did until those blasted reporters swooped down on the town."

"Reporters?"

"Yeah, they work for a sleazy magazine. Harlan convinced them Bigfoot was in the area."

"The man I met who has the two-headed snake?"

He grimaced. "That would be the one. I mean, Bigfoot, get real. There's no such thing. Now he's convinced an alien landed on my property."

She looked anywhere but at him. "And this Big-foot? What is a Bigfoot?" Much better to talk about something besides aliens.

"A mythical creature someone made up. It's sup-posed to be half man and half beast. Don't they real-ize that if something like that actually existed we'd have seen it by now?"

A shadow moved in the stand of trees they passed. She turned her attention to the movement, her eyes adjusting as she followed it. The shadow stepped into a small circle of light and she saw the beast was at least seven or eight feet tall.

He turned and looked straight at her. Then he smiled.

Odd, it looked like a Hypotrond. They'd been ex-tinct on her planet for hundreds of years, but she'd seen holograms of them. Gentle creatures that wouldn't harm anyone. Man had exploited them in their wars until finally they'd died out—just like the male population. She wondered how they'd come to be on Earth.

"I want to show you something," Mason said, draw-ing her attention back to him. When she looked back, the Hypotrond was gone. "We'll have to go on foot. I promise it's not that far."

She nodded, wondering what he wanted to show her.

He dismounted and came to help her. When his hands wrapped around her waist, warmth spread through her. She slid down his length, her feet touch-ing the ground once again, but her legs were wobbly and she faltered. He grabbed her closer to him so she wouldn't fall.

"Sometimes it's like that when you first climb off," he said close to her ear. "Better now?"

The heat from his breath warmed her all the way

down to her toes. She nodded, closing her eyes and inhaling the musky fragrance he wore, before moving away.

How could something that felt so right be so wrong? It wouldn't be good if she started to like him too much. The Elders would never permit her to stay.

"Come on."

She pushed her dark thoughts away, vowing to enjoy what time they had together and not think about the future. She followed him down a well-worn path, through the trees. Sunlight filtered through the leaves like prisms of light dancing around her. The sun cascaded warmth over her.

"It's beautiful." She stretched her hands upward, catching the light.

He turned and smiled. "You look as if you're covered in jewels."

"I like your surprise," she said, twirling around.

"This isn't it, but I think you showed *me* something new today."

He caught her hand and pulled her after him. They burst through an opening, and for a moment she couldn't breathe. All she could do was stare at the waterfall and the pond in front of her. It wasn't as large as the one in the documentary, nor the waterfall as high, but it was close enough to what she'd seen.

"It's a little cool for swimming, but I wanted you to see . . ."

She dove in.

Coldness enveloped her, but she didn't care as she surfaced beneath the waterfall. She laughed and shivered at the same time. As she shoved her hair from her face, she turned and looked at Mason. He stood on the bank with his mouth open.

"Are you crazy? The water won't be warm for at least another month."

"It's wonderful now. This is everything I imagined except I don't have a white brick. If I'd known we were going to the waterfall, I would've brought it."

"White brick?"

"It's okay. I don't need it." She raised her arms, welcoming the water. "Come join me."

"I don't think so. I have no desire to freeze half to death."

She had a feeling it wouldn't be hard to change his mind. "Are you sure? It's quite invigorating."

He grinned. "You couldn't pay me enough to dive into the water." He sat down on a boulder and crossed his legs at the ankle. "But you go ahead. Don't let me intrude on your lunacy." He laughed to soften his words.

Maybe she couldn't talk him into joining her, but she wondered if she could seduce him.

Mason picked up a small rock and rolled it around in his hand as he watched Mala. She amazed him. Never in a hundred years had he expected her to dive into the pond. A shiver sent goose bumps up and down his arms just thinking about how damned cold the water must be.

Not that he had any intention of finding out. Nope, he was quite content to watch her play . . .

He swallowed past the sudden lump in his throat as Mala raised her knit shirt over her head and tossed it away. The lacy bra barely covered her full breasts.

She cast him a saucy look and turned her back.

Suddenly the lady turns shy? He silently laughed until her hands came up behind her and she deftly unhooked her bra, letting it fall into the water and drift away.

He sat forward. This wasn't fair. Not fair at all. Crap, that water had to be nearly freezing.

She faced him, her nipples hard little nubs.

Yeah, it was cold. The crotch of his pants got a whole lot tighter, too.

With eyes closed and looking like some damned nymph, she raised her arms, the water lapping her breasts.

He stood, then walked to the edge.

She didn't look his way as her arms lowered, moving beneath the water.

But he did. He looked plenty. In fact, he couldn't have *not* looked.

A few moments later she raised her jeans out of the water, then let them drop.

This was downright cruel. How could she . . .

Her hands went below the surface again and a few moments later a bit of pink lace floated on top of the water before drifting away.

She opened her eyes and looked right at him. Their eyes met, hers filled with barely restrained passion. If her stripping wasn't invitation enough, the look on her face certainly was.

Screw it. The water didn't look that cold. He stripped out of his clothes and tossed them into a pile before diving in.

Crap!

Son-of-a-bitch!

He surfaced, spitting out water. His dick was going to be too shriveled to make love.

"See, I told you it wasn't that cold."

"Cold? It's freezing!" His teeth chattered.

"Then let me see if I can warm you." She moved closer, her naked body pressing against him.

Soft breasts. Luscious curves. Her flat abdomen

rubbing against what he thought would never rise again. Okay, he was starting to feel a little warmer already.

"See, wasn't I right?"

"You were right." He leaned down and nuzzled the side of her neck. But at the same time he eased her away from the small waterfall. He wasn't a glutton for punishment and cold showers weren't conducive to making love—and that's exactly what he wanted to do with her.

When they were in waist-deep water, he lowered his mouth to hers. Had any woman ever tasted as sweet as this one? He didn't think so. His tongue delved inside, caressing hers. Long, sensuous strokes. She pressed closer. He cupped her bottom, moving his erection over her sex. She moaned, grasping his shoulders.

He ended the kiss, sliding his mouth along her collarbone, nipping and kissing.

"Make love to me now, Mason."

"I'll have to get protection out of my pants."

She leaned back and looked him in the face. "Protection? From what?"

"Disease. Pregnancy."

Her forehead creased. "Are you diseased?"

"No, I'm not."

"Neither am I."

"But you could get pregnant."

Just before she lowered her head, he saw a deep sadness lurking in her eyes. "I cannot have a baby."

"I'm sorry."

"So am I." She raised her head, desperation lacing her words. "Make love to me, Mason. Now. I want to feel you inside me."

He hesitated before lifting her up then sliding inside her. He held her close for a moment as her body closed around his, her legs circling his waist.

Tight, wet.

Liquid heat that intensified by the second. When he looked into her face to see if she felt the same thing, she was biting her bottom lip and there was a look of pure pleasure on her face.

He began to move inside her: long, gentle strokes. The water lapped around them. He moved faster, clasping her bottom, bringing her even closer.

The air around them seemed to crackle. Mason closed his eyes, savoring the feel of her body, plunging deeper, moving faster until she grabbed his shoulders and cried out. He grunted, tightening his grip as he came inside her.

It was all he could do to move them to shallow water. He sat down hard. She kept her legs wrapped around his waist, keeping the connection between them. They sat there, snuggled in each other's arms, and Mason knew he'd never felt this blissfully happy with another human being.

He opened his eyes and happened to glance up at the sky. And frowned. There was an odd blue and pink light above them, swirling and blending colors.

What the hell?

He closed his eyes and looked again. It was still there.

"Is something wrong?" She pulled away and looked into his face.

"Yeah." He nodded toward the sky, but the lights had faded and were gone when she glanced up.

"It's beautiful," she said and sighed. "Almost as if you could reach up and touch the white puffy clouds."

Maybe he'd have the doc check his eyes the next time he was in town. Especially if he was going to start having optical illusions.

"It's cold, Mason." She burrowed in closer, her body shivering.

Now she was cold?

He'd finally gotten used to the water—sort of, and she was freezing. He wrapped his arms around her. "And what might I ask are you going to do for clothes? Yours are somewhere at the bottom of the pond. I hate to tell you this but the ride home might be a little chilly, Miss Lady Godiva."

Her bottom lip protruded prettily. "But you'll share, won't you? And who is this lady you talk about?"

He laughed. "Yeah, I'll share. And Lady Godiva rode naked through a town."

Her forehead puckered. "And why did she do that?"

"To drive all the men crazy."

She looked up at him. "And do I drive you crazy?"

He kissed her lips, holding her closer. "Yeah, and I hope you never stop."

She laughed. "Then I'll make a point of continuing to drive you crazy."

"Yeah," he sighed. "I had a feeling you would."

Chapter 11

Mala snuggled against Mason as she sat on his lap. It was much warmer sharing his horse. Shasta seemed content to follow.

"If you don't be still, Dancer is going to throw us both."

"Yes, Mason," she dutifully answered, but she didn't think he minded her moving against him so very much. He'd risen again quite nicely.

She looked down at the ground. She didn't think it would be a soft place to make love. Maybe she would be still—until they arrived home.

Besides, she was getting chilled wearing only Mason's shirt, and he couldn't be much warmer wearing only his pants and boots, but it was warmer riding together rather than being on Shasta all by herself.

She closed her eyes and let the gentle motion of Dancer's gait lull her into a feeling of peace and contentment. Earth was so much more than she'd expected. Just wait until she told Barton everything she was seeing and doing. Everything she was feeling.

Her pulse skipped a beat.

Telling Barton would mean leaving Earth . . . leaving Mason. She worried her bottom lip with her teeth and pressed closer to him. The thought of leaving caused her chest to hurt, and a strange emptiness filled her.

What if she didn't go back? Never saw Nerak again? And Barton? Her cousin Kia?

Pain like she'd never before experienced ripped through her. They were a part of her. How could she give them up?

But the thought of never seeing Mason again hurt even more.

Who was she trying to fool? The Elders would never allow her to stay. They would find her no matter where she went. Their powers were strong. And they were very wise.

She'd always respected their wisdom. She still did. Except now she didn't particularly care about what was the wise thing to do. She only knew what she felt in her heart. How could wanting to be with Mason be so wrong?

"Looks like we have more company," Mason said, his breath tickling her face. His arms tightened around her.

She raised slightly. Not the man in the big brown craft, but then she hadn't ordered anything else.

There were two men and a woman spilling out of a small white van as she and Mason approached on the horse. Emblazoned on the side were the words *The National Gossip.*

"Son-of-a-bitch. Reporters," he said under his breath. "This is all I need."

"These reporters are not good?"

"Not in the least."

They rode up to the house and Mason climbed off Dancer then helped her down.

"You're on private property. I'll ask nicely that you leave. The next time I ask, I won't be smiling."

Mala didn't think it would be prudent to tell him he wasn't smiling now.

The only woman in the group stepped forward with a predatory gleam in her eye. "We have every right to be here. "I'm Alice and this is Aaron." She nodded to a younger man. "And the other one is Perry." She didn't even look at the older man she'd just introduced, as if he might be beneath her.

"Is this the alien? What planet did you come from? Is it in this galaxy?" Perry asked,

They pressed closer, clasping tablets of paper, pencils hovering as they waited for her to speak. Mason stiffened beside her. She didn't think she liked the way they were badgering her, but she'd been taught force was never the answer. She was afraid force was exactly what Mason was thinking.

She stepped away from the safety of his arms. "Another planet?" Her words were softly spoken. "Do I look like I've come from another planet?"

"Well, no . . ." Perry said. He had a dusting of gray at the temples, but he didn't appear as wise as one of the Elders. She didn't think she liked the way he was ogling her, either. As if he wanted to gobble her right up.

Their gazes connected. He finally drew his eyes away from her and looked down at the paper he grasped in his hands. His face turned a bright red.

"I . . . uh . . ." He cleared his throat.

"Where are you from . . . Miss?" Alice asked. Tall, with dark hair and wearing a hard edge, she pushed past the younger man and Perry. Her gaze didn't waver. Mala didn't like her. She couldn't say why exactly, but there was something mean about her.

Mason stepped closer, putting his arm around Mala's shoulders. "Like I said, you're on private property, and since you're speaking to the sheriff it might be wise to turn around, climb in your vehicle, and leave. Do I make myself clear?"

"Awful evasive for a man who has nothing to hide," Alice said, then added, "And . . . woman?"

"It's okay, Mason. I understand their curiosity." She directed her comments to the older man, not liking the predatory gleam in Alice's eyes or the younger man's shifty glances toward her and Mason. Perry was the least of the three evils.

Her gaze rested on each one of them, until she knew she had their full attention. She didn't want to take a chance they would discover she was an alien or that Mason would somehow be blamed since she was staying with him. Fear for his safety trembled inside her. She was about to do something she found distasteful.

She was going to lie, but it seemed she'd been doing that a lot since coming to Earth.

She raised an imperious eyebrow. "Do I *look* like an alien? I mean, really. Do you see two heads? Four arms, three legs?" When she swept her arm down her body, she noticed the two men's gazes lingered far longer than necessary on her legs. Mason's shirt just scraped the middle of her thighs. She almost reached to tug it down a little, but shrugged away the uneasy feeling. She wouldn't give them the satisfaction.

"Looking human doesn't necessarily make you human," Alice said, her eyes narrowing. "Maybe you're here to discover something about Earth so you can destroy it."

Mala chuckled, even though she could barely breathe past her fear. She forced her gaze to drift over the men and planted her hands on her hips. The shirt she wore raised by a couple of inches.

"I'm a woman," she began in a fair imitation of the

woman on the sexy television show. "—who's just had the best sex she's ever experienced in her whole life. Right out in the open, beneath the trees. Right after a dip in the pond." She raised her hand and ran the tip of one finger over the smooth surface of the top button on her shirt. "And we were quite naked when we were swimming. You see, Mason is only trying to protect me. It's not good sometimes to . . . talk about one's sexual adventures."

"Maybe we were wrong," Perry sputtered, his face an even deeper shade of red. "Come on." He dragged on the other man's arm as he turned toward their craft. "Alice, we're leaving."

She stood her ground. "There's something strange going on here. I feel it in my bones. Call it gut instinct, but you're not from Earth."

Mason tucked Mala behind him. "Call it whatever the hell you want, lady, but my gut is never wrong either, and it tells me that if you don't have yourself back in that van within the next minute you'll find yourself in jail sleeping on a hard-ass cot tonight. Now, which is it going to be?"

"You might have fooled the men," she directed her sneer at Mala. "But not me. I don't work on testosterone and I'll be watching and listening." She spun on her heel and tromped to the van. The door slammed shut after she climbed inside. Dust swirled behind them as they sped down the road.

"Damned reporters," Mason mumbled.

She turned, wrapping her arms around him and holding him close. "They're gone."

"But I have a feeling they'll be back."

Cold chills ran up and down her arms. He was right, they'd be back, and Mason would be in danger of losing everything he held dear. They would lock them both away and, as Mason had said, throw away the key.

The Elders were right to forbid interplanetary travel. She'd only managed to put Mason in danger. He would not like being locked away.

The telephone rang.

"I'd better answer that," Mason said. "With all the craziness going on lately it could be something important." He squeezed her close before letting her go.

She watched him as he walked away. A cold loneliness washed over her. She drew in a deep breath and followed inside, already missing him.

He spoke on the phone for a moment, then hung up. "I'm sorry, I have to go into town. A meeting I'd forgotten about. Do you want to go?"

She shook her head. "I think I'll rest a bit, if that's all right."

"Don't let the reporters scare you. I can handle them. Who the hell is going to believe you're an alien?"

He chuckled, but his laughter stopped when his gaze met hers. He lowered his mouth, his lips brushing hers. She accepted his kiss, knowing this might be her last, savoring his taste, inhaling the musky scent that clung to his body and hoping it would be enough to last a lifetime, but knowing just one minute away from him would seem like forever.

He ended the kiss and went to his room where he changed clothes. She followed, not wanting to be away from him for even a second.

As soon as he left, she would climb on Shasta and find her craft.

Then she would leave . . . forever. She clamped her lips together, stifling her sob.

Her gaze fixed on him as he peeled off his damp clothes. He was a magnificent male specimen. He was perfect. She couldn't have created something as wonderful as Mason.

"If you keep looking at me like that, I might end up late for my meeting." He grabbed his pants and slipped them on, tucking his shirt inside.

"Would that be so bad?" She would love to tumble on the bed with him and make love one last time.

"Not for me, but Cal might not be too pleased. Since he helped get me elected, I don't want to piss him off. I kind of like my job. Besides, he's also a friend."

"Then you must go." She would be brave.

"As soon as I put the horses up."

"No, I can do that. I watched closely this morning."

"Those saddles are pretty heavy."

She needed Shasta saddled and she didn't think she could do that part of it. "You're late already. I can unsaddle the horses. Please."

He hesitated. "Okay, but if you have any trouble just leave them saddled."

In a few minutes he was gone. She wanted to call him back, beg him not to go, but to do so would be taking the chance she would destroy him. She couldn't do that.

It took her longer to unsaddle Dancer than she'd imagined. He was very good about standing still, and when she closed the stall door, he whinnied. A sad sound. As if he knew she was leaving.

She sniffed, hating the misery that filled her. She'd never felt sad on Nerak.

Or the kind of happiness she'd felt on Earth.

Her feet dragged as she went back inside the house. This didn't feel at all right, but she had to protect Mason.

She scribbled him a note. Just one sentence— "I'm so sorry, but I have to leave"—and signed it simply, "Mala."

What else could she say? I really am an alien? Nerak is not another country, but a planet in another galaxy? No, he would think she'd lost her mind and would be desperate to find her so she didn't come to harm. This was best this way.

She removed his shirt, hugging it close to her, inhaling his scent one last time before slipping her dress over her head. The house was quiet without his presence. She trudged through it, her footsteps heavy. There was nothing to say that she'd been there. Mason would forget about her before the sun passed overhead seven times. A tear ran down her cheek.

She swiped the back of her hand across her face and sniffed again. It wasn't fair, she thought, as she went to the cabinet and took out the bag of chocolate, holding it close to her.

Not fair at all.

Climbing on top of Shasta was a little harder without Mason to help lift her, and holding the bag of chocolate didn't help, but she finally made it on top of the horse and they set off at a brisk pace.

"Good bye, Mason," she said, and sniffed again.

The tears were streaming down her face as she aimed Shasta in the right direction. Every clip-clop of the horse's hooves seemed to chant—don't go, don't go, but how else was she going to keep those horrible reporters from discovering she was an alien? She couldn't put Mason at risk. His safety was worth more than her happiness.

She unwrapped a chocolate bar and devoured it.

But it didn't stop the hurt. Oh, Barton was so right. There was pain on Earth, but not from stepping on a thorn. No, the wound went far deeper than that.

She dried her eyes one last time and reined Shasta

toward where she thought she might have stumbled out of the woods, then climbed down.

"Go home," she told the horse, then hugged Shasta's neck. The horse snorted. She sniffed and hurried into the dense forest.

Returning to Nerak was going to be so hard. She touched a tree, careful not to get insects on her. She would take all these memories with her. That would be enough to sustain her until her lifeblood drained.

It would have to be.

She unwrapped another chocolate bar and ate it. Oh, the pain was so great inside her.

She didn't have far to walk. Her craft was as she'd left it. She slipped inside and finally managed to manually close the door. "Good bye, Earth." Her bottom lip trembled. She waved her hand over the control panel.

Nothing.

She waved her hand again, her pulse speeding up.

Nothing.

"Well, hell." She plopped down in her control seat and wondered what she should do now.

The control panel should at least light up. How else would she be able to leave? If she stayed, Mason could be in danger of being locked up and the key thrown away. That couldn't happen. She wouldn't let it.

There should be tools to open the panel. She looked around, discovered the hatch and opened it. The tools were outdated, but nothing she couldn't figure out.

It took her a few minutes to get the top off the panel, and when she did, she could only stare at it. Wires were melted and fused together. How would she be able to sort it all out?

She already knew the answer. She wouldn't be going home on her own, but she could enjoy Earth until someone came to get her. Odd, but she didn't feel quite so put out at the thought of staying.

She ripped open another chocolate bar and began eating, pondering her situation.

"Umm, this is so good," she said while savoring the taste. The lights flickered and fizzled on the panel. Maybe . . . no, she'd have to eat several bags to jolt the aged craft into flying, and even she didn't think she could eat that much chocolate without getting sick first.

So, what was she going to do? She couldn't live in the woods as the Hypotrond was apparently doing. She'd starve. There was only one thing to do: go back to Mason's and hope the reporters stopped bothering them.

The thought of returning to Mason was vastly appealing. Her pulse sped up again, but this time it was fueled by anticipation.

She grabbed the bag of candy and hurried back out. If she beat Mason home, he wouldn't even have to know she'd left.

When Mala stepped from the trees Shasta was still there, munching grass as if she knew no one would be leaving today.

"I don't like the idea of doing random drug checks, but we at least need a policy, and as the president of the school board I thought you'd be the one to get us a comprehensive plan together that isn't going to anger a lot of parents." Cal leaned back in his chair.

"I'll have you something ready by the end of the week." Mason watched his friend, knowing there was something else on Cal's mind. He had a feeling he wasn't going to like hearing it. "Spit it out," he finally told him.

Cal cleared his throat. "Rumor has it you have a woman living with you and it isn't exactly a platonic relationship." He shifted in his seat.

He cocked an eyebrow. "And your point is?"

"Come on, Mason. Don't get pissed at me."

"And just who should I get pissed at?"

Cal sighed. "I tried to tell the board you wouldn't like anyone butting into your private life."

"And you were right." Mason rested his hands on the desk. To the casual observer he seemed calm, but on the inside he was fuming. This job didn't pay enough for people to get moral on him. Hell, he knew stuff about the good people of this town that would make a sailor blush. If they wanted to get moral, he'd get moral right back.

"Now don't take this the wrong way," Cal said. "I don't care what the hell you do with your life. You know how Hazel is, though. Those reporters were at her house this morning asking her all kinds of questions about you and that woman staying at your place. As soon as they left, she called me. Damned woman wouldn't shut up until I promised I'd say something to you."

"And you want me to . . ."

"Oh, hell, Mason, forget I even said anything."

"Okay, I will, and if Hazel says another word about my personal life, let me know. Her grandson got off pretty easy when I caught him drinking behind Herschel's barn last month. I'll go head-to-head with her about morals." He looked pointedly at his friend. "And anyone else that has a mind to interfere in my private life."

Cal's face turned a rosy hue. "Ah, jeez, Mason. I wouldn't have brought it up, but I am the president of the school board and I have a duty, same as you."

Cal was right. The trouble was, Mason knew it.

They talked for a few more minutes, then Cal left.

Mason clenched his fists. Cal had said the board was worried about improprieties. They should look at their own lives before making judgments.

And those damn reporters and Harlan. He snorted. Mala—an alien. Yeah, right. Where in the hell did people get crazy ideas like this?

As the idiocy of it all hit him, his anger vanished and fear set in. She was still a defector and he could get into deep shit harboring her. The thought of turning her in didn't sit well with him, either, but damn it, he was risking his job. He couldn't just sweep it all under the rug.

He swiveled his chair around until he faced his computer. Nerak. He typed the name of Mala's country into the search engine and pushed *enter*. A few seconds later he got his reply. Nothing found other than conveyor systems. He wasn't the most technical person when it came to computers, but he knew someone who was.

He picked up the phone and bumped Francine's key.

"You need something, boss?"

"Yeah, see what you can find out for me about a country called Nerak."

"You planning a vacation? It's about time. You haven't taken one in years."

"I'm thinking about it." It probably wasn't wise to disclose more than that right now.

He turned the computer off and stood.

"Damned reporters," he mumbled as he left the

sheriff's office by the back door and climbed into his Jeep. It roared to life when he turned the key.

Just let one of them step out in front of him. He could claim it was an accident. He was the sheriff. The townspeople would believe him.

He was losing it.

A vacation. Francine was right, that's exactly what he needed. Somewhere in the mountains—Colorado maybe. There would still be snow. He could easily imagine a roaring fire and Mala snuggled up against him, furs draping their naked bodies.

He left town behind him and headed toward the ranch. If worse came to worse, he would think of some way to keep her with him. He would not send her back to a country where she wasn't allowed to think for herself.

She was getting under his skin, he knew that, but there was so much about her to like.

And to think, the stupid reporters thought she was an alien. They'd been watching too many old movies. *Aliens from Mars, Attack of the Aliens* . . .

He shook his head and glanced at his watch. He'd been gone a little longer than he'd planned. He hoped Mala had found something to occupy her time.

Chapter 12

Mala stood beneath the waterfall in Mason's bathing room. It wasn't as nice as the pond, but it was a whole lot warmer. As she ran the white brick over her body she thought how much nicer it would be if Mason was gliding the white brick over her skin. But she was starting to wrinkle so she turned off the water and stepped out.

She quickly dried herself and slipped on some of the black lacy underclothes that Carol said would drive Mason over the edge. She wasn't sure she wanted him to drive over anything, but she had a feeling that wasn't what Carol meant. It would be interesting to see what happened, she thought as she pulled the black dress over her head and ran a brush through her hair.

He was still gone so she'd decided to watch his television. What was showing didn't excite her, though. In fact, it was scaring her. A lot! She sat down hard on the edge of the lounging sofa, gripping the empty bag of chocolates.

This was terrible!

Where was the couple having sex from the other night? The ones rubbing naked against each other?

This was barbaric!

Is this what humans would do if they captured her,

locked her in a room and threw away the key? Would they slice her open with a shiny sharp knife?

She drew in a deep shuddering breath, her gaze locked on the television.

> *"We have to open him up. I'm the chief of staff and I have to protect the world!" He swung a knife above his head.*
> *"But it will kill the alien," the nurse pleaded, clasping her hands to her chest.*

"Yes! Let the alien live!" Mala sat forward, almost tumbling off the sofa. She grabbed the cushion and held on.

> *"We must do it. This . . . this thing isn't human. It will destroy our race. We must cut it open."*

Oh, she couldn't watch any more. She turned off the television and jumped to her feet. The sound of Mason's Jeep had her running to the door.

"Mason," she called as she hurried out the door.

He looked around, his eyes narrowing, as he climbed out of the Jeep. "Is everything okay?"

"They were killing an alien on television! Cutting it open! It was horrible!"

"It's okay," he said as he walked toward her, his words soothing away some of her fears. "It was only a movie. It wasn't real. Just because a handful of crazy reporters try to convince people you're an alien it doesn't make it so. Normal people don't believe that sort of thing."

"They don't?"

He shook his head. "Nope, not even a little."

"I missed you," Mala told him as she ran down the

steps and into his arms, arms that snuggled her close to him.

"I wasn't gone that long."

"Almost a lifetime."

He held her tight and she felt safe again.

"You look beautiful. Is it a special occasion?"

Yes. She was still here. At least, for a little while longer, but she couldn't tell him that she'd almost left him today . . . but *she* knew.

Would her heart flutter like this every time they were together?

"Even a minute is too long to be away from you," she told him.

"You smell nice," he murmured against her neck, sending tremors of excitement over her body.

She stepped out of his arms. "I used the white brick."

"Soap."

"Soap?"

"That's what the white brick is called. Soap."

His mouth lowered to hers. She closed her eyes and accepted what he offered. The world swam around her with dizzying speed as she lost herself in his taste— smoky . . . musky . . . he tasted like Mason.

And when his tongue caressed hers, heat spread through her body, starting an ache inside her that only grew stronger.

He was breathing hard when he ended the kiss. "Let's get away from here. Get out of town. I need to be alone with you. No phones ringing. No pagers . . . no radios."

"Where will we go?" She'd already learned it wasn't easy to escape the noisemakers. The bedroom sounded good to her. Or maybe the porch. The floor wasn't *that* hard.

The sooner the better.

He put his arm around her shoulders and pulled

her close as they walked toward the house. "I want to take you out. Show you the town."

She met his eyes. "But I've seen the town." The bedroom would be much better.

"No, not Washboard. I want to get away from here. Let's go to San Antonio. Maybe take in a play or something."

Her curiosity rose. "A play?"

"You've never been to a play?"

She shook her head.

A slow grin tilted one side of his mouth and curled her toes. "Then lady, we'll paint the town red."

Paint? She looked at the barn. The wood had been painted red. She looked down at her dress. "Should I change if we're going to paint San Antonio?" She was losing her new clothes at an alarming rate, and rather liked the black dress.

He chuckled as they walked up the porch steps and went inside. "That's an expression. We won't actually be painting the town, just seeing the sights." His gaze roamed slowly over her. "And you look just fine to me. Better than fine. Sexy as hell in fact. Remind me to compliment Carol on the type of clothes she stocks the next time we're in her boutique."

When his gaze returned to her face, a warm glow started in the pit of her stomach and spread outward. What was this emotion? The longer she was around him the greater it became. Leaving was going to be difficult.

"I'll just change and make a few calls."

She nodded, watching him go.

The Elders would come for her. That was a certainty. They would soon realize she was gone and question Barton. Even though he was loyal to her, he couldn't defy the Elders. As soon as he told them where she'd gone, they'd come after her.

She would be in trouble, but they wouldn't vaporize her or anything. The people on Nerak were peaceful. They hadn't vaporized anyone for hundreds of years.

She bit her bottom lip. Of course, that didn't mean they couldn't start again. No, she wouldn't even think like that. For now, she would enjoy her time with Mason.

It didn't take him long to change. When he returned, her breath caught in her throat. A dark jacket covered his broad shoulders, and beneath that was a deep blue shirt and something silver around his neck. She liked it, but then, she liked him.

Her gaze lowered to the dark slacks, the pleated front and the way they fit his lower half. Her mouth watered and she wondered if she'd ever seen a male specimen as attractive as Mason.

She doubted it.

They walked outside. Blue jumped in the back of the Jeep, but Mason told him to stay. He whined but jumped back out.

"Next time, boy." He ruffled the top of the dog's head.

Once they were on the highway, Mala rolled her window down, marveling at how well she had mastered the technical side of Earth. The mechanisms were quite dated, but she had conquered them.

"You're going to mess your hair."

She smiled at him. "I don't care. I love the wind on my face. It makes me feel so alive."

"You're the first woman I've ever met who would take wind over a perfect hairdo."

Well hell, she'd apparently made another mistake.

"I like that about you," he continued. "You're not afraid of looking convention in the eye and laughing. You would've made a great hippie—a free spirit. Most people want everything to fit in a nice, tidy box."

Her shoulders relaxed as she leaned against the seat. So, maybe she hadn't made an error. Mason said he liked her this way. Good, she wanted to enjoy tonight.

"And this tidy box. This isn't a good thing?"

He shook his head. "People should learn to think beyond their circle."

"As in aliens from other planets?"

"I never would've thought you were a big sci-fi fan. I'm afraid that's stretching my boundaries of belief. Remember, I told you no one will believe those reporters or Harlan. You have nothing to be afraid of. No, what I'm talking about is more like I never thought I would become a sheriff. When I realized what I wanted, I went for it and didn't let anything stand in my way."

She sighed. He still wasn't ready to believe. Would he ever be ready for the whole truth?

As they drew closer to San Antonio, she sat forward. "It's bigger than Washboard."

"Just a little." He grinned and her stomach did a little flip-flop. "Washboard has a population of around three thousand. San Antonio is closer to a million."

That many? It seemed impossible. They were overcrowded on Nerak, but the whole planet wasn't more than one million five hundred thousand at the most. That's why they had to regulate the birth rate. Only certain females from each family unit were allowed to have their eggs taken for fertilization, but then, once the child reached gestation and came home, all the members of that unit were assigned with raising the child.

She blinked back the moisture in her eyes. She hadn't been chosen to reproduce.

Not being able to have children didn't really matter as long as she was here with Mason. But the emptiness was never very far away.

Chapter 13

Mason couldn't stop staring at the look of pure pleasure on Mala's face. The only tickets he could get were for *The Lion King*, but she seemed mesmerized by the musical play unfolding in front of her.

Suddenly she turned to him, tears in her eyes. "Scar is so very bad."

He lightly caressed her arm. "Don't worry, the good guy always wins."

"I hope you're right." She shook her head. "But it doesn't look like he will."

Later, when they were eating dinner, Mala was still talking about the play.

"The circle of life. Do you believe each one of us has our place?"

He was so caught up in watching the lights from the chandelier catch strands of her hair and turn them to a golden brown that at first he hadn't realized she'd even spoken. When he did, it took him a moment to respond. Damn, she was just so beautiful.

"What?" he finally asked.

"Like in the play. The circle of life. Do you believe we each have a . . . destiny to fulfill? That there's a place for each person?"

He'd never really thought about it. He supposed

there was something to it if you wanted to get deeper into the meaning of life and all that stuff. He lived one day at a time and never really thought about the other stuff that some people liked to get into. Hell, he was just happy to wake up every morning. That is, until those damned reporters came to town.

She continued before he had a chance to answer. "And what if we venture out of our circle? Like with Simba. He upset the balance of the circle of life."

She moved the food around on her plate, then looked up, meeting his gaze.

"Do you think someone could wreak havoc on someone else's life if they wandered out of their territory?"

Ah, she was worried about being deported and the scars she might leave behind. So far they hadn't discovered anything about her background. No missing persons that fit her description. Nothing on the international front. It was like she just appeared one day. Still, she had to be worried about her future.

"I'll do everything in my power to keep you from being deported." He reached across the table, taking her hand in his. "You're safe with me."

"They'll find me."

The sadness in her words broke his heart. "There's ways to keep you here. Laws that will protect you. I have one of my deputies looking into what recourse we can take." He also had Francine finding out as much as she could about Nerak. He didn't want any surprises.

But even as he assured her that he was doing everything within his power to keep her safe, he wondered if he was telling her the truth. Could he keep her safe? Ah, damn, the alternative wasn't even thinkable. He wasn't prepared to let her go.

She opened her mouth, then closed it. "I've brought

unhappy thoughts to our wonderful evening." She squeezed his fingers. "I won't spoil the rest of it."

"You could never spoil anything." He motioned for the waiter to bring the check, and after the bill was taken care of they left.

"Nighttime is beautiful," she said as they climbed back into his Jeep. "I wish our evening didn't have to end." She sighed, leaning her head against the back of the seat.

"Who said it did?"

She glanced in his direction, raising her eyebrows in question.

"The Riverwalk at night is beautiful." And romantic. He could picture her curled next to him, the heat of her body snuggled against his. For the first time in his life, he wished he had a vehicle without bucket seats.

"What is this Riverwalk?"

"I'll show you. It's easier than telling you about it."

When she smiled like a child about to open another Christmas present he knew there was no way in hell he'd let anyone take her back to her country. He didn't care who they were.

He gripped the steering wheel. Damn people for forcing their beliefs on others. Making them do what *they* felt was right. It wasn't fair. And hard as hell to believe it still happened in this world. He shook off his anger, determined to make Mala forget her anxiety about the future.

The traffic wasn't bad as he drove through the streets of San Antonio. He parked in one of the garages and they got out. Hand in hand they strolled to the Riverwalk, letting the peacefulness of the evening wash over them.

"I think you'll enjoy the ride. There's a lot of history about San Antonio that's interesting."

He paid for their ride on the barge. As they climbed aboard, Mala held his hand for support. Odd how right it felt being with her. As if he'd been waiting for her all his life. He wondered if she felt the same way.

Mala liked the way Mason's hand offered gentle strength and guidance as he assisted her into the craft. She would remember this day forever. That's probably all she'd have—a memory of her time spent on Earth. She knew the Elders would never let her stay. Mason didn't understand. They were all-powerful. She would try to repair her craft so she could return before the Elders came looking for her.

But she had tonight.

Their guide pointed out the landmarks. She listened intently, especially when he boasted one place had the best margaritas on the Riverwalk.

Margarita?

It had a nice ring to it. An almost musical sound, the way the man had rolled the R off his tongue. She turned to Mason. "What's a margarita?" She tried to roll the R but it twisted and came out sounding more like a gurgle.

"A drink." He smiled.

She thought he might be laughing at her on the inside, but she didn't mind. Tonight was a night for pleasure. And this drink would be something else to try. Maybe it would taste like chocolate.

"I would like one, please." It had been a while since she'd had chocolate.

"Are you sure? They're pretty potent." His expression was skeptical.

Potent? Ahh, strong. Not that she was exactly sure what that meant, but she wanted to see and do everything Earth had to offer before she had to leave. Besides, her curiosity was getting the better of her. Now she had to taste this margarita.

They got off at the next landing and strolled back to the little café with the umbrellas over the tables. They sat at an empty table outside, where they could still enjoy the view.

A young man came over and while Mason ordered their drinks, she took in all the sites. Four men strolled among the tables, singing and playing odd-looking instruments. It was very festive. They wore wide-brimmed hats and their black jackets sparkled.

Couples walked hand in hand, gazing at each other with such adoration. There was one young woman with a protruding stomach. Pity washed over Mala, for there must be something terribly wrong with her, but the man walking beside her seemed to care deeply as he hugged her close to him and tenderly ran his hand over her disfigurement.

Imperfection, but it didn't seem to matter. She loved this place. She loved Earth and all it had to offer. And she had a feeling that she was falling in love with Mason.

Something caught in her throat. She would never have this on Nerak. She would be forced to spend her life with women as friends, or Barton. It wasn't fair.

No, she'd promised herself not to think about the future. She bravely smiled at Mason as the waiter set their drinks on the table. Tonight was their night to enjoy. She planned on making a lot of memories to sustain her after she left.

She raised her glass and took a sip. Words she'd heard Mason mumble whipped across her mind.

Hell! Crap! Damn!

Heat seared her throat as the tart crystals along the rim of the glass clung to her lips. Just as quickly the heat turned into a warm mellow glow inside her stomach. She liked this feeling it left behind.

"It burns just a little, but it's good." She quickly

downed the rest of the drink, set her glass on the table and licked her lips. "Can I have another?"

Mason's eyes widened. "You finished that kind of fast. Tequila can pack a punch and it hits you when you least expect it. You don't want to go overboard."

"No, I think I want another, please." Her mouth was watering for another. She'd never experienced this all-consuming need. The strong desire to have another drink was almost more than she could stand. She had to have one—now!

He watched her, apparently noting the look on her face. She really wanted another margarita.

With a sigh of resignation, Mason motioned toward the waiter. A few minutes later the young man set another margarita in front of her.

"Maybe you should drink this one a little slower." Mason's brow furrowed. "They add a lot of tequila here."

She nodded, then downed her drink, licking the last taste off her lips as she set the glass back on the table. She loved tequila. Warmth filled her, starting as a little bubble and spreading to her arms and legs.

The lights above their heads began to flicker as her gaze met Mason's. She could almost visualize him without his clothes on. Naked, sitting across from her—his legs slightly parted, letting her see all he had to offer.

She bit her bottom lip, her hands grasping her thighs.

He would be hard and so ready to have sex, and he wouldn't care they were in full view of the other humans as he raised her dress and pulled off her panties.

The warmth inside her burst into flames as she imagined what he would do. Her thighs trembled.

"What?" Mason laughed but it kind of choked out. "You're looking at me like you could . . ."

"I could what?" Her gaze devoured him. "Like I could get down on the sidewalk and scoot between your legs? Like I could slowly unzip your pants and release you? Like I could run my tongue over the tip of your erection before sucking you inside the heat of my mouth? Is that how I'm looking at you?"

Under the table, she inched her foot closer until she could caress him with the toe of her shoe.

He jumped, hissed in a breath. "Son-of-a . . ." Dropping a bill on the table, he grabbed her hand and stood. "I think you've had enough alcohol."

"I want you." She hurried beside him as they left the café. Never in her life had she wanted something as badly as she wanted Mason right now.

No, it was more than want.

Her body itched and burned. Every part of her tingled with awareness.

The tequila was doing something very strange to her. Everything around her was heightened. A woman dropped some change and it sounded like loud bells ringing as each coin pinged on the sidewalk. A man and woman at an outside café clinked glasses and it became cymbals crashing together.

The world around her slowed.

She looked at Mason as he hurried her along and could feel the blood pulsing through his body. His engorged penis aching to plunge inside her.

She drew in a sharp breath. Her nipples hardened to sensitive pebbles and she began to burn for his touch. She couldn't stand it any more. She had to have him.

Now!

"Mason," she pleaded.

"We'll be to the Jeep soon," he panted.

"No. Now. I'm hurting so much. I have to have you now. Please."

He stopped and looked at her. "Oh, crap. There's no place . . ." He scanned the area. "Why didn't you tell me alcohol affected you like this?"

She shook her head. "I've never had alcohol." Her gaze swept over him. She pressed against him. "Don't you want me, too?"

The sidewalk was practically deserted where they were. He pulled her toward two buildings, slipping between them. It was dark enough so that she could barely see him, but there was at least four feet of space.

More than enough room.

"I've never had sex in an alley. I'm sorry, but it's the best I can do."

She slipped the straps of her dress off her shoulders, undid her black lacy bra, pulled it out of her dress and tossed it away. Any second now she knew her body would go up in flames. Only ashes would be left to mark her stay on Earth.

Reaching up, she cupped her breasts in her hands. "Mason, make love to me."

A low growl erupted from him. He caressed her breasts, the pad of his thumbs rubbing the taut nipples before he leaned down and took one into his mouth.

She gasped, pressing herself closer. Nothing had ever felt this wonderful. He massaged one breast while sucking on the other. She leaned against the brick wall, pulled his head closer as her other hand undid his pants and released him. She shivered with excitement as she clasped him in her hand, drawing the foreskin up, then gliding it back down.

He raised his head, but didn't stop teasing her breasts. "Damn, that feels so fucking good," he moaned close to her ear as he slid his hand under her dress and caressed her sex through the thin material of her panties.

She pressed against his hand. "More," she moaned. The fire inside her was burning hotter.

"Turn around."

"Can't," she gasped. She couldn't move. Could barely stand.

He moved his hand away. "Turn around," he softly commanded.

She whimpered, but turned, facing the wall. "Don't stop touching me," she begged, planting her palms on the bricks.

Before she even got the words out of her mouth he was pushing her panties down, slipping one finger between her legs.

"You're so damn wet and hot."

She wiggled against him. He didn't disappoint, but began to move inside her. He found the tight little button and massaged.

"Damn, I'd like to take you in my mouth. Kiss your hot sex. Run my tongue up and down your clit."

She closed her eyes, her breath coming out in little puffs.

"I can't hold back any longer." He bent her over at the waist and pressed the tip of his erection against her sex. He held it there for a moment, teasing, before sliding deep inside her.

She bit back the moan that threatened. His fingers continued to fondle her clit as he slid out, then back inside. He filled her, stroking her even as she clenched her inner muscles, tightening herself around him, keeping the heat inside her as long as possible.

She closed her eyes, losing herself in the sensations he created. Lights danced behind her lids. Wild gyrating colors: deep blues and purples.

And still he slid in and out of her. Faster and faster. Harder and deeper. All the while rubbing his fingers against her sex.

Spasms washed over her in waves. "Ahhhh," she cried out, clenching her legs. He jerked seconds after her as he came, leaning his head against her back.

They drank in gulps of air as if their bodies were starving for oxygen. Still, it didn't feel as if it were enough.

Finally, she opened her eyes. Darkness wrapped around her like gentle arms in a warm embrace. She glanced toward the sidewalk, but the lights were out.

Mason pulled out of her, turned her around and lowered his mouth. His kiss was gentle, sweet.

"You are something else," he said after he ended the kiss.

She smiled, then frowned as she felt the beginning of heat building inside her, the familiar need to have sex.

"Mason, maybe it's better I don't drink any more tequila."

"Why's that?" He nuzzled her neck.

"Because I want you again. I want to feel you buried deep inside me." She turned her face toward him, running her tongue over his lips.

"After what we just shared? I mean, you can't want it again so soon."

She nodded even though he couldn't see her. "It's like a burning need. It's not that I want it, but more like I have to have sex. If I don't, I'm afraid of what might happen."

The ache inside her began to build. Would she disintegrate if her body wasn't satisfied? Go up in a poof of smoke? Not fair! Her grandmother hadn't mentioned anything about consuming alcohol.

"You're serious, aren't you?"

"Yes. I can't help it, Mason. We have to have sex again."

"We'd better get a room. I have a feeling this might be a long night." He bent down, then straightened. "Damn power outage. All I can find is your panties and you might want to . . . uh . . . clean up a bit before I try to get us a room at one of the hotels." He tugged on the straps of her dress, pulling them back in place.

She wearing only her strappy sandals and her dress, he with his rumpled clothes, they strolled into the Hilton as if they were meant to be there and asked for a room.

He raised an eyebrow when the man behind the desk looked twice at them. Mason out-stared him, though. It always worked, whether it be a prisoner he'd brought to justice and was questioning or a haughty employee at a four-star hotel.

The only thing that kept him from being totally convincing that they should be there was the fact that he knew Mala didn't have a stitch of clothes on under her dress—and he was almost positive he was sweating.

Why wouldn't he?

Any red-blooded man would be drenched with sweat if he were standing in his place—and knew the only thing covering Mala's bare breasts was a thin piece of black lace that clearly outlined her tight nipples.

He almost groaned just thinking of the cool air creeping under her dress and caressing the lips of her sex. He wanted his mouth there instead: kissing and licking her.

Damn, and now he would have to walk from the lobby to the elevators with a world-class boner. He didn't dare look in her direction.

"I'll need a credit card," the man behind the desk spoke imperiously.

Mason fumbled inside his back pocket, withdrew his wallet and slid his card across the counter.

Mala delicately cleared her throat. He knew she was about to speak. Gut instinct never failed him. He also knew there wasn't a damn thing he could do about stopping her from saying exactly what was on her mind.

Oh Lord, he had a feeling this wasn't going to be good.

"Could you please hurry," she said. The man looked up, arching an arrogant eyebrow. "I really, really need to have sex and unless you want us having it on the floor in front of your desk, then I suggest you move faster."

Mason had never been thrown out of a hotel before. He guessed there was a first time for everything.

Chapter 14

Mala bit her bottom lip and stared at the man behind the desk. He'd better do something really fast. The itch was growing stronger. The heat between her legs was almost unbearable. She really needed to have an orgasm.

The clerk opened his mouth, then snapped it closed, apparently noticing the desperation on her face. "Yes, ma'am." He turned toward Mason with a look of envy. "Here's your keycard." After a brief hesitation he asked, "Do you realize just how lucky you are?"

"You better believe I do," he mumbled, scratching his name on a paper before grabbing the card out of the man's hand.

"Have a lovely evening," the clerk said before they could escape. "It's a good thing the power came back on," he continued, wearing a deadpan expression. "The top floor was all we had left. I have a feeling you wouldn't have made it up all those stairs."

"Smart ass," Mason grumbled as he took her elbow, aiming her toward the elevators.

She flung herself into his arms as the door closed. Her nipples strained against the lacy material of her dress as she rubbed herself against him. Even that one little caress sent spasms over her. She couldn't wait. Her body burned with the need to feel his touch.

His hand snaked up her dress, stroking her, fondling her sex as he backed her into the corner. Yes, this was what she needed. Delicious sensations swirled around her as she gave herself up to the erotic pleasure he was creating inside her with his touch.

She swallowed hard. "Yes, this is what I need, Mason." She melted against him. He would put the fire out that threatened to consume her.

"Kiss me," he said against her neck. The warmth of his breath caressed her skin.

She raised her head, meeting his lips halfway. His tongue stroked hers, just as his hand continued to massage her sex. Ahh, it felt so good.

He brought her leg up to his waist, moving his hand away even though she moaned in protest. Her moan turned into a sigh of pleasure as he pressed himself against her. She could feel his hard erection through his slacks. She pressed closer, until there was nothing between them except his clothes.

He ended the kiss and nuzzled her neck. "Damned if I don't want you again just as badly as I did in the alley. What the hell have you done? Cast some kind of spell?"

"No spell. This is real." She moaned. "Ah, Mason, take me now. I need you so much."

"Almost there," he croaked.

The elevator came to a stop. Her pulse was beating erratically when he moved away. He kept a tight hold around her waist. It was a good thing. She didn't feel very steady on her feet right now.

The doors swished open.

He tugged her along behind him. She looked back over her shoulder with a yearning that was hard to control.

What was wrong with the elevator? They could've had sex there. Hard, thrusting, bone-jarring sex. The

kind that ended in a satisfying climax. Not this frus-
trating I-need-to-have-sex kind of desperation that
made her want to scream!

Or what about this hallway? Mason could press her
against the wall, drive deep inside her body right
here . . . right now.

A shiver of lust washed over her. She needed him
this very minute . . . and he was stopping? Couldn't
he see how bad she was hurting?

"Hurry, Mason." She was going to explode. Or in-
cinerate. Or worse. Although she didn't know what
could be worse than incineration.

He inserted the small plastic card into the door.
Green lights flashed and he shoved it open.

She stepped inside, pulling her dress over her head
and flinging it away as she did. The cool room did
nothing to cool her body. If anything, the tempera-
ture in the room had risen several degrees when she
stepped across the threshold. She whirled around,
standing in front of him wearing black, strappy, four-
inch heels and nothing else.

"Damn . . ." Something close to a gurgle erupted
from him as he slammed the door shut. He yanked
his jacket off and his shirt open. Buttons flew everywhere but he didn't pause as he flung them toward
her dress.

"Can you hurry, Mason?" She really needed him
to hurry.

She closed her eyes. Her hands moved over her
breasts, cupping them, tweaking the nipples before
sliding over her abdomen and down to the vee of her
legs. She massaged the ache, but it wasn't like when
Mason massaged, and she really wanted his touch.
She licked her lips and opened her eyes.

Why had he stopped undressing? Didn't he realize she was in physical pain? She needed relief.

Sure, his pants had joined her dress on the floor, but he still wore his briefs. And he was just staring at her.

She wanted him naked.

She wanted him inside her.

She wanted him sliding in and out and making her even hotter.

Her legs trembled. "Mason?" Her voice came out high-pitched, and no wonder—her nerves were stretched past the point of endurance. Any minute she might snap into tiny little pieces.

"What the hell do you expect me to do when you drive me crazy like this? Wearing only those sexy heels and nothing else, touching yourself like that. Damn, I want you so bad it drives me over the edge of reason." His words were husky, ragged with his need as he tore out of his briefs and hurled them away.

They didn't even come close to her dress. She didn't think he cared as he strode toward her, scooped her in his arms and carried her to the bed.

As soon as he laid her down, she spread her legs open. "Now, please. I can't stand it any longer."

He positioned himself between her legs, sliding deep inside her. She arched her back, wrapped her legs around his waist and pulled him still deeper.

"I love it when you tighten up on the inside," he said on a groan. "It feels so fucking good when your heat contracts around me."

Tremors of delight rushed through her body. Knowing she brought him pleasure was a potent aphrodisiac.

He began to move inside her. Slowly at first, letting the pressure build. Yes, this was it. This was what she wanted and needed. He began to move faster, thrusting deeper and harder. She arched toward him, needing to be closer, feeling the slap of his skin against hers.

Sweat shimmered over their bodies. Their gazes locked. Their ragged breathing filled the room as the tension built. Ah, damn, she was going to snap in two. She couldn't stand the pressure inside her, but at the same time she wanted it to keep building, taking her higher than she'd ever gone.

Lights swirled behind her lids. Bright, exploding colors: bright yellows, vibrant blues, deep pinks and bold greens. He pumped harder, faster. She rose to meet each thrust, her body straining closer and closer.

Her orgasm crashed over her in waves. She arched her back, crying out and opening her eyes. She wanted to see. Didn't want to miss one moment of the look on his face when he climaxed.

She knew the exact moment he came. He wore a look of such intense pleasure. She wasn't a bit disappointed.

His body melted into hers and she truly felt as if they became one person. One heartbeat between the two of them, one breath, then slowly they became separate again.

He rolled to his side, but took her with him, kissing her forehead, her cheeks, then his lips landed on her mouth in a gentle, all-consuming kiss. Almost as if he were branding her. Strange, but she rather liked knowing she was his. She nipped him on the shoulder. Why shouldn't she mark him as well?

"I didn't think anything could top the last time, but I think we just proved me wrong."

She laughed as she ran her hands over one shoulder and down his arm. "I enjoy sex with you, Mason. It's quite pleasurable."

"You think so?" He chuckled. "Come on, off to the showers, then bed. I think you've worn me out."

She crawled over him and slid out of bed. "I hope not," she said over her shoulder as a familiar heat began to build inside her.

As she went inside the bathroom, she thought she heard him groan. Maybe two margaritas wasn't such a good idea. Could humans die from too much sex? She certainly hoped not.

The waterspouts were somewhat different on this waterfall, and there were funny little knobs on the inside of the big basin. "Mason, what are these?"

"Jets," he said, coming up behind her.

"And what are they for?"

He leaned past her and pushed a button. To her disappointment the waterfall stopped, but the basin began to fill. When it reached halfway, he pushed a button and the water churned.

"Oh, how wonderful!" She climbed in and sat down. Water vibrated around her in the most sensuous way, tickling her sex and making her nipples tingle. "This is very nice, Mason," she told him in a low throaty voice.

"Oh, no," he moaned.

She picked up the little brick . . . no, he'd called it soap. This was very nice soap and smelled even better than Mason's soap. She began to rub it over her breasts and between her legs.

"Mason?"

"You're going to be the death of me, woman, but damned if you're not making me hot watching you. I swear you've bewitched me." But she noticed he was getting in, scooting behind her. He took the soap and began running it over her already slick body. The heat began to build to alarming degrees.

She turned around in one quick movement and straddled him, noticing that he wasn't dead yet.

"I love feeling you inside my body." She rose above

him, then lowered herself, feeling him sinking inside her deeper and deeper.

He closed his eyes and rose to meet her. Water sloshed over the side of the tub. She grabbed his shoulders, biting her bottom lip.

"Yes, this is good. Oh, Mason, don't stop!"

He cried out as she climaxed. She brought her knees in tight to his body, clenching her legs against his strong thighs, and laid her head against his chest as she tried to bring her breathing under control.

"No more alcohol for you."

"Yes, Mason."

Mason slowly opened his eyes, blinking several times as he tried to bring everything into focus. Where was he? Hotel? Yeah, hotel. He pushed up on one elbow and swung his legs off the side of the bed.

"Damn." He grimaced. He was so sore he could barely move. How many times had they made love during the night?

Seven?

At least.

It was great, terrific, the best sex he'd ever had. But after a while it began to feel as if his dick might fall off. He'd have to remember about alcohol and its effect on her.

Maybe only half a glass next time.

The bathroom door opened and Mala stepped out, a towel wrapped around her. A small towel. One that barely covered her.

"You're killing me," he moaned and fell back on the bed, flinging his arm across his eyes. He couldn't look. He wouldn't look!

She had the gall to chuckle.

"That's not a damn bit funny."

She tumbled onto the bed, scooting close to him. "I've had such fun in San Antonio. I wish we could stay here forever and ever."

How could he resist her? She was cute . . . and funny . . . and sexy . . . and sexy . . . He rolled to his side and kissed her nose before trailing his lips down to hers. She eagerly opened her mouth, accepting him.

Her tongue stroked his. He captured it, sucking. She moaned as her body pressed closer. He moved his hand downward, fondling the damp curls between her legs.

"Ow," she said, drawing away from him. "Oh, Mason, I'm so sore."

"Want me to kiss it and make it better?" He knew his grin was more than a little suggestive. It served her right for nearly killing him last night . . . and half the morning.

She sat up in the bed, tugging the towel tighter around her, a frown puckering her forehead. "That was cruel."

"Like you didn't deserve it." He laughed lightly. "I'm not sure I can even make it to the bathroom. Why didn't you tell me alcohol affected you like that?"

She shrugged. The towel slipped, falling to her waist and exposing her perfectly shaped breasts. The ones he'd caressed and fondled all night.

He swallowed, staring at the dusky areolas, the way her nipples puckered. And all she did was casually bring the towel up and tuck it back into place.

"I didn't know," she told him.

She didn't know what? Oh, yeah, alcohol. "Have you never had a drink before?"

"Not one that had alcohol."

Talk about Communism. He'd hate for someone to have that much control over his life.

He stood. "I'm going to take a shower."

Her intake of air made him look back at her. Damn, he hadn't meant to embarrass her. Even though they'd had wild sex, he'd discovered women were usually shy in the light of day.

"I should've warned you that I'd be standing. Sorry," he apologized.

She shook her head as her gaze slowly came up to meet his. "Looking at you makes me want you all over again. It causes a burning down deep inside me. Do you understand this?"

He reached down, running his hand through her hair, cupping her chin and placing a light kiss on her lips. "Yeah, after last night I'm starting to understand it all too well."

Before he did more than kiss her, he went into the bathroom. Standing under the cool spray of the shower didn't do a thing to stop the fact he wanted her again. He was so damned sore, yet he wanted to bury himself deep inside her. What did that tell him?

That making love with Mala wasn't such a bad thing? She damn sure made him feel alive . . . and damned sore.

When he finished and walked back into the bedroom, she was dressed and standing in front of the window. The morning light cascaded over her. Damn, she was so beautiful it made him ache.

As if sensing he'd come into the room, she turned and smiled. "You look good in only a towel."

He grinned.

She frowned. "My stomach feels empty."

"I'm hungry, too. As soon as I dress, we'll grab a bite to eat and head home."

"I think it'll take more than a bite to fill my stomach."

It took Mason a few seconds to realize she was serious. He chuckled, going to her and wrapping her in his arms. He held her close as he looked down on the Riverwalk.

Lazy boats filled with tourists moved slowly across the water. For the first time in a long time he felt whole.

Was this what love was all about? It was still too soon for him to tell, but he knew being with Mala was becoming a habit he didn't want to break. And maybe he'd been by himself far too long. Suddenly he didn't feel quite so alone.

"Can we eat soon?"

He grinned. "Yeah, we can leave as soon as I get dressed."

She leaned away from him and looked up, her gaze meeting his and melting his heart.

"I'm very hungry."

He was still smiling when they were in the Jeep headed for home. He'd stopped at a fast food place and Mala had discovered the chocolate malt. She was in heaven. Not exactly his idea of a good breakfast drink, but the look on her face made it okay in his book.

And now she had the window down again. The wind blew through her hair. Her eyes were closed but there was such a look of rapture on her face. Suddenly she opened her eyes and smiled. Her smile turned to laughter. Damn, she was amazing, beautiful, and he wanted her so bad he could hardly stand it.

The Jeep hit the wake-up bumps on the passenger side of the road. He swerved back on the pavement, heart pounding. He really had to pay more attention to his driving. Reaching over, he turned the radio on, hoping that would keep him focused.

"Nice!"

"You don't have music where you're from?"

She hesitated briefly. "Not music this wonderful."

True, how many singers in her country sang about a cheating woman and a bottle of whiskey? He doubted there were very many.

The song ended and the DJ began to talk.

> *"Anyone living in or visiting San Antonio last night will probably be asking themselves what the heck was going on with the electricity."*
>
> *"A very strange night indeed, Phillip," the co-hostess chimed in.*
>
> *"The electricity went off no less than seven times," Phillip stated.*
>
> *"And those blue and red hazy lights dancing around in the sky. An odd night to be sure."*

Mason frowned. Lights swirling in the sky. That was strange. He'd seen lights the day he and Mala went to the waterfall.

"There's the ranch," Mala said, drawing his attention away from the newscast. She looked worried. As if she might have had something to do . . . He shook his head.

You're losing it, man.

"Home sweet home," he said and smiled.

But when he turned down the long dusty road leading to his house, his smile disappeared. There was a man standing on his front porch.

If it was another reporter, he'd shoot the bastard. He was the sheriff. He might be able to get away with it. Damn it, why couldn't they leave him the hell alone?

From the passenger seat Mala sucked in a deep breath. He turned and looked at her. She sat straight up in her seat, shoulders back, body stiff. He glanced back at the man on the porch.

Well, hell.

He'd thought nothing else could complicate his life, but he had a feeling the man on his porch was going to do a whole lot more than just cause him a few headaches. In fact, he had a feeling they should've spent the day in San Antonio.

Chapter 15

Mason pulled to a stop in front of his house, glaring at the man standing on the porch. He looked creepy if you asked him. Suit pressed, shirt starched. Nothing out of place. What kind of man dressed like that?

IRS agent? Couldn't be, his taxes were all paid up. Still, a sense of foreboding sat in his stomach like a lead balloon.

His gaze swung to Mala when she groaned. Apparently she knew him.

Ex-lover? Ex-boyfriend? Ex-husband? He drew in a shaky breath. *Current husband?*

"Do you know him?" he asked.

She didn't meet his gaze. "You could say that." She nibbled on her bottom lip.

"Exactly how do you know him?" he asked, trying to stay calm—but calm was about to fly out the friggin' window.

"I sort of own him?"

"You sort of . . . what!"

As soon as he'd cut off the engine, she slipped out of the Jeep, ignoring him as she hurried straight to the guy on the porch.

"What are you doing here?" she frantically whispered, but Mason was right behind her and heard every word. It sounded damned suspicious to him, too.

Mason glared at Blue, who was lying on the porch, half asleep, as if it wasn't his job today to protect the ranch from intruders. Great watch dog he was. He might as well trade him in for a Chihuahua.

"I've come to take you home," the man told Mala.

"Like hell you are." Mason stormed up the steps, bristling when the man looked at him with more than a touch of condescension.

"Mason . . ."

He turned when she spoke. What the hell was going on? "Mala, I want some answers and I want them now. Who is this guy and don't tell me you own him. People don't own other people." He clenched his fists, trying to stay calm, but calm had never been his strong suit. The look he gave the other man should've had him begging for mercy.

It didn't.

The guy was cool, calm, and collected. Everything he wasn't.

She glanced from one to the other. Her mouth opened but no words came out.

"Is this Sheriff?" the stranger asked.

Mason spun toward her, disbelief filling him. "You've been talking to him about us?"

"No!"

He'd interrogated a lot of criminals in his time. He could tell when someone was lying to him. His gut told him Mala was genuinely upset. Or was his heart the one telling him not to convict without a fair trial?

"Don't you remember that first night when I saw you?" she babbled. "I called you Sheriff because you were wearing a star just like the one in the documentary I'd watched. I came here looking for Sheriff . . . and found you."

"So this isn't Sheriff?" Barton said.

"Yes, this is *a* sheriff," she explained.

"Have you copulated with him?"

"Yes."

Mason choked.

"No!" she quickly amended.

"Then you haven't copulated with him?"

"Yes . . . Barton, please be quiet!"

Mason glanced between the two. Mala looked as if she wanted a hole to open up so she could crawl inside. He hated to be the one to tell her this wasn't earthquake country and he wasn't going anywhere until he had a few answers. Crap, he'd never felt so used in all his life.

He closed his eyes and counted, but only got to five. That's when he remembered something. That first night, she'd said the name Barton.

Maybe he *was* her husband. Hell, he didn't know anything about the customs in her country. He opened his eyes and studied the man in front of him. Jealousy ripped through him like a sharp knife.

He looked at Mala. "Are you going to explain?" Mason demanded, but before she could answer Barton began to speak.

"If you're going to copulate with him I would advise you that it might be prudent if you hurry. You don't have much time."

Who the hell was this guy? Definitely not a lover or husband . . . unless he was damned understanding. It didn't matter. She wasn't leaving.

"Listen, Bud, no one is going anywhere except maybe you. I don't care if you're an ex-boyfriend, ex-husband, ex-lover or current anything. Mala isn't leaving." His gaze roamed over Barton. When he raised his head again, he knew his expression held more than a little distaste. "And certainly not with the likes of you."

Barton raised an imperious eyebrow. "Exactly what do you mean by, 'with the likes of me'?"

"She's not going anywhere. That's what I mean." He planted his fists on his hips and squared his shoulders.

"I beg to differ. She has no choice but to leave."

No choice? Mason wasn't about to let this stranger force Mala to leave. "We'll see about that."

"Mason, please don't . . ."

Mason raised his fist. In a split second, Barton clamped a hand over it in a vise-like grip. Mason couldn't have moved if he'd wanted.

"Barton! Don't hurt him."

"As you wish." He nodded and released Mason's hand. "Please forgive me. I wish you no harm."

Mason shook the circulation back into his hand. Okay, so he was tougher than he looked. Damn, the guy had a grip. It still didn't change anything. "I don't care who you are or what you do. Mala isn't leaving unless she wants to."

He wouldn't keep her against her will, but God, being without her would leave a hole inside him that he didn't think would ever be filled.

He had to know how she really felt. "You don't want to, do you?"

Tears welled in her eyes. "I told you once that I might not have a choice." She sniffed.

"You do." He went to her, gathering her in his arms. "Don't go," he whispered.

"I have to."

Barton cleared his throat. "Actually, we do have seven rotations before we need to return. I would like to explore this place. When I landed, I discov-

ered many things. Like trees . . . and bushes . . . and
little black bugs that crawl on the trees. And a Hypotrond." He looked at Mala. "Were you aware there
are Hypotronds in the surrounding woods? They've
been extinct for many, many years. I would like to
gather more data on them and this place."

"Now I know I won't let you go with him. The
guy's crazy."

"He's my companion unit."

"Companion . . . what?"

"Unit. He sees to my needs."

"Nerak must be one strange country." It dawned
on him what she was trying to explain. The guy
worked for her? Relief left him weak. At least she wasn't
married to him.

Mason shook his head. "I've never heard a butler
called a companion unit before. Hell, why didn't you
explain he works for you?"

"I take care of her and I serve her, seeing to her
every need. I also protect her."

Bodyguard, butler, valet all rolled up into one. He
didn't trust the guy as far as he could throw him. "How
did Jeeves get here? I don't see a car or anything."

"In an aero craft."

High-tech plane. Things were getting more complicated than he liked. If she was wealthy, he might
not have a choice except to let her go. Not everyone
could afford their own bodyguard.

What if it got political? He studied her for a moment. "You're not a princess or anything?" When she
still looked confused he continued. "In line to in-
herit a throne or something?"

She shook her head.

He expelled a deep breath. "Then you don't have
to leave." And especially not with this Barton guy, he
didn't add.

"Barton is more of a . . . friend. You'll like him," she said, as if guessing his thoughts.

"We'll see." He eyed the other man. There was still something odd about him. Sometimes it was better to keep the enemy close enough to observe his moves. "You can stay, but cause any trouble and you're out of here. Got that?"

"You have a very strange way of speaking, but yes, I understand you perfectly well." He looked from Mala to Mason, then back to her.

This isn't good, Mala thought to herself. Not good at all. Barton was very perceptive. He would guess she had feelings for Mason. Not that it mattered that much. If he'd been told by the Elders to bring her back, she wouldn't have a choice but to return.

At least he'd managed to give her a little time before she had to leave. That would be enough time to convince Mason what she had to do.

But would it be enough time for her to mend a broken heart? It would have to be. There was no other choice.

First things first. She needed to speak to Barton alone. Find out exactly what the Elders had said. She had a feeling she was in big trouble.

She didn't have long to wait. As soon as they went inside, they heard beeping coming from the machine connected to Mason's phone. A reprieve. While he called the sheriff's office, she grabbed Barton by the arm and pulled him into the other room.

"Okay, just how angry are the Elders?"

"Oh, they're not angry," he told her.

Okay, this might not be as bad as she first thought.

"I would say they were more furious. Certainly way beyond anger."

She'd love to remove all his chips. "Why didn't you say that in the first place?"

"You asked: Are the Elders angry? They're quite beyond that point. In fact, I can't remember ever seeing one of them this upset. It wouldn't surprise me if . . ."

"Enough! I don't want to hear any more." She covered her ears with her hands. Barton waited patiently until she lowered them.

"But you've always been a favorite of theirs so I doubt they'll vaporize you."

"You think I'm a favorite?" She couldn't stop the warm glow from spreading through her.

"Of course."

"Let's just hope you're right."

He let his gaze roam over her. "You look different." He fingered the silky material of the dress she'd worn to San Antonio. "Odd fabric . . . but nice." His eyes narrowed. "No, it's more than that. You're practically glowing."

"Oh, Barton, I love Earth. There's so much to see and do. Last night we went to San Antonio. It was big and wonderful. We saw a play and then I had alcohol and then we found a hotel room and made love all night. But we're not supposed to talk about sex openly so you can't say anything. But this is the most fabulous place."

"You know you can't stay," he gently reminded her.

She dropped down into one of the chairs. "I know."

"You care for him?"

She nodded. "I didn't want to. I came down to experience sex with a human. That's all I planned to do."

"I don't believe you."

Her brow furrowed. "You're calling me a liar?"

"Not exactly."

"That's what it sounds like to me."

"I think you came here looking for an emotion. You wanted to experience love."

She folded her hands in front of her. "Well, do you have a quick remedy to fall out of love?" She stood and paced across the room. "It wasn't supposed to hurt this much. I don't want to leave him."

"You're a Nerakian, not an Earthling. This isn't your planet. Have you thought about what kind of chain reaction you could set off just by being here?"

"But you don't understand. How could you?" The words had slipped out. Oh no, she hadn't meant them the way they'd sounded.

"If you cut me, I don't bleed," he began hesitantly. "But I hurt just the same as you."

She rushed to him, throwing her arms around his neck. "I'm sorry. I didn't mean it that way. I'm just so confused." Never in her life would she hurt Barton intentionally. He wasn't just a machine.

He patted her on the back. "It's all right. I understand." He drew in a deep breath. "Does Mason know you're from another planet?"

"No."

"Don't you think that is something he should know? You might want to inform him before we have to leave."

She shook her head. "I tried—the first time we had sex. He didn't believe me. I think we're a little beyond his realm of comprehension."

"We'll need to rectify that situation."

Cold chills swept over her. Mason would hate her. She couldn't let Barton tell him. Sometimes he was a little too . . . blunt.

"Let me try to explain once more," she told him.

He eyed her dubiously.

"I promise I'll tell him, but it has to be in my own way and my own time." She held her breath.

When he gave her a resigned nod, she breathed a sigh of relief.

Mason came back into the living area. "It was nothing. The deputy took care of the problem."

Mala didn't like the way Mason was looking at Barton. As if he wanted to do bodily harm. This wasn't her kind and gentle Mason. The man who made her laugh, took her to a play, made sweet love to her.

Was this what wars were like? She'd never realized men could be so territorial.

"Would you like to see the horses?" she quickly spoke up. There would be no war in Mason's house or anywhere else for that matter. Not between the two men who meant so much to her.

"So, it was a horse."

She grabbed Barton's hand and pulled him toward the door before he could say anything else. Mason followed right behind them. Did Earth women have to go through this?

They went inside the barn, leaving the double door open so that light streamed in.

"It has an unusual smell," Barton said.

"Welcome to the real world," Mason said under his breath, but Mala heard him. He was being quite confrontational.

The cat meandered from the back. Mala smiled, relaxing for the first time since she'd seen Barton standing on the front porch.

"This is Stripes, Mason's cat." She bent and picked the animal up. "And those are her babies. Kittens."

"How strange." Barton bent and picked one up. "It's quite soft." He rubbed the animal against the side of his face.

Mala glanced toward Mason, who was feeding the horses. She didn't think he was paying attention to them, except for the occasional glare he'd cast in Barton's direction. She could tell Mason wasn't at all pleased with the turn of events.

As soon as the horses were fed, Mason leaned against one of the stalls, but he didn't look relaxed. More as if he was ready to pounce. She didn't think she wanted to take Barton over and show him the horses, but she was afraid that's exactly what he'd want to do next. Unless she could tempt him with something better.

"Mason has a computer where you can learn all about . . . the area. Come, I'll show you." She hurried Barton toward the house. Mason didn't say a word, just followed behind them, still glaring. This wasn't good. Not good at all.

"I'm terribly thirsty, Mason. Would you mind getting me something to drink? I'll join you in a moment."

He hesitated before going toward the kitchen. Her legs felt like rubber. She had a feeling she'd averted a war. At the very least, a battle.

Barton followed her into the room Mason called a study. When she pulled up the history of Earth in the encyclopedia, his eyes fairly glowed with excitement. She knew for the next few hours he would absorb everything in the computer. His storage chip would hold a considerable amount.

She, on the other hand, needed chocolate. Maybe then she would be able to come up with a solution to her current problem. She never would've guessed Earth would be such a complication.

Mala was being evasive, Barton had been holed up in the study glued to the computer all afternoon and into the evening, and Mason was getting more and more pissed.

"How the hell can he stay this long at the computer?" Hell, the guy hadn't even taken a break, not even to come out to eat. "He isn't normal."

Mala wrapped her arms around his neck and hugged him tight. "Barton is a friend. Nothing else. But he's very dear to my heart. Can't you like him even a little? He means us no harm. Truly."

"He wants to take you away from me. How can I like him?" His arms went around her and pulled her close. "I won't let him do that."

Her body melted against his, but he knew it was more from emotional stress than anything. He suddenly realized what kind of toll this was taking on her. Damn, he hadn't thought how she must be feeling. What did that make him? Certainly not a protector. How could he be when he was so blasted jealous? He'd hit the nail on the head. That's exactly what was wrong. He didn't want Mala to have had a life before him. Ridiculous thinking.

He'd try harder.

"Let's go to bed. Things will look differently in the morning."

She nodded.

Later, when she snuggled her naked body against his and sighed deeply in her sleep, he knew he really would try to be a little . . . nicer to Barton. For her. He lightly brushed away the hair from her face, marveling at the smoothness of her cheek.

A commotion from outside drew his attention. He slipped out of bed, grabbing his jeans.

Damn, he'd left the barn door open. Some of the ranchers had been having trouble with a pack of wild dogs. Dogs that had once been pets that people had decided they didn't want or need for one reason or another. The country was a good dumping ground. It didn't take the animals long to turn mean. Slowly starving to death could do that.

He hit the front door at a run, grabbing the shotgun off the wall as he went, and ran toward the barn.

Most of the noise was coming from around the side. Blue barking. Unfamiliar barking and howling. His blood ran cold. Blue wasn't a young pup—they'd tear him to shreds.

He slid around the corner—and froze. Barton stood in the middle of four dogs, Blue by his side, the dog's haunches raised.

"Stay real still," Mason warned. He expected them to rip into Mala's friend and Blue any second. If he could get off one good shot it might scare the wild dogs and just might save Barton's life.

"Whatever for?" Barton asked.

When Barton reached a hand out toward one of the dogs Mason cringed, but rather than bite Barton's hand off the dog whimpered and licked his hand. Slowly, Mason lowered the gun. This couldn't be the same pack of dogs that had been terrorizing the countryside.

"I believe they require nourishment. Would you happen to have sustenance for them? They seem quite pitiful. Why would anyone abuse such friendly creatures?"

There was a note of sadness in Barton's voice that Mason couldn't ignore. So maybe the guy wasn't so bad. Like Mala had tried to tell him, except he hadn't wanted to listen.

"Yeah, I think I have some dry dog food in the barn."

A couple of hours later the dogs were still hanging close to Barton. They'd been fed, and animal control had been called and was just arriving to pick up the strays and hopefully find good homes for them.

"This certainly looks like the bunch that's been causing so much trouble," Micky said as he loaded the last dog into a cage. "At least they fit the description. Took down one of Weston's cows. If he hadn't been out checking fences, they would've killed her." He glanced at the black and white collie mix that was licking Barton's hand. "They sure don't act like killers now."

He got inside his pickup and drove off.

Damn it, Mason didn't want to like Barton, but there was just something about a man who had a way with animals. Mason's grandfather had been like that.

Mason's father used to tell about the time grandpa came upon a wild boar out in the woods. Mason's father was with him, just a boy at the time. He said that old boar had razor-sharp tusks and a deadly gleam in his eyes. But the boar didn't do anything. It was almost like grandpa and that old boar silently communicated with each other, then went their own way.

You just automatically knew someone was a good person when they could communicate with animals. People might not see the good, but an animal did. Mason's jealousy had kept him from seeing the kind of man Barton was, but he knew Mala meant more to him than anything. Sometimes that made it hard to be fair.

Barton interrupted his thoughts. "I don't want to take Mala away from you. You've made her more happy than I've ever seen her."

"Then go away. Pretend you didn't find her."

"I wish it were that easy. They would find her."

"They who?"

"Mala has the answers you seek. She is the one you should ask."

Mason nodded, knowing he was right. Damn it, the guy was starting to grow on him.

Chapter 16

Barton was already giving Mala a headache. The next day he wanted to know even more about Earth. The computer had only whetted his appetite.

And what was this with Barton and Mason? Maybe a good night's sleep had made him see more clearly this morning. Mason acted as if he actually liked Barton. The Elders were right when they said men were a very different breed.

"This is all very interesting," Barton said as they walked inside the sheriff's office. "It's brick and mortar, right?"

"It keeps the big bad wolf from blowing us away, so I guess it'll do." Mason walked to the dispatcher's window and took the papers Francine handed him.

"From the fairy tale, right?" He beamed as he followed Mason. "I read about it on the computer. Amazing facts, and fiction, were stored on the machine."

"That must be why the light was on all night. Didn't you go to sleep after we came inside?" Mason asked.

After they came inside? Now she was confused. The last thing she remembered was being snuggled against Mason's back. What had they been up to?

"I don't need sleep," Barton said before she could ask.

Oh no. "How about if I show you some of the

town?" Before Barton had time to say anything more, she grabbed his hand and pulled him out of the office. "See you later, Mason."

"Earth is a strange place," he pointed out once they were outside. "Did you notice his craft never took off? The ride was quite bumpy."

"They don't fly."

He raised an eyebrow. "How barbaric."

"Just different." Barton could act so superior sometimes. Damned attitude chip. And she didn't want to talk about crafts. They had more important things to discuss.

"What happened last night after I went to sleep?"

"Mason realized I was no threat and that for the moment you won't be leaving." He stopped, turning to the right, then to the left. "What are these?"

Well, that explained absolutely nothing, and as engrossed with his surroundings as Barton seemed to be, she doubted she would get any more out of him.

She looked down the street. His gaze was riveted on the stores. "A clothes store, a place where they sell flowers, a candy store, and the other store we have to stay away from. The owner thinks I'm from another planet."

"But you *are* from another planet."

"Yes, but we're not supposed to talk about it. They'll lock us up and throw away the key if we do."

He looked thoughtful as he gazed across the street. "I would like to go into one of the stores," he abruptly said. "I believe I read about them. Reading and actually exploring a place are two very different things."

She'd known he'd want to look around and she had to admit being rather proud she'd been here first. That, and she hadn't had any chocolate in a few hours. She wanted to see Barton's reaction to the tasty treat.

He functioned like any normal Nerakian so he could digest food capsules and drink without shorting out any wires. The Elders had made the companion units as close to her species as they could get. She and her cousin had . . . tweaked him a bit.

They walked across the street and entered the candy store. Anna looked up, smiling when she saw who it was.

"Out of chocolate already?"

"And I've brought . . . a friend."

"The more the merrier is what I always say. What suits your fancy?"

"Fudge. A lot."

Anna smiled again. "That's what I like, a woman who isn't afraid to sink her teeth into chocolate and not worry about gaining a few pounds."

Gaining pounds? She doubted it would be anything for her to concern herself with. She'd always been quite comfortable with her size.

As soon as they left the store, she dipped inside the sack and broke off a chunk of fudge and gave it to Barton. "You eat it," she explained.

"Do you realize the harm you can cause to your body by consuming human food? It could create all manner of dysfunctions. The food capsules are meant to provide you with all your daily requirements."

"Just try it."

He gave her a long-suffering sigh but put the piece of chocolate in his mouth. His eyes closed. "Oh, my, that's quite delicious. So much tastier than a smoothie or a food capsule." He reached for the bag but she moved it to her other side. "Later. I thought you wanted to check out the other stores?"

His brow furrowed. "I don't think you like sharing."

She ignored him and began walking toward the

flower shop. "You'll like this store. It smells really nice."

"Like the candy store?"

She shook her head. "Different. And you can't eat the flowers but they smell nice just the same."

A few minutes later they emerged, Barton's nose buried in a rose. When he came up for air, he was smiling.

"This next store is more for women, but it has pretty candles and you'll like Carol. But don't try to eat the candles. They don't taste as good as they smell."

He nodded as they went inside. "This is rather pleasant," he stated, sniffing the air.

No sooner had the words left his mouth than a stricken Carol hurried out of the back room, followed by an angry-looking man. She skidded to a halt when she saw Mala and Barton.

"Oh, I'm so sorry. I didn't hear the bell." She cast a wary look at the man who came up behind her.

The stranger studied them for a brief moment, then turned back to Carol, effectively dismissing them. He grabbed her arm. "Carol was just locking up. Weren't you, babe?"

She grimaced, her hand clamping onto his in an attempt to remove it, which failed.

"I do not believe this woman wants your hand upon her," Barton stated.

The man grinned. "It's not like you'll be able to do a damn thing about it." His gaze slithered over Barton. "Pansies. The whole fuckin' world is full of 'em."

"Scott, please," Carol pleaded.

Barton grabbed the man's hand. Scott's knees buckled, his legs barely holding him up.

"Pansy." Barton looked thoughtful. "That's a flower."

He raised the rose to his nose. "Is it as fragrant as a rose?"

Scott swung his arm. Quick as a flash, Barton dropped the rose and grabbed Scott's other fist. "I must warn you that if you continue your attempts at bodily harm I will be forced to inflict pain upon you and you really don't want me do that."

"No limp-wristed bastard is going to . . . Owwwww!"

"With just a small twist," Barton explained, "you can cause minimal damage, but still exert a high degree of discomfort."

Mala smiled. This man called Scott had no idea just how much pain Barton could inflict. She was quite proud of him.

Carol rushed to the counter and slid open a cabinet. When she straightened, she was holding a long black stick with two holes in the end. "I think it's time you left, Scott."

"Tell him to let go," he ground out.

"Of course." Barton released him.

Scott rubbed his knuckles, hurrying toward the door, but paused after he opened it. "Don't get so high and mighty, Carol. This guy won't be around all the time. You owe me."

"I don't owe you a damn thing."

When Barton stepped toward him, he slammed out of the store without another word.

"Are you okay?" Mala went to her new friend and hesitantly put her arm around her shoulders. Carol surprised her by setting the stick on the counter and turning into her arms, sobbing. Anger shot through Mala as Carol's emotions washed over her.

"Do you have a work station?" Barton asked.

Carol raised her head. "Oh, I'm so sorry to start blubbering like that. Thank you so much for helping me." She took a deep breath and stepped away from Mala and looked at Barton. "What were you wanting?"

"A mixing station?" His words were soft, meant to calm.

Mala looked between the two. She'd never seen Barton act so . . . tender.

"I have a small kitchen in the back."

"I'm sure that will suffice." He walked past her and disappeared behind the curtain.

"He's with you?" Carol asked.

"A friend."

"So, you don't have amnesia anymore?"

"No."

"It was kind of him to take Scott down a notch. Your friend is a surprising man. I mean he doesn't look like he would be so strong. But then who am I to judge anyone? It's not like I'm good at recognizing a person's true character or anything. Scott really . . . really . . . fooled me."

She sniffed. Then sniffed again. Tears began to roll down her face. She dug into her pocket until she brought out a white cloth.

"I'm so sorry for breaking down like this. It's just that I thought he was finally out of my life, and then to have him walk into the store this afternoon." She wiped away her tears with the cloth.

"Shh . . . it's okay now. He's gone."

Barton joined them again. "Here, drink this."

She took it from him without question and began to drink. The glass was empty when she set it on the counter. "Oh, that was good. What was it?"

"A smoothie. It will calm you."

"Are you a doctor?" Carol's smile was a little lop-sided when she grinned up at him.

He returned her smile with a shake of his head. "No. I'm a companion unit."

Oh, no. Mala didn't think it was wise for Barton to tell her he wasn't quite real. Close, but not quite. She'd only warned him about not telling Mason.

"A companion unit?" Carol's brow wrinkled. She looked at Mala.

"He takes care of me. Like a . . ." What was the word Mason had used? "Butter! He's my butter."

Carol giggled. "Oh, that was a strong drink. I could've sworn you called him your butter." Her gaze moved around the room. "I never noticed what a lovely store I have. All these pretty colors: blues, pinks, and look at that purple color." She reached her hand into the air, swirling it around absolutely nothing.

"I don't think smoothies act the same way here as they do on Nerak," Mala told Barton as they took Carol's arm and together led her to a chair, which the woman immediately plopped down onto.

"I think you could very well be correct in your assumption. She seems quite . . ."

"Drunk," Carol supplied, then giggled again.

The door swung open and Mason strode inside. "Carol, are you all right? Someone said Scott was in town." He quickly assessed Mala, then knelt beside the chair and took Carol's hand.

"Come and gone." She pulled her hand loose and waved it about the room, almost clonking him upside the face.

Mala flinched when Mason glanced up, a question in his eyes. Oh no, now what was she supposed to tell him? That they had made her tipsy? It was an accident. But at least Carol wasn't nearly as upset as she had been.

"Barton came to my rescue," Carol continued. "My knight in shining armor. He scared away the dragon and made my world safe."

"He seems to do that a lot. With animals, with people. But you're acting awfully strange." Mason sniffed. "Have you been drinking?"

Barton straightened. "Actually, I mixed her a smoothie. I didn't realize the effect on her system would be this strong. I only wanted to make her happy."

"I'd say it worked . . . and then some." He stood, went to the door and turned the sign to *closed*. "So, you took care of Scott?" His expression said Barton might have earned a little more respect from Mason.

"He had his hand upon her and she didn't want it there," Barton explained. "I simply suggested he remove it."

"You should've seen him," Mala told him. "Barton was quite efficient. He made the bad man go away."

"I'm not sure Scott won't come back." Mason slipped a protective arm around Mala's shoulders. "Carol, I don't think it would be wise if you stayed here by yourself tonight."

Carol looked at him with a lopsided grin. "Didn't I tell you? I have my knight in shining armor. Barton can stay with me, can't you?"

Barton squared his shoulders. "I will stay with her and see to her protection."

"Sorry, fella, but I don't really know you," Mason said.

Mala rested her hand on Mason's arm. "He'll protect her. Trust me, this I know. He won't let any harm come to Carol."

"I'm still not sure about this."

"Oh, poo, Mason. Barton can stay in the spare bedroom. He's Mala's friend and if she'll vouch for his character then I don't see what the harm would be."

"Yes, Mason. Don't you trust my word that Barton will have only Carol's best interests in mind?"

"I think everyone's ganging up on me."

Mason ran a hand through his hair, then stared for a long minute at Barton, as if he was deciding whether or not he could be trusted. Something seemed to pass between the two men. Mala would still like to know what happened after she'd gone to bed.

Mason finally nodded and looked at Barton. "Watch out for Scott. If he shows up, call 911. Don't wait for him to get ugly. He was born that way." Then he looked at Carol. "We'll only be a phone call away if you need us."

"I'm sure Barton will be all I need." Carol was looking at Barton like she could eat him up.

This might not be such a good idea.

"You ready?" Mason asked.

Mala nodded and followed him out the door, but at the last minute she looked at Barton. He smiled at her. She certainly hoped everything went okay tonight.

Chapter 17

Carol knew the room would stop spinning any second. She just didn't think it would be in the next second . . . or the one after that. "You make a good smoothie." With smoothies like that, the whole world could stay healthy . . . at the very least, extremely happy.

"Would you like to rest?" Barton asked.

She returned her attention to Mala's friend. Had she really invited him to stay the night? Her protector? Tingles of anticipation ran up and down her body.

No, he wasn't there to provide anything more than a safeguard in case Scott returned.

Her gaze lingered on his face and just how handsome a man he was. Barton had the perfect good looks—as if he'd just stepped off the cover of *GQ*. Very polished. Certainly the opposite of Scott.

But her mind was really wandering now. What had Barton asked? If she wanted to lie down? Oh, don't even go there.

She drew in a deep breath. "That sounds like a good idea." It might just get her mind off Scott . . . and thinking the kind of thoughts she was starting to think about Barton. Not wise at all.

She attempted to stand, but wobbled when she got to her feet. Her knight scooped her up in his arms.

The room really swam then.

Whoa, when was the last time a man had picked her up without wheezing? Not that she was very big, but Scott had tried once and turned blue in the face, then promptly accused her of gaining weight. She hadn't. She still only topped the scale at one hundred and twenty-seven pounds, and on her five-foot-six-inch frame that was a good size. Scott had been an ass. Barton made her feel as if she were as light as a feather, though. It was a good feeling for her bruised ego.

"Which direction?"

"Sorry." She nodded toward the back. "Through the kitchen and up the stairs, but you don't have to carry me. I'm perfectly capable of walking." At least she hoped she'd start to feel her feet again. Right now her whole body was sort of numb, but in a good way. A really good way. Numb and relaxed. Why else would she let a complete stranger carry her upstairs to her bedroom?

"You're frowning," Barton pointed out.

"I don't know you. Other than you're Mala's friend." A twinge of uneasiness rippled down her spine. What had she let herself in for?

"I will not hurt you, if that's what troubles you."

She snorted. "Yeah, well, Scott made promises too, and I was stupid enough to believe him. Mark my words, I won't fall for another man's lies." But it did feel rather nice snuggled next to a manly chest. Her tummy felt like there were butterflies fluttering inside. She hadn't felt this giddy in a long time.

"But I'm not exactly a man," he said.

Well, crap. She should've known he was too good to be true. "You're gay?" Damn, what a shame. The guy was starting to grow on her. He was carrying her up the stairs as if she weighed nothing.

And look at all the pretty colors that floated along

with them. They swirled all around them, blending with the sparkling stars.

"Gay? As in happy?"

She pulled her gaze away from the colors and looked at him. Oh, this was nice too. Barton was a very handsome man. Such a waste.

"No, gay as in you like other men . . . sexually." She couldn't believe she was even talking like this. It had to be the drink he'd given her.

He smiled and her toes curled. "Then no, I'm not gay."

She nodded toward her bedroom door as heat spread up her face. First she'd warned him she wouldn't fall for any lies, then accused him of being gay. He, on the other hand, probably thought she was deranged.

And the biggest problem—she really didn't care! Maybe it wasn't a problem after all, she thought to herself as the colors floated into the room ahead of them.

What the hell was in that drink? She certainly wasn't upset anymore that her ex-husband had stormed into her shop demanding money. Relaxed, that's what she was. Very relaxed.

And a little horny.

No, not horny. She'd gotten her fill of men after Scott disappeared with most of her money and a cute little nurse's aide from the local hospital.

No, she was not horny.

Barton laid her on the bed with seemingly no effort, then straightened. "Would you like me to draw you a bath?"

Oh, God. She closed her eyes as visions filled her mind of Barton stripping her clothes off—slowly, sensuously, one layer at a time. Filling the tub with warm water, coconut-scented bubbles rising to the top. He'd pick up the soap and begin to lather . . .

"Carol, are you awake?"

Damn, she'd been right at the good part. She opened her eyes and frowned. Barton waited patiently. What had Mala said? He was butter? Her eyes widened. "You're Mala's butler!" That explained so much.

"I take care of her," he stated.

"Oh, more of a valet."

"If you like."

God, he had a wonderful smile, beautiful blue eyes and a mouth-watering broad chest that had been so terrific leaning her head against. She couldn't have picked a more handsome man if she'd chosen him from a catalog. Lucky Mala!

"You don't have to wait on me. I appreciate that you got rid of Scott, but you don't have to wait on me." God, she sounded so lame.

"I want to."

He turned and went into her adjoining bathroom and a few moments later she heard water running. A man who waited on her. Life couldn't get any better than this. Where the hell was he from?

A few minutes passed before he returned. "Would you like me to lay out your nightwear or do you sleep nude?" He stood very tall as he waited for her answer.

Heat spread through her like a fire out of control. He was killing her. He wanted to take care of her and all she could think of was jumping his bones.

"Really, I can manage." She swung her feet off the bed, but when the room tilted, she grabbed the mattress to steady herself. In turn, Barton grabbed her.

She found herself staring into his eyes again. Everything about him was perfect. "God, you're gorgeous." Did she just say that? When he smiled, she knew she had. "Sorry," she mumbled.

"You're quite beautiful, too."

Why hadn't Mala scarfed him up for herself? But then, she'd seen the way her new friend looked at Mason and the way Mason had looked at her. There was definitely something going on.

"My bath water should be ready." When she stood this time, she was a little more steady on her feet. *Please don't let me fall flat on my face,* she prayed.

Concentrate.

Straight line.

She breathed a sigh of relief when she made it all the way to the bathroom without even a stumble. She went inside and shut the door, leaning against it with her eyes closed until she could catch her breath.

No more smoothies. She snorted. Not like any smoothie she'd ever had.

Pushing away from the door, she opened her eyes and began stripping out of her clothes. She needed to get sober. Pull herself together.

Warm fuzzies wrapped around her. Okay, they could stay. She liked feeling as if nothing could ever harm her again. She wasn't worried about Scott at all. That was a first in a very long time.

But then, the smoothie had been pretty potent.

Barton wasn't so bad, either.

She walked naked to the tub, turning the water off and climbing in. She sank so low that the water covered her from her chin downward. As the water swirled around her, she felt herself totally relax. This was nice. Would that she could afford a butler all the time. Mala must have loads of money.

"Would you like me to soap your back?"

She shoved with her heels, shooting upright with a whoosh that sloshed water over the side as she fought to cover herself. Oh, God, he was in the bathroom with her. A total stranger, and she as naked as the day she was born. She didn't even have bubbles to hide behind.

"Get out!" She glared at him, reaching for a towel, but the closest one was out of arm's reach. "Do you always sneak into a room when a woman is trying to bathe?"

His brow furrowed. "I've upset you. I'm terribly sorry. I assure you that wasn't my intention." He bowed at the waist and turned.

Oh, damn, she'd made a mess of everything. Barton had saved her from Scott, and was only trying to take care of her. Then what does she do? Bites his head off.

She hugged close to the side of the tub. "Wait. I'm sorry." When he looked back she wanted to sink all the way down into the tub and drown herself. She was so embarrassed. "That is, I mean . . ." She took a deep breath. "Men don't usually walk into a woman's bathroom when she's taking a bath."

"I understand." He lowered his gaze and stepped from the room.

She wanted to die. Absolutely die. The only man who'd ever seen her naked was Scott, and he told her she was flat-chested and her hips too round.

Now Barton had seen her.

This wasn't good. How could she look him in the eye ever again?

As much as she'd like to, she couldn't hide in the bathroom forever. She quickly washed and climbed out.

Every noise from the next room made her jump. She was being ridiculous. She was a grown woman. He was a valet who was apparently used to taking care of naked women. She swallowed hard.

But Mala was cute and sexy. She probably didn't have any flaws.

As she dried off, she caught a glimpse of her reflection in the full-length mirror on the back of the door.

Taking a deep breath, she dropped the towel and stared. Really stared. Her breasts didn't look that small or her hips that round. She faced the mirror. When had she started thinking her boobs were small?

Yeah, like she didn't know the answer to that. She'd never thought there was anything really wrong with her body until she'd married Scott.

He'd brainwashed her. And she'd let him. She glared at the mirror. Her shoulders slumped. What if she was wrong, though?

There was only one way to find out.

Sometimes a woman had to do what she had to do. With back straight, she marched to the door and flung it open.

"What does my body look like?" Her bravado quickly began to falter when Barton looked at her without saying a word. Slowly, his gaze moved over her and she wanted to die, but she raised her chin instead. If he thought she needed a body bag then she'd swear off men entirely.

"I think you're a beautiful, vibrant female with a body meant for making love."

Her knees grew weak as he walked toward her, but she wouldn't run away. Never again.

He stopped in front of her, raised his hand and lightly caressed her cheek. A sensuous shudder rippled over her. How long had she waited to feel the tender touch of a man? Way too long, but even now she didn't want a man's pity.

"I shouldn't have just barreled out here demanding to know what you think about . . . about my body. I've put you on the spot." She started to turn away, but he stopped her with a touch on her arm.

"It's not in me to lie. I can omit things, but I cannot lie. You are a beautiful woman and I want to make love to you." He cupped one breast, running his finger back and forth across the nub.

Oh, Lord, this was good. Her eyes fluttered closed as the roaring in her ears blocked out everything except what her body felt right now.

His words tumbled around inside her head: beautiful, vibrant, the most sexy woman—okay, maybe he hadn't said that last part, but he might as well have and oh, God, please don't let him stop touching me. She grabbed his arm so she wouldn't fall over, but he scooped her up again and carried her to the bed. She loved the way he scooped!

Snuggling closer to his warmth, she wrapped her arms around his neck, and when he laid her on the bed he slid next to her, his lips connecting with hers.

He even tasted great. Just like the chocolate Anna sold in her shop. Life couldn't get any better than this: a man who tasted like chocolate. Unless it was a naked man who tasted like chocolate.

She tugged at his clothes, her hands trembling in her anticipation. It had been a long time since she'd felt this eager to have sex.

He gently moved her hands and stood. Before she could complain, he began to strip. Oh, this was so nice. Someone had been listening to her prayers because she was getting them all answered . . . tenfold. Sometimes it paid to be good.

But right now, she was feeling really bad.

He removed his jacket and shirt. Her mouth began to water as he stood there, bare to the waist. She could only stare at his broad shoulders, biceps with just the right amount of bulge. Not so much that he looked pumped up on steroids, but enough that she could squeeze and caress . . . and just the thought of touching him made her damp.

"I want to please you," he told her, slowly drawing his belt from the loops and letting it fall to the floor.

How many times had she dreamed a man would say those very words? *He* wanted to please *her*. She almost had an orgasm just thinking about it. Hell, he was already pleasing her. Boy was he pleasing her. She rolled to her side and continued to watch him please her, as he undid his pants and let them slide to the floor before kicking out of them. His briefs followed.

Ah, Lord. She thought she might have just had an orgasm. Her first in what seemed like forever. He was so damn beautiful, though. It almost made her cry just looking at his total perfection.

"Do I meet with your approval?"

"You think? I mean, ohhhh . . . yeah." She forced herself to look up. "Yes, you more than meet with my approval."

He smiled. She was melting all over the place, and he smiled.

"Then let me please you." He lay down beside her and gently pushed her onto her back. Next, he lightly caressed her from the top of her chest to the top of her mound. She arched upward, wanting more.

"Sometimes, just the thought of what a person might do will cause heightened sensations within one's body." He ran his hand down her once more, then back up. "You want me to touch your breasts, to tangle my fingers in your curls, caressing your sex. You also know I will, eventually. It's that which causes the fire to build inside you."

She moaned. Her body was beginning to burn. Through the haze of passion, she heard his words and knew he was right. She ached for his touch, but anticipation was making her body burn even hotter.

"You can only go so far," he continued. "Only building a person so high before you have to offer them some release or your efforts will backfire."

When he cupped her breast, rubbing his thumb back and forth across her sensitive nub, she gasped.

"Knowledge is a wonderful thing. I have discovered many things from your information centers."

"Information center?" He squeezed her nipple between his thumb and forefinger just enough that it caused spasms of pleasure to erupt inside her. "Ohh, that feels nice."

"You call the information center a computer. A wealth of knowledge." He lowered his mouth, flicking his tongue across her tight nipple before gently sucking on her breast.

She ran her hands through his hair, over his back. Nice muscles, smooth skin—rock hard ass, and that wasn't the only thing nice and hard. His erection rubbed against her. She bit her bottom lip, pressing against him as much as she could.

Release . . . she had to have release.

He moved his head to her other breast and began to suck. She whimpered. At this point she didn't care if he thought she was desperate because she was.

"Make love to me," she moaned. "I need you . . . now."

He raised his head, moving down to the end of the bed.

What was he doing? He wasn't leaving, was he? No, thank goodness. He settled himself between her legs. Release, yes, finally. This was a good thing. A very good thing. She closed her eyes.

Nothing happened. Had she done something wrong? When she opened her eyes, he was staring down at her sex. The heat of her embarrassment flooded her face.

"The heart of womanhood," he said, reaching out to fondle her.

At the first touch of his fingers, she cried out and jerked forward.

"You're wet," he said when he inserted two fingers.

She rocked her hips against his fingers, crying out again when he removed them, but he quickly replaced them with something that gave her even more pleasure. Damn, it felt good having him inside her. Yes, this is what she needed.

For a moment he didn't move, letting her get used to his size. She wrapped her legs around him for a tighter fit.

He began to move inside her, slowly at first—a moist, vibrating heat thrusting in and out. Her vagina contracted and released against him.

"Oh, jeez, ohhhhhh . . . yesssssssssss!" She tightened her legs around him. He thrust faster, the vibrations intensified. The heat intensified.

She was coming. Oh, yes, oh yes! Her body tightened. She screamed, jerking forward as her whole body convulsed. The air around her exploded as she came.

Panting, she relaxed once again. When her world came back into focus she looked into his face, saw the happiness, and laughed for the pure joy of it.

"Where the hell are you from?" They needed more men like him!

"I'm from the planet Nerak. Just on the other side of your galaxy."

She slowly deflated. Damn, he was crazy. She'd just had the best sex in her whole lifetime and it was with a lunatic.

Tears filled her eyes.

Life just wasn't fair.

Chapter 18

Mason stood on the back porch, surveying the land in front of him. This ranch had been in his family for a long time. He'd lived in Washboard all his life. Most of his relatives were buried in the local cemetery. Some still lived here or at least within driving distance.

He had a sister in the next county. She was happily married with two boys. Every holiday they all got together. Traditions built on love and respect—on the fact they were blood, and that mattered a lot to him.

But right now he was contemplating giving it all up for a woman he barely knew. Just run away with her and never look back. Then her family, her country, couldn't touch her. They could hire anyone they wanted to come looking for them, but he knew lots of places where they could get lost.

Soft footsteps padded outside, slender arms came around his waist and lightly hugged, her cheek resting against his back.

How had he fallen under her spell so quickly? But then, he knew the answer. He'd been waiting for Mala all his life. He just hadn't known it until she'd stumbled into his heart late one night.

"It's cool outside. And there's an odd smell in the air—pleasant, though."

The rumble of thunder followed her words. She stiffened, sliding under his arm and snuggling against his side. "What is that? Are there warriors about to attack?"

He laughed until he realized she was shivering. Was she serious? "It's just thunder." He brought her around to face him, studying her. She was teasing. He relaxed. Yes, that had to be it. He loved her sense of humor.

He pulled her against him, lightly running his hands up and down her back. "The smell of rain. We can use it, too."

"Rain. It sounds wonderful."

"Barton is trustworthy, right?" he asked, changing the subject. He needed her to confirm it one more time. Even knowing people might lie, but animals didn't. Barton was still better than taking a chance Scott would return.

"Barton will let no harm come to your friend. He will keep her safe."

"He's an odd fellow, though. I've only seen a few people with an ability like he has to connect with animals."

"Barton is very special."

"Did he come from England? I mean, he's kind of proper."

She took a deep breath. "Yes, from England." Oh, there she went again. Mason wasn't going to like that she lied to him. But would he believe Barton wasn't flesh and blood? He was as close as anyone could get, but he still would never be human. Telling Mason wasn't going to be easy.

Tomorrow, that's when she would explain everything.

Mason's stomach rumbled. Her fear disappeared and she laughed.

"I'd forgotten we skipped supper," he said.

"I rather enjoyed the substitution." Making love with Mason was very good.

"A shame we can't live on sex alone," he interrupted her naughty thoughts. "How about I rustle us up a late-night breakfast? Fried eggs, toast with gobs of butter and strawberry jam . . ."

Now it was her stomach's turn to rumble, but in a different way. She could feel the color draining from her face as a cold sweat drenched her body.

Oh, no, Barton had warned her not to eat the food on Earth. Just the thought of it made her . . . oh, no . . .

"Mason, I think . . . I might be dying." With those words, the contents of her stomach exited her body.

He lifted her into his arms and carried her toward his room. "What's wrong? Should I call a doctor?"

"No!" She couldn't afford for the doctor to take her lifeblood. She might very well need every drop. Besides, she didn't think she would still be breathing by the time he arrived. Not the way she felt right now.

He nudged the door open to his room and carried her across to his bed. When he laid her down, he sat next to her, laying his hand upon her forehead.

She curled on her side. This was just awful. The horrible rumbling in her stomach wasn't going away.

"I'll be back in a second." Mason hurried from the room and returned in a few minutes with a wet cloth, placing it on her forehead. "My mother always said it would help."

She dragged her eyelids open, hating that she'd caused him to worry. "I'll be fine." He didn't look like he believed her. That was okay because she didn't really believe it herself.

"Maybe some chicken soup?"

Her stomach lurched.

"Please, no."

She moved the washcloth to her mouth and pressed it against her lips. Just the thought of food was too much to bear.

"I need Barton." He was the only one who could help her. Or at the very least, explain to the Elders that her lifeblood had drained away and she was no more. She could only hope it would come soon, as the sickness gripped her in its clutches, refusing to let go. "Hurry," she moaned.

He grabbed the phone and dialed Carol's number. Busy signal. Damn it, she'd probably taken it off the hook since Scott was in town. He'd made a habit of calling her and making threats. There was only one thing to do. Go get Barton and pray on the drive over that he could cure whatever was wrong with Mala.

"I'll hurry," he said right before he dropped a kiss on her forehead. He grabbed his keys off the dresser, noting that his hands were shaking. He hadn't been this scared in a long time. It wasn't a good feeling.

Carol looked up at the ceiling as she lay in bed. The bathroom light was on and there was just enough light that she could count the square tiles. But it wasn't enough to take her mind off what had happened.

She'd just had sex with a man who was crazy. How much worse could her life get?

But then again, she thought to herself, Scott was pretty much certifiable and sex with him had been lousy. So what was the big deal about having fantastic sex . . . the best sex she'd ever had . . . possibly the best sex she'd ever have again in this lifetime . . . with someone who didn't have all his marbles?

But on the other hand, how could she have a relationship with a man who thought he was from another planet?

Her body tingled. Damn, it had been the best sex she'd ever experienced, though.

What if she told him to tell people he was from a foreign country? That might work.

No, no, no. If he was crazy enough to think he was from another planet he might be crazy in other areas as well, and did she really want that kind of person in her life?

Yes.

No, no, no!

But where was she going to find another man like him? She'd never heard of anyone . . . vibrating when they had sex. And the heat. Ah, damn, that had been . . . sooo fantastic! She was getting hot just thinking about it.

"Did I give you pleasure?" he asked.

Laughter bubbled out of her, she couldn't hold it back. "Did you give me pleasure? Oh, yeah, you gave me enough pleasure to last a lifetime." She rolled over, half lying across his chest and staring into his eyes. "You gave me a *lot* of pleasure." She scooted forward until her lips were against his.

Closing her eyes, she lost herself in his kiss. The way his tongue stroked hers. She'd never been aggressive in the bedroom because Scott hadn't liked it, but she was feeling more than a little aggressive at the moment and climbed on top, straddling Barton, enjoying the fact he was aroused, enjoying the fact that her sex was pressed intimately against his and it was stirring all kinds of wonderful sensations inside her.

It was great being on top and looking down at him. She rubbed against him. He closed his eyes and raised himself just slightly. A surge of power rushed through her.

"So, what's it like on your planet?" She might as well see how crazy he was.

He opened his eyes and looked at her. "It's very bright." He moved his hands to her thighs, running his fingers up and down the insides of her legs and causing wonderful tremors to explode inside her body.

"And you're Mala's valet." She closed her eyes, biting her bottom lip when he brushed his hands through her curls and up her clit. "That feels good."

"I take care of Mala. That's what I was programmed to do."

She opened her eyes. "Programmed? As in robot?" This was worse than she thought. Of all the luck in the world, she had to have the worst.

"Not exactly. Nerak's technology is far superior. I'm highly intelligent, but I can also feel—much like the people on your planet."

"So, if I did this . . ." She scooted down his body, met his gaze, then grinned mischievously before lowering her head and taking him in her mouth. He groaned, raising his hips. She closed her eyes and gently sucked.

In the beginning she'd wanted to experiment with Scott, but the one time she'd suggested going down on him, he'd called her a whore, so she'd curbed her desires. She'd learned to curb a lot of things.

This was wonderful, though. Everything she'd imagined. His skin was smooth and he tasted yummy . . . almost like Anna's chocolate fudge. Odd, but wonderful.

She raised her head, sliding back up his body. "And you liked that? I mean, you felt it?" She wiggled against his erection and it quivered beneath her. Oh, yeah, he'd felt it all right.

He gasped when she slid him inside her. "I can feel everything a human feels. I can give you whatever pleasure you like."

"I like this. Does it bother you that I'm on top?"

He shook his head.

"And if I ask you to touch me?" She stopped moving, waiting to see if he would do whatever she asked. He didn't disappoint, reaching forward and cupping her breasts, tweaking the nipples. She moaned, savoring the feel of his hands. "And if I asked you to touch me . . . lower."

Was she being so bold? She hardly recognized the husky voice. But they were the only two in the room so it had to be.

She held her breath as his hands caressed their way down her body, until they parted the folds, exposing her sex. He rubbed lightly. She whimpered, running her hands through her hair, excitement coursing through her veins. He said he would do anything. Was he lying? Would he do anything she asked? Anything she'd ever dreamed about?

"I want your mouth where your hands are." She opened her eyes. Their gazes met. He took her into his arms and rolled her on her side. She took a deep, shuddering breath as she imagined his mouth sucking, his teeth pulling on her sex. But . . . "You don't have to if you don't want to," she whispered.

"I'll please you any way you like. Pleasing you gives me pleasure."

He scooted downward, his mouth just above her sex. "You smell so sweet." Then he lowered his mouth.

She cried out as his tongue slid down her length. She gripped the sheets in both her hands so she wouldn't fly off the bed as heat engulfed her body. This is what she'd been wanting. "Oh, yes," she moaned.

He sucked her into his mouth while his fingers splayed on either side of her sex, massaging, bringing her to climax. Before she could think even one rational thought, he entered her.

Vibrations and sensuous heat swirled around inside her and she could feel the passion building again. Another orgasm. Oh, yes, this was soooo good! Yes! Yes! Yes! Her body jerked upward as she wrapped her legs around his waist and clung on as the orgasm swept over her in wave after wave of sensuous release.

As her breathing slowed, she floated back into the mattress. This was good . . . life was good. Who the hell cared if he wasn't exactly real? He was the most real man she'd ever been with.

And he vibrated. My gawd! How cool was that!

Her breathing finally began to slow. Her pulse steadied to a more regular rate. Exhaustion swept over her, making her body tremble.

"Sleep," she heard him whisper from a long way off. "Sleep." She closed her eyes, emotionally and physically drained, and let the darkness close around her.

For the first time in her life, she was sexually satisfied.

For the first time in her life, she knew she'd sleep without worrying about one damned thing.

And for the first time in her life, she knew she was going to hire herself a valet—no matter what the cost!

Mason pulled into the narrow alley behind Carol's store and jumped out of his Jeep. Mala should've let him call an ambulance. Damn it, she'd been so pale.

His heart skipped a beat. If anything happened to her before he returned with Barton, he'd never forgive himself. He killed the engine and jumped out.

A staircase led to the outside entrance of Carol's apartment. He took the steps two at a time and pounded on the door. "Carol, open up."

"Go away," was the barely distinguishable reply.

"I need Barton."

"No, you can't have him!"

He heard something that sounded as if Carol might be stumbling around in the dark, followed by a muffled curse and the door being jerked open.

"What are you doing here at this hour of the night?" she asked, shoving her hair out of her face.

Mason opened his mouth, then snapped it shut, at a total loss for words. Never in his life had he seen Carol in such disarray. At least, not since she'd been married to Scott. She'd always been soft spoken . . . demure . . .

But right at this moment she looked like a woman who'd been having sex all night.

"Are you through staring?" She tugged her robe closer to her body.

He cleared his mind and remembered why he was there. "I need Barton. I mean, Mala needs him. She's sick and won't let me call a doctor."

"Go home. We'll be right behind you." She shut the door in his face.

Breathing a sigh of relief, he hurried down the stairs and jumped into his Jeep. All the way back to the ranch he silently prayed Mala would be okay.

Ten miles had never seemed so long. His foot grew heavier on the gas with each mile. When he took a corner a little too fast and almost lost control, he knew he had to slow down if he was going to make it back to Mala at all.

The long stretch up to the house had never looked so good. He slid to a stop and turned off the engine before getting out and running inside. He went straight to his bedroom.

It was an effort just for Mala to raise her head. "Oh, Mason, you didn't bring Barton. My life is draining away. Soon I will be gone. I'll miss you so much."

"He's on the way. Carol's with him. I'm calling the doc. I'm not taking any chances."

"No." She grabbed his hand. "Barton will know what to do." She just wanted it all to end, but as kind as the doctor was, she didn't quite trust him not to take her lifeblood. He wouldn't understand how much she needed it. "My mouth, it's so dry."

"I'll get you something to drink." He hurried from the room as if he were glad to have something to do.

Oh no, her stomach contents were coming up. Surely there wasn't anything left inside her.

Without raising her head, she eased off the bed and onto the floor. The cool wood felt good against her face so she lay there for a moment catching her breath.

Her stomach rumbled.

She clamped her lips together.

This wasn't good. Getting to her knees, she crawled toward the bathroom. She was halfway there when Mason came around the corner with a glass of water. She slumped to the floor.

"I'll never regret coming to Texas and meeting you." She sniffed, sucking up her tears.

"Shh, you're not dying. You've caught some kind of bug. Probably when I took you into the hospital. You'll be all right before you know it."

"I'm going to be sick," she whimpered.

He set the water down and picked her up, carrying her to the bathroom, but it was like she'd thought: there was nothing left inside her. After rinsing her mouth and wiping her face with another cold wet cloth, Mason carried her back to bed and tucked her in.

"I've never felt like this before."

He paused with his hand on the blanket. "Never?" His smile was gentle. "Surely you've been sick before."

She shook her head.

"Childhood diseases?"

"No."

"Never?"

"Uh-uh."

"Well, I promise you it will get better. Just rest."

She hoped he was right, but he didn't realize she was from another planet. He didn't believe her. Their anatomy was almost the same, but in some ways it was different.

And being sick on Nerak was unheard of. No one became ill. They had minor problems that could easily be fixed with a smoothie.

She hadn't taken into account what Earth would do to her system. She was probably dying.

Well, hell. Life was so unfair sometimes.

She closed her eyes and tried to calm her fears. After a few minutes, she heard the front door opening. Voices. Carol, then Barton. Her old friend would be here to see her off into the deep sleep. She sniffed.

"Mala?" Barton hurried to her side. He looked at Mason and Carol. "Leave us for a few minutes while I examine her."

She heard the door shut, but didn't open her eyes. A cool hand touched her forehead.

"Normal." Barton felt her pulse. "Steady." He laid a hand on her heart. "Strong."

She opened her eyes and stared into Barton's beautiful face, saw the worry. He was so near to perfect that it would be easy to forget he wasn't completely Nerakian.

"What is happening?" he asked.

"I'm going nearer to the deep sleep." She sniffed.

"Explain."

"I've emptied the contents from my stomach several times. There is nothing left. I'm fading away."

He pushed the covers down to her legs and placed his hand upon her stomach, then immediately jerked it away.

It was as she had thought. There was something horribly wrong inside her. The room even began to grow darker. She sniffed again, not wanting to leave Mason now that she'd found him. Or Earth. Or chocolate.

Her stomach roiled. Okay, maybe she could leave chocolate right now.

She drew in a deep, shuddering breath. "You can tell me. What's wrong?"

He slowly brought his hands toward her again and gently placed them on her abdomen. A look of wonder crossed his face.

"What?" she asked.

He met her gaze, a smile curving his lips. "You're going to have a baby."

Chapter 19

"I'm what?" She sat straight up in bed, holding her stomach as it rumbled and rolled. The room began to spin as the sickness threatened to come upon her again. She didn't think she had anything left in her stomach that might come up.

Except for the baby.

But no, that couldn't be possible. Barton was wrong. She wasn't going to have a baby. That's all there was to it. He was simply misdiagnosing.

"You're going to have a baby." He laid his hands on her abdomen again, as if he sensed she didn't believe him the first time.

"But how is that possible? I wasn't the chosen one in our family unit."

"Mason impregnated you."

She didn't understand. Her eggs were not taken from her and matched with Mason's. None of this made sense. It still didn't stop the giddy feeling inside of her, though. A baby. She'd always wanted one all her own.

She suppressed her excitement. Something still wasn't right. "If I'm going to have a child, then why am I so ill?" None of this made sense.

"Because the baby grows inside of you."

"What!" It grew inside of her? A child? But if it

grew inside of her surely she would explode as it gained in size.

Mason hurried into the room. "What are you doing to her? Mala, are you okay?"

"You will not explode," Barton explained, ignoring Mason. "Your body will adjust."

She drew in a deep breath and nodded. It was a lot to take in. Her body would adjust as the baby grew. She frowned. What did he mean . . . adjust?

"Mala?" Mason's expression showed concern.

She smiled, a little wobbly, but still a smile. "We're going to have a baby."

He laughed. "But you can't know that. . . ." he sputtered. "Besides, you told me you couldn't . . ."

"Oh, but you see, it is quite possible," Barton explained. "On Nerak, the planet we come from, females are chosen to have children. That way the population is controlled. The eggs of the female are taken and joined with that of artificial male sperm, where the DNA has been manipulated so that only girl children will be produced.

"When Mala came to Earth and copulated with a male specimen, you, she was outside of her controlled environment and became impregnated."

"Barton! I told you not to say anything."

"Nerak another planet? Aliens? Yeah, right. I think someone should explain." Mason looked between them. "It would be nice to have the truth this time if you don't mind."

"The first time we made love I told you the truth. You didn't believe me."

"What truth?"

"That I'm an alien. Don't you see, Nerak isn't another country, it's another planet."

"But you were joking."

"On the contrary, she was telling you the truth," Barton supplied.

"If it's a planet populated only with women then how the hell did you come into existence?" Mason growled.

"Mala and Kia, her cousin, created me."

Mason didn't look happy receiving the information. He seemed quite angry in fact. When would he accept the truth? She had a feeling it might take a while.

"So, you're telling me that you're . . . you're what . . . some kind of machine? A robot," he snorted.

Barton stood. "Mala and her cousin created me, but I am no robot," he replied disdainfully. "I have all the good qualities of any living person, without any of the bad ones."

"I'm not so sure about that," Mala mumbled. When Mason looked at her, she continued. "I gave him an attitude chip. I thought it would be interesting. I didn't have anyone who would get into debates with me." She shrugged.

Mason's glare only grew darker as he turned back to Barton. "Listen, you might work for her family and you might want to help Mala, but you're only hurting her by feeding this . . . this delusion that she's from another planet."

"I don't think he is, Mason." Carol spoke from the doorway.

"Carol! Not you, too?" He ran a hand through his hair and let out an exasperated sigh. "They're not from another planet. Trust me. Barton thinks because Mala has amnesia he has to play along with her fantasy."

"Then explain how they got here. Where are they from? You know darn well they don't act like us."

"Well they're damn sure not from some planet called Nerak! Mala was in an accident. Probably running from her crazy family. All this nonsense with the lunatic reporters, idiotic sci-fi movies . . ." His frown was directed toward Barton. "And a bodyguard that perpetuates the delusion, because he thinks he's helping Mala, has only confused her. I don't want to hear any more of this nonsense." He turned on his heel and stormed from the room.

"I have to go after him." Mala swung her feet off the bed but another wave of nausea swept over her, draining her energy. She fell back on her pillow with a groan. How long would this sickness last?

"Let me," Carol said. "I've known him a long time. Mason is stubborn and doesn't believe in something he can't see or touch. Life on another planet would fall into that category." She started from the room, but looked back at the last minute. "You did everything right when you created Barton." Face flaming, she rushed out.

Mason breathed in deeply of the night air. How could his life be going so well, at least reasonably well, then this happen? Maybe Doc missed something, but he'd run every test, even a CT scan.

But yet the woman he loved, and he did love her, thought she was an alien. How could he have a normal life with someone—he swallowed past the lump in his throat—who thought she was from another planet?

He didn't even turn when he heard footsteps join him on the back patio. He knew they belonged to Carol.

"Don't try to convince me there's life out there,"

he told her before she could say a word. "Mala is . . . confused. It doesn't help that Barton feeds her fantasy."

"She's not confused."

He swung around and glared at her. When she took a fearful step back, he immediately stopped scowling. Damn it, he never wanted a woman to be afraid of him. He closed his eyes for a moment, forcing himself to calm down.

"There's an innocence about her that I can't quite explain." He thought about the way she'd acted with the stray cat that lived in the barn, the way everything excited her as if it was something new, something she'd never seen before.

So maybe she wasn't quite so innocent in some things, like making love, but in others it was definitely there.

Carol sighed deeply, gazing up at the sky. "Who knows for sure what's out there? All I ask is that you keep an open mind."

"Yeah, okay." He nodded toward the house. "This Barton guy treating you okay?" He'd just started to like him and now this load of crap.

If he'd done anything to hurt Carol . . . He remembered the guy's grip. It didn't matter. He wouldn't tolerate anyone else harming Carol. They'd known each other since they were in diapers and she was like a sister to him.

"Barton has treated me very well."

"Good." He cleared his throat. "You don't really think she might be pregnant, do you?" The thought of becoming a father scared the hell out of him. What did he know about fatherhood? That could be the reason she thought she was an alien, though. Her hormones might be all out of whack.

"How should I know if she's pregnant?" Her eyes widened innocently. "I would think you'd be a better judge about that than I would."

He frowned. "You know what I meant. Damn it, you're a woman, aren't you?"

"A woman, yes. A doctor, no. If I were you, I'd buy one of those home pregnancy tests. Now, if you don't mind I think I'll head back to the shop."

He watched her go back inside the house, then pulled out an iron lawn chair and sat down heavily. What if Mala *was* pregnant?

No, this couldn't be happening. Women didn't know this soon if they were pregnant. They couldn't. Barton was just feeding into another one of her fantasies. That's all it was.

But why was she throwing up? Flu? She might have caught a bug at the hospital. But *he* didn't feel a bit queasy.

As soon as he heard a car start, he knew Barton and Carol had left so he went back inside. "How are you feeling?" he asked, standing in the doorway of his bedroom.

"Better," Mala said, raising her hand and showing him some saltine crackers. "Carol said when her sister was pregnant she ate crackers and they helped."

He drew in a deep breath. "I thought you couldn't get pregnant?"

"It's controlled on . . . where I live. Just like what Barton was saying. I truly didn't think I could. Are you upset about our making a baby? I'm not. I want this child more than anything."

"I've never really thought about having a kid," he spoke truthfully. "It might take a little getting used to." He paused. "It would probably be better if I slept in the other room tonight."

He left faster than he needed to, but damn it, what could he say? He went into his room and sat down hard on the side of his bed. Mala thought she was an alien. He ran a hand through his hair. He'd finally met the woman he wanted to live the rest of his life with, and she thought she was an alien. Oh, God, now *he* was going to puke.

When the wave of nausea passed, he stood and went to the window, staring out at the land. His land. He'd always wanted a family. Someone he could leave the ranch to. The right woman had never come along.

He closed his eyes and thought about the first time he'd seen Mala—when she'd fainted at his feet. The way she felt when he held her in his arms as he made his way back to the ranch. The first time he'd looked into her eyes. The way his heart sped up.

It was too soon . . . wasn't it? Did people fall in love this quickly?

What would his life be without her, though? A cold chill ran down his spine. He didn't even want to contemplate Mala not being around.

There was something he could do, though. Force her to confront her delusions. Make her see they weren't real.

He stripped out of his clothes and lay back on the bed. Maybe if he could make her see that this Nerak didn't exist, she would come back to reality. It would be worth a try.

And he'd buy a pregnancy test tomorrow. Hell, he wasn't sure what was real anymore.

Mala didn't think Mason was taking the news about her being pregnant very well. *Now* he wanted to talk. A question and answer game. This was getting monotonous. He didn't believe her when she told him the truth. He just looked at her like she was crazy. Okay, she would humor him.

"Tell me more about Nerak?" he asked as she sat down on the lounging sofa.

She noticed he didn't sit beside her but instead chose the chair. Fine. "What do you want to know?"

He opened his hands. "Anything you want to share." His smile was just a little too fake.

Nerak was all about fixing any problems that arose. The Elders wanted the people to be happy. She was a sensitive. Had been a sensitive for as long as she could remember. She could tell when someone wasn't happy, or was angry. Not that she'd ever truly run across that emotion until she came to Earth. On Nerak everyone was happy. Her profession was practically obsolete.

What she did know was when someone was humoring her—which Mason was now doing. "Why do you want to know about Nerak?" she asked, with more than a touch of suspicion.

He smiled. It didn't look like a real smile, though.

"I want to know where you come from. Is that so difficult for you to believe?"

Yes, it was, but she wanted to know why, so she decided to play his game.

"Nerak is a small planet," she told him. "Just on the other side of your galaxy."

He nodded. "Go on."

"Not much bigger than San Antonio."

She leaned back on the couch, wiggling until she found just the right position. What if she was wrong? That Mason truly did want to know more about her planet. Okay, she would tell him more about where she came from.

"Nerak is the planet of light. That's what the name

means. We have two bright suns that rotate opposite each other, so there is never any darkness."

"And you like the sunlight? A planet where no darkness can invade your space. Interesting."

She looked at him. He was analyzing her. That meant he didn't believe her. A rush of emotion bristled through her. So, this was what anger felt like. She knew all the emotions, but as suppressed as they were on Nerak, she'd never actually experienced all of them.

What would revenge feel like? She thought it might be rather sweet.

"Yes, always light," she told him, her eyes narrowing.

"And the people?"

"Only women. There are no men."

He raised eyebrows at that. "None whatsoever?"

She shook her head. "We killed all of them."

He visibly swallowed.

"Yes, we found they asked too many questions."

His eyebrows drew together. "That's not funny. I was trying to learn more about you."

She sat forward. "No, you were analyzing me. I should know, it's what I do—did."

"You're a therapist?"

"You find that so hard to believe?"

"Well . . . no."

"Give me your hand."

He hesitated, but finally gave in and reached his hand out to her. She took it in hers and closed her eyes. At first she felt nothing. Too many emotions running around inside her. Taking a deep breath, she cleared her head, humming under her breath.

He snorted.

She dropped his hand and glared at him. "You find something amusing?"

"Of course not."

He pasted a deadpan expression on his face that didn't fool her for one minute.

"Please, continue," he told her.

She took his hand again, closed her eyes and began to hum. She could feel her muscles relax as the essence of who Mason was seeped inside her mind, filling her body with heat. It felt nice having him there.

Soft colors swirled around her as she went deeper. She liked what she saw, even knowing he didn't believe in Nerak, or that other races even existed beyond Earth. What she saw was that he cared deeply for her. That he loved her, but he wasn't quite sure of the emotion yet.

"What do you see?"

She opened her eyes, pulling away from him. She would've liked to have seen more, but whether intentional or not, his colors were clouding. People could do that, shut themselves off.

"Well?" he prodded.

"You don't believe there is such a place as Nerak. You're hoping I'll face my delusions."

"I . . . uh . . ." He leaned away from her. "You're only guessing."

She shook her head. "Nerak does exist."

He scooted out of the chair and knelt in front of her, taking her hands in his. "It doesn't. I don't know what you're running from, but let me help you through this."

If he wasn't so cute and so sincere—she'd smack him upside the head. No wonder there were no men on Nerak!

"Why won't you believe me?" She stood and stomped her foot, and it felt good. Maybe anger wasn't such a bad emotion. It felt fabulous telling him what she really thought.

He stood, towering over her, but she didn't back down. Not one inch.

"Because there are no such things as aliens!" He fisted his hands on his hips.

"Are, too!"

He drew in a deep breath but snapped his mouth shut and glared at her. Something tingled inside her. The way he was looking at her was rather sexy. It was all she could do to keep her hands to herself.

"Prove it," he blurted out.

It took a few seconds for his words to sink in. Her thoughts were more on making love than the fact she was exactly who she said she was. But they did eventually make their way to her brain. Prove it? Why hadn't she thought of that?

"You can't," he continued, placing his hands on her shoulders. His eyes looked so sad.

"Yes I can."

His hands tightened. "Stop. You know you can't."

"But I can. I came in a spacecraft. It's a little dented but it should prove that I'm from another planet."

His eyes narrowed. "And if we don't find this spacecraft? You promise to stop talking nonsense about coming from a far off galaxy?"

"It's not that far off. Only a few hundred thousand . . ."

"Mala? Do you promise?"

"Yes, of course, but when we do get to my craft will you finally believe me?"

"There is no spacecraft because you're not from another planet."

She stomped her foot. "Mason!"

"Yes, I promise."

"Good." She smiled smugly. She would finally be

able to prove where she was from. He would have to believe her. "We can leave right now."

A rumble overhead made her jump. Then something began to ping on the roof.

"What's that?"

"A reprieve."

"I don't understand." She went to the door and looked out. The sky was dark and it had opened up to let droplets of water fall down to earth. "Oh, this is wonderful." She opened the door and started to step out at the same time a streak of light crashed to earth.

"I don't think so," he said as he grabbed her around the waist and hauled her back inside. "You'll have to wait to show me your spaceship. It's not safe going outside with the lightning."

"Then what shall we do?"

He smiled, and she had a feeling she knew what he was thinking—and she didn't even have to be a sensitive to guess what was on his mind.

Chapter 20

Carol snuggled against Barton as thunder rumbled overhead, followed by a crack of lightning. "I'm going to have to get up. I don't want to, but I have to make a living." It would be nice to just stay in bed and let the storm rage outside. Lying in Barton's arms made her feel safe and secure.

He absently caressed her back, and she wondered if she could get away with opening an hour later than usual. A nice thought, but it was all she could do to make ends meet now. If things didn't improve, she might have to close the shop for good by the end of the year.

And Scott had wanted money. What an imbecile.

"I read about wages and earnings on the Internet," Barton said.

"Then you know if I don't open I can't make money." Reluctantly, she swung her feet off the bed and sat there for a moment.

"You will show me how you run your business?"

A man who showed interest in what she was doing. This was a novelty, to be sure. "It would give me great pleasure." Turn about was fair play. He'd certainly given her pleasure last night . . . and early this morning.

He smiled and stood.

Just as he was giving her great pleasure now. He was magnificent. Her gaze slowly roamed over him. A familiar ache began to build inside her. She glanced at the clock. Damn. If she dallied any longer she would be late. A shame. A smile formed. But there was always tonight. For a moment she indulged in erotic visions.

"I'm going to take a quick shower," she mumbled, and hurried from the room. If she gave in to her fantasies the store would never get opened today. Lord, they were very good fantasies, though.

Barton wasn't in the bedroom when she finished her shower, so she dressed and went downstairs to open the store. She unlocked the door and turned her sign around. She was ready for business. The rain had even stopped and the sun peeked from behind the clouds.

She went in search of Barton, and found him in the tiny kitchen in the back part of her shop.

Oh, man, this guy was really something. The coffee was ready and he'd set some of her tiny muffins on a plate. "Are you for real?" she murmured as he pulled out a chair for her to sit down. Tears filled her eyes. She'd never been treated like this.

"Technically, no," he told her.

She clasped his hand before he could move it off her shoulder and placed a kiss on his palm. "You're more real to me than any man I know."

He squeezed her hand. "Thank you."

"Please, sit," she told him. "Can you . . . I mean . . . do you . . ." She was making a mess of this, but she didn't want to insult him.

"If you'd like to know if I eat, then the answer is yes, I can if I so desire, but it isn't necessary. I have taste buds just like you, although there wasn't any need for them when I was on Nerak."

"What, don't they have food?" She reached for a knife and buttered her muffin.

"They have food capsules."

"That sounds pretty boring."

"Boring, yes. But quite efficient." He sat across from her. "We have no need to work the land, which is good, since there's a scarcity. We have no need for animals. In fact, there is little that we do need. It's the perfect place to live."

"I'm not so sure about that. Apparently neither was Mala, if she chose to come to Earth."

"Mala wanted to have sex with a human."

Carol choked. She quickly swallowed some of her coffee to wash down the muffin.

"I think she got what she wanted," he said.

"I think you're right." She chuckled. "We don't usually discuss sex quite so openly on Earth. At least, not in Washboard, Texas."

He nodded. "I understand. She has mentioned this oddity."

"What, it's okay on Nerak to discuss one's sexual experiences?"

"Of course. The women are quite open, but I have to admit sex has become rather dull."

She could feel her face heat. "Not if the companion units are all like you."

"But I did not realize there was anything missing until I read about sex on your Internet."

"I bet that gave you a lot of ideas."

"Yes, it did. Would you like me to show you?"

Would she like him to show her? Oh, Lord, this was good. If she was dreaming she hoped she never woke up. "Tonight," she told him. The heat moved from her face and settled lower in her body.

Robot or not, she could really fall for Barton. But what did it matter that he wasn't . . . human. The way

Scott had acted during their brief marriage, anyone would question whether he was human.

Besides, she would never guess Barton wasn't human, so what difference did it make?

The bell over her door jingled.

"Time to go to work." She stood, brushing the crumbs from her blouse. She paused at the curtain. "Join me when you're ready."

She squared her shoulders and pushed the curtain to the side. This was a small town. There were some people who might not like the fact she had a lover.

And one was standing in the middle of the store right now. Oh . . . oh, hell!

Taking a deep breath, she pasted a smile on her face and stepped forward. "Margaret, how nice to see you. It's been a while." She would've liked to keep it that way, too, if the truth be known.

Margaret shook out her umbrella and placed it by the door. "Hello, dear. You're right, it has been a while. I wouldn't have come out today with the rain and what have you, but it was a necessity. Besides, it seems to have stopped for the moment." She adjusted the blue hat on her head a little more to the right.

"New hat?"

"Yes." She beamed. "I bought it in San Antonio. The prices are so much better there. Oh, not that yours are so very high."

Always the little digs. Deep breath. Don't let her see she's gotten to you.

"You get what you pay for, I suppose." Okay, maybe one little dig back at her. She was tired of people walking all over her. Maybe it was time they stopped.

"I rather like this green dress," she said, fingering

one of the dresses that had just arrived yesterday. "Albert and I are planning a trip, you know. To Italy. I'll need a few more things, but I'm just not sure that this would work." She dropped the hem of the dress, and it fell softly back into place on the metal rack. "Maybe this blue one," she said on a sigh.

"The red one." Barton spoke from the back of the room. Slowly he walked toward them.

"What? Who said . . . Oh, you have a man in your shop, Carol." Margaret's eyebrows rose all the way to her hairline.

"Yes, I do." Oh, Lord, there went her business. Margaret was the biggest gossip in town. Everyone would know about the man in her store and be wondering if he was also in her bed.

So be it. She raised her chin and dared Margaret to do her worst. Before she could dwell too long on her business going down the drain, Barton spoke again.

"The red one," he said in a low husky voice.

"What?" Margaret's words hit soprano levels. Not a good sign.

Barton took the red dress from behind the green one and brought it up to her chest. "Look into the mirror."

As if he were hypnotizing her with his words, she did as he'd requested.

"Do you see it?" He spoke the words softly.

"Why . . . yes . . ." Her eyebrows drew together. "See what?" she whispered.

"Only a bold color will do for such a bold woman." He looked down into her eyes. "You *are* bold, aren't you?"

"I suppose . . ." She squared her shoulders. "Yes, I am. I'm the president of the Women's League."

"Yes, I sensed that about you. That you're the type who takes charge—a leader. It's almost as if you have an aura of fearlessness about you."

She looked back into the mirror. "Yes, I do."

"You have to buy the red. See how it will look on you?"

She nodded.

He stepped away from her.

"Carol!" She held the dress above her head. "I must have this red dress. Does it come in my size? And shoes to match. What about a hat?" She turned back to Barton and fluttered her eyelashes. "I'm sorry, I don't believe I caught your name."

He took her hand and raised it to his lips, bowing at the waist. "Barton," he told her as he straightened. "At your service."

"Oh, my." She giggled.

Carol couldn't believe what had just happened, but she had seen it with her own eyes. Margaret had actually fluttered her eyelashes at Barton. She hadn't thought it possible for the woman to flutter anything. She'd always thought Margaret sucked on lemons all day. Yet here she was at the cash register, with more items than she'd bought since the store opened last year, and the woman was smiling from ear to ear.

"He's not from around here, is he?" Margaret whispered behind her hand.

Her head jerked up. Barton was busy arranging some slips. What should she tell her? The truth? It was worth a shot. "He's from Nerak."

Margaret slapped a hand to her heart. "Oh, one of those foreign countries! I just knew it." She lowered her voice. "He's of royal blood, isn't he? In exile? I've been reading the most delicious romance about this very same thing. The unscrupulous younger brother had his older sibling thrown onto a vessel bound for the West Indies. Dreadful affair, except for the young governess that he meets. She saves the day, of course, and they fall madly in love," She eyed Carol. "Your Barton would be quite the catch, if you know what I mean."

"I don't think . . ." Oh, no, what had she just gotten Barton into?

Margaret patted her hand. "Don't worry, I won't tell a soul, dear." She grabbed her packages and was out the door before Carol could correct her misconception.

"A very remarkable woman," Barton said as he joined her at the counter.

"I don't think remarkable is quite the word I'd use. Oh, Barton, I'm so sorry. Somehow Margaret got it into her head that you're of noble blood."

"A gimmick."

"Huh?"

"I read about this on Mason's computer. When marketing something you need a gimmick."

"But I don't want to use you as a gimmick!" She would never even dream of using him in that way.

"But you said your business has not been good. Is that not correct?"

"Yes, but I'm going to give Margaret time to get home and then I'm calling her and explaining you're not of royal blood and you're not in exile. I won't let anyone use you like that."

He put a hand on her arm. Was he really not human? The heat from his touch caused her body to tremble.

"But who is using who? Your sales should increase. Speculation will bring them into the store. Isn't that what you wanted?"

"But not at your expense."

"Is it my expense? It gives me pleasure to make

you happy. And I am not hurting anyone. Margaret is a bold woman, is she not?"

"Oh, yeah, Margaret is definitely bold."

"Do you not think the red color suited not only her body but her personality as well?"

"Yes . . . but . . ." She'd been trying to get Margaret to try red for months now and the other woman had brushed away her suggestions. "Okay, so you're right."

He smiled and her heart did cartwheels. "Of course I am. I'm programmed to be correct."

"Oh, you are, are you?" She sauntered over to him. "And what color would I look good in?"

He brushed her hair behind her ears and stared into her eyes. "Why, flesh colored, of course."

"Oh, good answer," she purred. It was like she'd been waiting for Barton all her life. She hoped Mala didn't want him back because she was growing very attached to him.

The next hour slipped by and Carol was starting to have impure thoughts. Okay, she'd been having them all morning, but she couldn't stand not being close to him for one more minute. He apparently sensed what she was feeling and pulled her into his arms.

"You look very sexy today," he told her before lowering his mouth to hers.

Her thighs trembled as she pressed closer. His mouth was hot against hers. His tongue probing . . . stroking . . . igniting the flame inside her.

With more than a little disappointment, she stepped out of his arms and ran her hands down the front of her slacks when the bell above the door jangled.

"Hello, Carol!" Ms. Darcy said as she came simpering into the shop.

Carol smiled. She liked Janet Darcy, a rather plump

woman in her late fifties, with rosy cheeks and a wide smile. From the way her eyes darted around the room and came to rest on Barton, she knew Margaret was heating up the phone lines with her gossip.

"Margaret said you had some new dresses in?" Janet asked, but couldn't take her gaze off Barton.

"They're over here." Carol walked to the woman and physically turned Janet until she faced the rack and not Barton.

"Oh." Janet giggled like a young schoolgirl. Then in a loud voice continued, "What color do you think I'd look good in?"

"Now, I'm not exactly sure. Maybe we should ask the color expert." She looked across the store. "Barton, in your expert opinion, what color do you think would look good on Ms. Darcy?"

Barton strolled over, staring at the now blushing Ms. Darcy. He stopped in front of her, raising her chin and turning her head from one side to the other.

"Definitely pink."

"Pink?" She seemed to deflate before their eyes. "My mother used to dress me in pink. I haven't worn pink since I was sixteen years old."

Barton smiled. "She wouldn't have let you wear it if she'd known what the color brings out in you."

Ms. Darcy perked up. "Oh, what does it bring out in me?"

"Pale pink and you're a cute little kitten wanting to be cuddled."

Her cheeks turned an even darker shade of red.

Barton whipped out a dress in a deeper shade of pink, a dusky-rose color. "But this says you want to do more than cuddle." He held it up to her, turning her until she faced the mirror. "This is a sultry shade of deep pink that would look perfect on you."

"Yes." She sighed. "Sultry." She patted her hair. "I wonder if Kathy would have time to do my hair today?" she murmured.

"Have her bring it away from your face." He demonstrated by pulling her hair back. "Much more sophisticated."

She nodded and turned to Carol. "I'll take it and shoes to match. What about a purse and a hat?"

"No hat." He shook his head. "You shouldn't cover anything up."

She gulped. "Thank you . . . Barton."

He bowed in front of her, then took her hand and lightly kissed it.

After she'd paid for her purchases and left, Carol turned toward him. "I predict by the end of the day you'll have every female in the county eating out of your hand."

"But there's only one I want to please the most."

"Good answer." She smiled as she wrapped her arms around his neck and pulled his mouth down to hers. A very good answer.

Chapter 21

"Mason, I swear, it was right there." Mala fanned back some brush . . . nothing.

He'd known they wouldn't find anything. He wrapped his arms around her and drew her close. He wanted to tell her it would be okay, but how did he do that when he wasn't sure himself? All he knew was that he'd fallen in love with Mala and he didn't want to lose her to anyone or anything—including insanity.

"There are doctors who can help . . ."

Something close to a growl came from her as she shoved away from him.

"I am not crazy!" She stomped her foot and glared at him. "But I'm getting really angry."

"Then how do you explain the fact there's no spacecraft as you claimed?" He had to make her see reality.

She stuck her hands on her hips. "Why don't you tell me?"

"I think when you had your . . . accident, you hit your head and now you believe you're from another planet."

"And what about Barton? Explain his existence."

This was getting them nowhere, but the only thing he could think to do was talk reasonably and rationally to her. He had to make her understand that she lived in a fantasy world. There were no such things as aliens or Elders. Barton was not a robot.

But he did want to strangle the guy. If Barton cared for Mala as much as he said he did, then he had to realize he was feeding her fantasy by agreeing that he was some kind of machine. It damn sure didn't help that Carol was buying into their warped world.

He drew in a deep breath. "Barton is a man—just like me."

"Yeah, well maybe they gave you one too many attitude chips, too," she grumbled. Then her eyes brightened. "I can prove he's not human."

"How?" He didn't think he was going to like her answer.

"We can slice him open."

It was worse than he'd thought. She harbored latent killer characteristics. This wasn't good. He had to make her see what she wanted to do was wrong.

"Mala, you can't cut Barton open."

Both eyebrows rose. "Why not?"

"Because you'd kill him."

"No I wouldn't. I might short out some of his wires though, and I'd hate for that to happen just to prove he's a machine, although a highly intelligent one. I'm sure he wouldn't mind. If I'm really careful I can even rewire him. It couldn't be that difficult."

What was she in her other life—a car thief? Just hot wire that baby and take off.

And Barton would probably let her slice into him since he was going along with her fantasy. Come to think of it, slicing and dicing him was starting to sound doable.

He had to clear his mind. He was the sheriff, and slicing and dicing was against the law.

"But we do have another problem," she said.

He didn't think he'd want to hear about this one, either. "And what would that be?"

"Someone must've stolen my craft. That means they

know I'm here and that I'm an alien. We could both get into a lot of trouble. I really don't want to be locked into a room and the key thrown away."

He pulled her back into his arms and held her close.

"I think I need some chocolate," she said. "So I can think better."

A sad smile formed before he could stop it. "Then let's go back to the ranch." Maybe he could call Dr. Lambert. He'd be discreet. It could be a medical problem that hadn't shown up that first night.

Damn, other than thinking she was an alien, Mala seemed perfectly fine. He only wished he knew how to fix what was going on inside her head. Surely it all began with her accident.

Mala felt Mason's frustration. This wasn't good. She had a feeling he thought she was crazy. She'd been so close to proving to him she wasn't.

Who had stolen her craft?

She gritted her teeth. Wait until she discovered the culprit. She'd vaporize him. Not that she would know how to go about vaporizing someone. It wasn't like she carried a manual she could refer to: how to vaporize obnoxious humans in three easy steps.

Having her craft stolen wasn't the worst of it. She'd felt Mason's horror when she'd mentioned they could slice Barton open. Barton really wouldn't mind, but she'd bet Mason would certainly have something to say. He acted like she went around chopping up people all the time.

Now what did she do?

She really did need some chocolate.

They climbed on the horses and started the trek back to the ranch. She cast furtive glances in Mason's direction. He looked deep in thought. The kind of deep in thought that didn't bode well for her. Sometimes the Elders looked at her like this when she would talk about space exploration. Mason was probably trying to think of the best way to go about locking her up and throwing away the key.

"I'm not crazy," she finally said, breaking the silence before she started screaming. Then he would really think she'd lost her mind. Frustration was one emotion she could do without.

He smiled at her, but it didn't quite reach his eyes. She could guess what he was thinking. Yep, he thought she was crazy. Well, hell.

She exhaled a deep breath. This wasn't good, but without her spacecraft how was she going to convince him otherwise? It wasn't like she had any kind of special powers or anything. She had noticed the lights flickering when she ate chocolate, but she didn't think that would be much proof.

The rest of the ride back to the ranch was quiet and uneventful. As soon as they arrived, she slid off the horse and hurried inside.

She really did need chocolate and the immediate sense of euphoria that went along with that first taste. Maybe then she would be able to think of a solution to her problem. If nothing else, she would at least be a little happier eating some of Anna's fudge.

But as she walked through the house to the kitchen, someone grabbed her from behind and clamped a sweaty palm over her mouth. She tried to scream but no sound came out.

Mason! She had to warn Mason there were intruders. Before she could do more than wiggle against the hands that bound her, she heard him walk inside, letting the front door slam behind him. The thud of a body landing on the floor reverberated through the house. A sickening dread worked its way through her.

What was happening?

"Tie her hands," someone said.

She squirmed and wiggled until she was loose and made a mad dash through the house. Her feet skidded to a halt when she saw Mason on the floor, his lifeblood draining from his body. The world around her grew dark, but she welcomed it. Anything to block the pain rising inside her.

Carol wrapped her arms around Barton. "I can't believe it," she said. And she still couldn't. She'd been trying to digest it all morning—when she had a moment, that is. Laughter bubbled out of her.

"You've been very busy with customers," Barton said. "According to my calculations your profit margin has far exceeded your daily quota."

"I would've been lucky to clear this much in a week." She looked up at him. "It's all because of you. I'm not sure exactly what you're doing but it's definitely working."

"It's quite simple, actually. I'm giving customers the perspective from a male point of view. At least, they view me as a male."

"But I've tried to tell them the same thing, and they wouldn't listen to me." She narrowed her eyes. "No, I think there's more to it. I think it's because you're really good-looking." It suddenly dawned on her what he was doing differently. "You've been seducing them!"

Oh my God! That's exactly what he'd been doing. Flirting with the women, telling them what looked good on them, how to enhance what they already had . . . he'd played a game of seduction with them.

"Seducing them is a bad thing?"

She looked at him, saw the confusion on his face. Had she hurt his feelings? Could she hurt his feelings? If she could, it was the last thing she wanted to do. And really, was it so wrong that for just a little while he'd made a few women feel good about themselves? That he'd given them a little more confidence?

"No, I think it's a very good thing. If more men would do the same there would be a lot of happier marriages."

"Then you're pleased?"

"Oh, yes. I'm very pleased." She would be more pleased if they were making love. The clock on the wall reminded her that she still had four hours until closing time. Could she last that long?

"Your eyes reflect your lust. Would you like to have sex?"

She choked back a cough. Would she like to have sex? Oh, yeah. On the floor, in the back room, on the stairs, in her bedroom. Yeah, sex with Barton was a good thing to contemplate. And she would have to remember how good he was at detecting her thoughts.

"Sex would be nice," she told him, "but it's the middle of the day and I do have a store to run."

"Then tonight we'll have sex."

Heat spread up her neck and over her face. "Tonight would be nice." She lowered her head.

"Your face glows a bright red. Is this blushing?"

She was going to die of embarrassment. "Yes, this is called blushing."

"Did I embarrass you?"

"A little." A hell of a lot, but she wasn't going to admit to it. He might not be exactly human but he was close enough that she considered him all man.

"I read about this on your Internet. Some women get flustered when they speak about sex."

"Yeah, well, I guess I'm one of them."

"Sex is a normal body function. There is nothing wrong in the act of copulation."

"Yeah, as long as you're with the right man." Sex with Scott hadn't been so great. Now that she thought back, it hadn't even been good. A few sweaty grunts from him and he was through. A loud belch, up to the bathroom, and then back to bed so he could go to sleep. No words, no cuddling . . . just sleep. Sex with Scott had been an entirely different matter, and she didn't want to even think about that time in her life. Not when she had Barton to erase all the bad memories.

"You're so good for me."

"I think maybe you are good for me, too. I feel much more productive when I am with you."

"And Mala?" She was jealous. She liked Mala, but she was jealous of her. It was a strange feeling. One she didn't particularly like.

"Mala and her cousin created me. I will always be grateful they made me as real as they could. Mala is a very good friend. But she does not need me anymore."

That was so sad. She knew exactly how he felt. She looked into his face. "I need you," she said with all the sincerity that was inside her. "I've always needed you. I just had to wait for you to get here."

The bell above her door jangled. Another customer. She couldn't help glancing at the clock. Three hours and forty minutes. Time had never dragged by as much as it did right now.

She caught Barton's eye and he smiled. A smile that said he knew exactly what she was thinking. She could feel the heat, but it wasn't just climbing up her face. It was settling low in her belly and starting an ache deep inside her.

For the first time in her life she thought she might be truly falling in love. Did it matter that Barton wasn't actually human? No, he was more of a man than she'd ever been with and she didn't care what he was made of. He had a heart and that's all that mattered to her.

Chapter 22

Her mouth was dry. And everything was foggy. What had happened? Where was she?

Mala opened her eyes, but the lights were so bright she had to close them. She waited a few seconds before she tried again. This time she could see more clearly.

She wiggled her fingers, but her hands were bound behind her and she was sitting in a very uncomfortable chair. Did Earth people not enjoy a soft cushion for their backsides? Apparently not.

The room was small and smelled musty. She looked around. Her heart began beating frantically when she spotted Mason slumped over, sitting in a chair in the corner. His lifeblood was dried where it had run down the side of his face and onto his shirt.

Deep breath. She wouldn't get hysterical. At least, not for a few more minutes.

Was he dead?

"Mason," she whispered.

When he groaned, she thought *her* heart would stop beating. He was alive. It didn't matter that they were tied to uncomfortable chairs as long as they were both okay. Somehow they would escape the terrible people who'd captured them. Her anger boiled to the surface. She didn't even want a smoothie. This emotion spurred her to find a way to escape.

She began rocking back and forth, but when the chair started to teeter, she quickly stopped. She didn't think landing on her face would feel very good.

There must be some way she could get loose and go to Mason. She needed to see how badly he was hurt. Not that she was a healer, but she could get him to the Elder doctor and he would make Mason all better.

She wiggled her hands, but the bindings were tight.

If she rocked just a little, maybe she could scoot closer to Mason, but when she heard heavy footsteps approaching she stopped, slumping forward as if she were still unconscious. The door creaked open and she held her breath, but when she started to get light-headed she silently exhaled.

"She's still alive, isn't she?" a female asked.

"I didn't hit her," a disgruntled voice stated. "She fainted."

"You don't really think she's an alien, do you?" another male chimed in.

"You saw the spaceship as well as me," Harlan said.

Mala recognized the voices. It was the reporters and the owner of the odd little store. The same owner Mason had warned her about.

She remembered them all very well. Alice hadn't wanted to leave without her alien story.

And they were the ones who apparently had her spacecraft.

This wasn't good. Mason had said they would lock them up and throw away the key, but he hadn't mentioned tying them up. Why hadn't she left Earth sooner? This was not good. Not at all.

"I think she's playing possum," Alice said, leaning

so close Mala could smell her awful breath. Ugh! She should point out that mouthwash might be helpful—as long as she didn't swallow.

Alice put her finger under Mala's chin and raised it. Mala's glared at her. Alice only chuckled. "Hello little alien. Are you quite recovered from your fainting spell?"

"How would you like to be turned into a pile of ashes?"

Alice looked unsure for a moment, dropped her hand away, and took a cautionary step back.

"Don't try nothin' funny," Harlan warned.

"If she were going to try something don't you think she would have already?" someone else said.

She didn't recognize the other man's voice, but when he stepped into her line of vision she saw it was Perry. Aaron stood back, as if he wasn't too sure about the kidnapping.

"Touch one hair on her head and I might not turn you into a pile of ashes, but I'll see you spend the next twenty years in prison."

Relief washed over her. Mason was all right. He was talking, and he was saving the day. Well, sort of. But once they were free of their bonds he would save them.

"Spend time in jail? For capturing an alien? I think not," Alice scoffed. "We're doing the country a service. This is a matter of national security."

"Not to mention the money you plan to make when you spew your lies." Mason glared at the woman until she took a step closer to the door. "What you'll get is jail time. Try these charges on for size: assault, kidnapping a sheriff and an innocent young woman and holding them against their will. I think that would get you at least twenty years in these parts."

"Not after we tell them you've been harboring an alien," Harlan sneered.

"Yeah, where's your proof?"

"We got her spaceship."

"Somewhere safe. Where you can't find it." Aaron finally spoke up, then ducked behind Harlan when Mason glared at him.

"There are no such things as aliens," Mason practically growled. "I don't know what you've found but it isn't a spaceship."

"Oh, I don't think *The National Gossip* will feel the same way," Alice purred. "Once we get pictures mailed off, you're going to have so many reporters in your little town you won't be able to throw a stick without hitting one."

"First we got to get that jammed door open," Harlan said. "I want to see what the inside looks like. And y'all better remember this is *my* spaceship."

When Harlan grinned at her, Mala's stomach turned over.

"I'm gonna put it on display in my store."

"Watch the green button," she warned.

"What green button?"

Now she had their attention. Teach them a lesson not to mess with an angry alien. She'd been perfectly happy to explore Earth and have sex with Mason, but no, they had to go and mess up everything.

"The green button on the control panel," she told them nonchalantly.

"What will it do?" Harlan asked.

"Poof."

He frowned. "Poof? What the hell's that supposed to mean?"

She shook her head. "Just what I said. Poof."

"She's lying," Alice said. "Believe me, ten years in the field and I know when someone is lying."

"You sure?" Mala asked.

"Positive. Let's go."

"Then if there's a green button you can push it 'cause I ain't," Harlan mumbled as he trudged behind the others, who were leaving the room. There was a distinctive click after the door shut behind them.

"I should've locked them all up and thrown away the key when I had the chance," Mason grumbled.

She frowned. "I bet you have a lot of rooms on Earth where you can't find the keys."

"It's a figure of speech."

"That's good." Her gaze swept over him. "How's your head?"

"It's down to a dull throb. I've had worse, so I guess I'll live."

She sighed with relief, then nibbled on her bottom lip. "They have my craft, Mason. What are we going to do? I don't want them to cut me open."

He began to scoot his chair closer to hers. "Why would they cut you open?"

"I saw it on your television. *The Alien From Outer Space*. The doctor was cutting the creature open to see if everything looked the same as earthlings. You won't let them cut me open, will you?" Unshed tears swam in her eyes.

"It was just a movie, I explained that to you. I won't let anyone cut you open. Honey, don't you see?"

"See what?"

"The trauma of your . . . accident, having amnesia, watching movies about aliens, Barton perpetuating this fantasy, Harlan and the crazy reporters—everything has fed into your brain so that you just think you're from another planet. But you're not. You're from Earth, just like me."

"I am?"

He nodded.

Could he be right? Maybe all this was concocted from what had happened to her. It sort of sounded plausible.

She brightened. If she were from Earth then she wouldn't have to leave. She could stay with Mason the rest of her life. She could eat chocolate forever and ever.

One thing puzzled her. "Why would they say I'm an alien? And that they had my spaceship?"

"Because they write for a sleazy magazine. That's how they sell magazines." He paused for a breath, their chairs practically touching. "I'm going to swing around and put the back of my chair against the back of yours, then I'll see if I can get these ropes undone. Okay?"

She nodded.

He wiggled his chair around. A few minutes later he was untying her ropes. As soon as her hands were freed, she brought them around to the front and rubbed her wrists. Her fingers tingled as the circulation was restored.

"Hurry," he told her. "We don't know when they might decide to pop back in."

He was right, of course. She stood and went to his chair. "The ropes are so tight," she said, grunting as she wiggled them loose. Then he was free. He pulled her close, hugging her to him.

"You ready to get out of here?"

"Very much."

"We'll have to be quiet," he warned as he went to the door and checked the knob. Nothing happened. He glanced around the room. There was another door. He went to that one and opened it. "Bingo."

"Bingo?"

"Wire hangers." He brought one out and began to straighten it. "This is a specialty of mine."

"What is?" she asked, as he knelt in front of the door and inserted the hanger he'd taken apart.

He looked deep in thought. There was a click, then he glanced up at her. "Opening locked doors." He stood, turning the knob and easing the door open.

"Oh, you did it!"

He put his finger to his lips. "Shhh . . ."

She clamped her lips together. He was right—silence, or they'd be caught before they ever escaped. But inwardly she laughed. She'd known Mason would save the day. He was one of the good guys.

He glanced around. "It doesn't look like anyone's home. Come on." He motioned for her to follow.

The house was definitely empty and when she glanced out one of the windows of the rustic cabin, she saw they were in the middle of nowhere.

"No phone. Figures. Looks like a hunting cabin." He walked into the next room, a small food preparation area, and began opening cabinets and removing food. "We'll take what we can carry. I don't know how far we'll have to walk before we get back to civilization. We might need supplies."

Chocolate would be nice, but she thought it best not to mention that. "I'll look for blankets." She discovered the nights could be quite chilly and although Mason provided nice body heat, they might need more.

When he nodded, she went to the other room. She found two blankets that were thin enough to carry, but looked as if they would provide adequate warmth. When she joined Mason again, he had a stuffed green bag, the handle slung over his shoulder. He glanced at the blankets and nodded. A feeling of accomplishment wrapped around her, even though she knew finding a couple of blankets was a small thing.

"We better make tracks. There's no telling how long they'll be gone."

Her forehead puckered as she followed him out the back door. "But if we make tracks won't they be able to find us?"

He laughed. "It's just a figure of speech."

"You have a very strange figure of speech."

"We'll have to hurry until we have some cover between us and the cabin." He pointedly looked down at her stomach. "You'll be okay?"

She smiled. "Yes. The baby and I will be fine."

"You'll tell me if there's any problems?"

She nodded. As she followed him over the rocky terrain and toward the cover of trees, she couldn't stop the pleasure that flowed through her. Mason hadn't said much about the baby. That he cared for their safety told her a lot. She had a feeling he'd make a good father.

They didn't slow their pace until they were a good distance from the cabin and were shielded by the trees. Mason eased his pace and they were able to talk.

"Where are we?"

"I'm not sure. I think that was the Millers' cabin. They're out of state right now visiting a daughter. Harlan would know that."

"And how long will it take us to get home?"

Silence.

"Is it *that* far, Mason?" She suspected the fact that he hadn't answered meant it was quite a distance and he didn't want to worry her.

"It's about fifteen or twenty miles. We're pretty far back from anything."

"Then we'll be able to explore much of the land. That will be good. When we return to town you can lock up the bad people . . . and throw away the key."

He stopped and looked at her.

"What?" she asked.

"We've escaped being held captive, we have a long walk in front of us, and you think of it as a chance to explore." He laughed. "Most women would be crying."

"But I'm not most women." She'd decided he was wrong about her only thinking she was an alien. It would be nice if that were true, and for a moment she'd wanted to believe it, but she was an alien. That was a fact. Mason was the one who didn't believe her. She wondered if she might ever be able to convince him.

But then she would also have to tell him their time together was dwindling. She didn't think he would like that any more than she did.

Chapter 23

Carol turned the sign around to *closed* and locked the front door of the shop.

"You're tired?"

She faced Barton with a smile on her face. "Exhausted, but in a good way. If things keep going like this I might even show a profit this year."

"Good. I'm pleased you are happy. Would you like to rest while I prepare your evening meal?"

"You don't have to wait on me." But putting her feet up did sound wonderful. The new shoes she'd worn today were rubbing a blister on her heel.

"You forget that it gives me pleasure when I can give to you."

She nibbled her lower lip. "Are you sure you don't have to get back to Mala? I mean, technically you were only here for the night in case Scott came back. I have a feeling he won't be returning anytime soon."

"Mala does not need me. She hasn't needed me for quite some time. You have given me a purpose again. Please do not ask me to leave."

She twined her fingers together. "I just don't want you to feel that I'm taking advantage of you."

His footsteps were silent on the carpet as he came to her. He took her in his arms and held her close. "You could never take advantage of me." He placed a kiss on top of her head before tugging her toward the kitchen. "Let me fix you a wonderful meal. I saw a cookbook earlier. It didn't appear too complicated. I thought you might like a simple soup along with a sandwich."

Thank you, Lord. Thank you, Lord. Thank you, Lord.

Barton didn't let her do anything while he prepared supper. She watched how he efficiently put everything together, then set it in front of her. The soup didn't taste the same as when she threw ingredients together in a pot. She felt like she was eating a gourmet meal in a five-star restaurant.

But she was still confused about something. "Mala *really* didn't like when you waited on her?"

"She's very independent and occasionally can be rather stubborn."

Her loss.

She finished eating and Barton carried her dishes to the sink. She closed her eyes but resisted hugging herself.

"I'll run your bath, then I would like to wash your body."

Her eyes flew open. "What?"

He helped her to her feet and easily picked her up in his arms. "I'm going to carry you upstairs and draw your bath. Then I'm going to slowly remove your clothes." He proceeded to carry her up the stairs with no effort whatsoever. "After you're in the tub, I'll run the bar of soap over your breasts and across your nipples."

Her nipples tightened as if he'd touched her.

"Then I'll slide the soap over your abdomen and down to your mound. The soap will be slick as I rub it against your sex. But I'll stop before you have an orgasm."

"Then what?" she croaked.

"We are here."

She looked around as if in a daze and saw they were in her bedroom. Lord, she hadn't even realized he'd opened the door. He set her on her feet, but her legs were a little wobbly.

"I'll start your bath."

She swallowed past the lump in her throat. Before she could do much more than expel a soft moan of anticipation, he'd returned. She could hear the water running in the bathroom. But rather than remove her clothes, he took off his.

This was better than she could've imagined. He slipped his jacket off, then his shirt. Her hungry eyes devoured his smooth chest, his fabulous pecs, then slid lower to his six-pack stomach.

His movements slowed as he unfastened his belt and slipped it out of the loops. He unbuttoned his pants next, then slid the zipper down.

She drew in a ragged breath.

He pushed his pants down and stepped out of them. His briefs followed.

Oh, man, he had a killer hard-on. She reached toward him, but he stayed her hand and began unbuttoning her top. Slowly, he undressed her until she was down to her bra and underwear. Her breasts strained against the lace of her bra, aching for him to strip it away and cover them one at a time with his mouth, sucking gently.

Barton didn't disappoint. He undid her bra, his gaze drinking in the sight of her bare breasts. It was almost as good. He knelt in front of her and peeled her panties over her hips and down her thighs. The warmth of his breath tickled her curls.

"Your bath awaits," he told her as he stood and led her into the bathroom.

And she remembered exactly what he'd said he would do. She let go of his hand and climbed into the tub. She wanted his touch so badly. He was becoming a fierce hunger inside her. One that needed to be appeased. The sooner the better.

He took the washcloth and wet it in the bath water, causing ripples of water to caress her breasts. She couldn't stand much more.

Her gaze was transfixed on the bar of soap as he picked it up, rubbed it against the cloth until he had a good lather, then placed the soap back in the dish.

She sucked in a deep breath as he brought the cloth to her breasts. The first touch of the rough cotton against her nipples sent a spark of desire through her, and she moaned.

She lay her head back against the tub and closed her eyes. Oh, yes, this felt good. Her body began to relax as she just lay there enjoying the sensations he created inside her, but when he slid the soapy rag down her abdomen, she tensed.

"Relax," he whispered. "I'm not going to touch you . . . yet."

"It's okay . . . I mean . . ." She swallowed past the lump in her throat. "If you want to touch me, it's all right," she said, her words running together.

"Soon," he told her.

He stood and she opened her eyes, lazily looking her fill. But then he took one of her legs and draped it over the side of the claw-foot tub. Then he went to the other side and draped her other leg over the side. Ah, damn, nothing was hidden from his view. Suddenly it didn't seem to matter.

"You are very sensual with your legs open and your sex exposed." He discarded the cloth and picked up the soap before kneeling beside the tub once more. "I'm going to touch you now."

She whimpered. At least that's what it sounded like. She was strung so tight that she would probably die if he didn't touch her pretty soon.

He slid the soap over her sex. She arched toward his hand. As soon as she eased back into the water, he began to rub the soap against her sex. Up and down, through her curls, over her clit. He applied more pressure. Her breath came in puffs. He reached up, massaging one breast, then the other.

"I want you to come against my hand," he told her. The soap slipped away from him, but his fingers continued the movement, rubbing vigorously against her sex.

"Oh, I think . . ."

"Don't think. Let go. Don't worry about anything. All that matters is the pleasure I can give you."

She bit her bottom lip, but it didn't stop the orgasm from washing over her. She arched her back, raising her hips. Oh . . . yes . . . it felt so . . . damn . . . fantastic. Her body quivered and jerked.

Her breathing slowed to a more normal rate. She closed her eyes and rested. Barton slipped her legs back into the tub, rinsed the soap off her body then helped her to stand. She felt like the soppy washcloth that had sank to the bottom of the tub. Not that it mattered, because Barton was doing everything for her. He dried her off then carried her to bed, lying down beside her.

"Don't ever leave me." She spoke so softly that she wondered if he'd heard.

"I may not have any choice," he told her.

Mason sat down on the ground, patting the place beside him as he leaned against a rock. "Let's take a break." He didn't want to tire her out. Especially if she were pregnant.

A pregnancy test would tell him for sure. But what if she wasn't? Damn, he didn't want to think of that possibility, either.

"I'm hungry. I don't suppose you put chocolate in the bag?" Her expression was hopeful.

"Sorry."

Her face fell.

"But we have an assortment of wonderful fare to delight the palate." He pulled out a can. "Tuna from the sea."

She made a face.

"Don't like tuna, huh?"

She shook her head. "You had a can in the cabinet. I tried some. It was awful. But Stripes seemed to enjoy it."

"I'm sure she did." He'd have to remember not to buy any more tuna or the barn cat would be dining like a queen. "Peanut butter and crackers it is then."

He fixed her a peanut butter cracker sandwich and waited to see what she thought.

"It's good, but it makes my mouth stick together."

He grinned and popped the top of a grape soda. "This is warm but it'll wash everything down." At least they'd have protein with the peanut butter, and if they ran out of soda they could always drink from the river that was close by. In fact, if they followed it they should make it back to town in a few days.

He looked up at the sky. The rain clouds had long since gone away, but that didn't mean it wouldn't cloud up again. He didn't even want to think about them being caught outside in bad weather.

Damn, when they got back to town he was going to lock Harlan and those dumb-ass reporters up, and they'd be lucky if they ever saw the light of day.

"You look angry."

Mason turned to Mala. "Huh?"

"Your jaw is twitching. Like when you're mad."

"Sorry. I was thinking about Harlan."

She looked away, not meeting his eyes.

"What?"

"I tried to believe that I might be from Earth, like you said. But all my memories are of Nerak."

She drew in a deep breath.

Oh, God, he knew what she was going to say. He hated that she believed she was from another planet. He could think of only one thing to do to stop her words.

He kissed her.

She tasted sweet. A little like grape soda and peanut butter. It seemed like forever since they'd kissed . . . since they'd made love. He wanted her so bad he ached.

Something rustled not far from them. He jerked away, his gaze narrowed as he scanned the area. It wasn't the rustle of a small animal. No, this was much bigger.

Human?

Would Harlan and the reporters have found them this soon? No, he didn't think so. They didn't strike him as the outdoor kind. But something big was out there, and he had a feeling it was following them. He didn't want to be its next meal, either.

"Mason?"

And he didn't want to worry her. They needed to keep moving.

"We should probably go."

She hesitated, then nodded.

He gathered up their supplies and stuffed them into the bag before zipping it closed. "It'll be getting dark soon. I don't want to be caught out in the open if I can help it. We need to find shelter for the night. Someplace where we'll be safe."

"Then we can have sex?"

Damn, she was going to be the death of him. He grinned. "No, then we'll make sweet love beneath a starry sky." Now he was waxing poetic.

What was his life coming to?

He wasn't exactly sure, but he liked it.

There was another rustle of underbrush. He grabbed Mala's hand and pulled her alongside him. "If something happens I want you to stay close to the river. If you always keep it to your left it'll lead you back to town. At least, close enough you should make it to a road."

She turned puzzled eyes up to him. "But what about you, Mason?"

He glanced over his shoulder. "I hope like hell I'll be with you . . . but you never know what might happen." He wouldn't let anything hurt her. Not as long as there was breath in his body.

"Nothing will happen," he said as he looked at her. "We're the good guys. You said the good guys always win. Remember?"

"You're right. I guess for a second I forgot."

But he hadn't taken into account there might be a hungry bobcat close by, just waiting for them to make a wrong move and become its next meal.

Chapter 24

Mala watched the flames reaching toward the night sky. The wood Mason had used to start the fire crackled and hissed because of the dampness from the recent rains. Sparks were sent upward and the sensuous smell of burning wood filled the small cave.

"Are you warm enough?" Mason asked.

She nodded and smiled up at him. "I like the open fire and the nice place you found for us to spend the night. It's almost as good as the hotel in San Antonio."

He laughed, the sound filling the interior of their small haven. She liked the sound of his laughter.

"I don't think you'll like the bed quite as much, but it'll keep us safe as long as we have a fire going. I've got enough wood that it should last us through the night."

"It will be nice making love here." She brought her knees up and hugged them close to her. Already her body tingled in anticipation of what would happen.

"You certainly aren't shy about sex, are you?"

She shook her head. "Should I be?" She still couldn't understand why something that was so much fun should be talked about in whispers. People should be shouting how much they enjoyed sex.

And that's one of the things that made Nerak different from Earth. Mason was going to have to understand and accept the fact that she was an alien.

"On Nerak we talk about the way we feel. We don't bottle it up inside us."

When he opened his mouth, she held up her hand to silence him. "Whether you believe I'm an alien or not, you should at least listen to what I have to say."

He sat down behind her and pulled her into his arms. "Okay, tell me about this planet you're from."

She leaned against him, snuggled in his warmth. When she caressed his hand she could feel the sadness inside him. He wouldn't believe her until she could offer proof, but for right now it was enough that he was willing to hear what she had to say.

"Nerak is as close to perfect as any place could be. We live in town bubbles, and when we travel we use aero crafts." She chuckled. "That first night, when you were taking me to the Elder doctor, I kept waiting for your Jeep to get airborne. I thought the bouncing would never end." She could feel his smile. It felt sad.

"Do you have farms . . . ranches?" he asked.

Now he was humoring her, but it didn't matter as long as he listened.

She shook her head. "We don't work the land. We take food capsules each morning to ward off hunger."

"Sounds kind of boring if you ask me."

"Now that I've had a taste of your food I have to agree."

"Especially chocolate?"

"Especially chocolate. That's a wonderful food."

"What do you do on Nerak? For fun, I mean. You've already told me you're some kind of therapist," he asked, his thumb stroking her hand. "Do you have family where you live?"

She smiled, sensing his need to think of her home as a distant place, but not so distant he couldn't drive or take an airplane to get there. That was okay.

He continued to stroke her hand, turning it until the palm faced up. For a second she lost her train of thought as delicious sensations swirled around inside her. She reined in her wayward emotions and focused once again. "We have holograms where we can go any place imaginable. I also have several cousins, and we like to visit with each other."

"Tell me about them."

A sudden longing swept over her. "Kia is older than me. She's a warrior. I'm probably closer to her than anyone else."

"I thought you said Nerak was perfect? If it's so perfect, then why would you need warriors?"

"We don't, really. Kia gets very frustrated at times. She has all this training on how to fight, but she has no use for it. Our planet is so small, and there's a lack of resources, so we're not worth the effort."

"Why didn't she come with you if she's so miserable?"

"I don't think she realizes she is." She sighed. "I miss her."

He stiffened. "How much?"

"Not more than I would miss you if I were to leave," she whispered. She turned in his arms. "Make love to me, Mason."

He lowered his head, the heat of his lips brushing against hers. A shiver of need swept over her. Oh how she wanted this man, how she never wanted to leave him. If they could stay here, in this cave, she would live the rest of her years in bliss.

She could even give up chocolate.

His hand moved to one of her breasts and she stopped thinking. A moan escaped as he scraped his thumb over her hard nipple.

"Damn, you get hot fast," he mumbled against her neck before licking across her skin. He swiftly unbuttoned her shirt, and tugged on her bra until both her breasts were exposed.

She wiggled around until she lay across his lap and gave him better access to her body. It still wasn't enough.

"Let's get naked."

A heart-stopping, slow grin lifted the corners of his mouth. "I like the way you think."

She scrambled off his lap and began to come out of her clothes. But when he stood and began to remove his, she stopped and unabashedly stared. He caught her looking and slowed his movements.

"So, you like watching me undress? Don't tell me you enjoy going to male strip joints?"

She dragged her gaze back to his face. "They have those? A place where men take off their clothes for women?"

"Yeah."

"Amazing. And did you ever strip at one?"

"Not my style." He unbuttoned the last button on his shirt and let it fall to the floor of the cave.

Her mouth began to water. The lights and shadows played across his sinewy muscles. Her eyes lowered to his low-riding jeans. He tugged on the top button with one hand.

"I think you have a very good style," she breathed as he undid the second button and the third.

"Does my undressing turn you on?"

She nodded, unable to speak, her gaze glued to his jeans as he began to slide them over his hips. He didn't get in any hurry, either.

Her chest constricted and she found it hard to breathe. The ache inside her began to build. Her thighs trembled as he kicked his jeans away from him. It was easy to see how much he wanted to make love. His erection was almost bursting out of his briefs.

Her gaze drank in the sight of him standing only a few feet away, but when he hooked his thumbs into the waistband of his briefs she thought she would fall over. She bit her bottom lip as he revealed the rest of his body.

Then he stood before her quite naked.

"You haven't taken anything off." His words came to her as if from a distance.

Now he teased her. She could see the twinkle in his eyes. He'd intentionally taken off his clothes in a way that would make her want him even more.

It worked.

She pulled at one of her sleeves but it didn't want to cooperate and she found herself getting tangled. It didn't help when Mason began strolling toward her in all his naked glory. He was a magnificent male specimen.

"Let me help."

All she could do was nod and drop her hand to her side. He slipped the shirt over her shoulders and down her arms. When he reached behind her and unfastened her bra she leaned against his chest, breathing in his smoky earth scent.

This was nice. She could almost stay in this spot forever, except he'd slid his hands down her back and cupped her jeans-clad bottom, squeezing and releasing. It started a chain reaction of sexy little eruptions inside her body as the rough material rubbed against her sex.

Nice as it felt, she wanted more, and there was too

much material between her and him. When she stepped away, her bra fell. She couldn't resist. She leaned a little closer and brushed her nipples through the light sprinkling of his chest hairs.

Ah, yes, that felt so good.

"Are you using my body for self-gratification?"

She grinned. "Yes, and it feels great."

"I feel so used."

There was laughter in his voice. She didn't think he felt used at all.

She unfastened the jeans she'd gotten at Carol's, and pushed them over her hips and down her legs. When she bent over, she was looking right at his erection. She wanted to give him what he'd given her.

She kicked out of her pants. Wearing only a pair of wispy blue panties and using her jeans to cushion her knees, she knelt in front of him.

"You're beautiful," she whispered before she ran her tongue up his length then back down. His skin was nice, the tip of his erection smooth against her tongue. She tasted him, taking him into her mouth and sucking. He groaned and clasped her head. It was a good feeling, knowing she gave him this pleasure.

All too soon, he pulled her up. She melted into his arms and against his hard body. Her legs trembled with her need, but she didn't have long to wait. He pulled her panties off and entered her.

"Wrap your legs around me," he said, bringing one of them up to his waist.

Her arms tightened around his neck as she brought her other leg up and clasped his waist. He sank deeper. She gritted her teeth, absorbing all of him as he plunged inside her body.

"I'm not hurting you?"

She shook her head. "Only if you stop," she managed to get out, wrapping her legs tighter around him, needing to take all he had to offer.

He slid in deeper, stroking her, caressing her. She tightened her inner muscles. He gasped with pleasure. She closed her eyes, biting back her cry of passion. He plunged into her again and again, faster and faster. The heat built inside her until she thought she would burst into flames.

This was very good! She opened her eyes—his were closed. Lights swirled around the cave: blues, purples, reds.

She held on, her eyes closed, as the beginning of an orgasm rippled over her. He groaned, squeezing her against him as he leaned back against the wall of the cave.

"Damn, making love with you is like riding a bull," he said.

She frowned. The bulls she had seen on his land were big, dumb-looking creatures. "I don't think I like being compared to one of your bulls."

He chuckled as her legs slid from around his waist. "Just the ride, baby, just the ride. You grab what you can and hang on for dear life, because it's going to be the most exhilarating experience of your life and you damn sure don't want to fall off."

"Okay, I like that much better." She sighed, leaning against him. "I love making love with you, too." And she knew, whatever it took, she wouldn't leave with the Elders when they came looking for her. They could . . . vaporize her if they wanted. She hadn't ruled that out. But getting vaporized would be better than living in a perfect world without Mason.

Carol frowned as she and Barton neared Mason's house. Something didn't look right. For one thing,

Dancer was saddled and bridled but the reins were trailing on the ground. It wasn't like Mason to leave the horse unattended like this.

"You're worried," Barton said.

"No, well, sort of." She bit her bottom lip. "Francine at the sheriff's office said it was Mason's day off, but something doesn't look right.

She pulled in front of the house and killed the engine. As soon as she opened her door, Blue began to howl, a low, mournful sound that sent a shiver of foreboding down her spine. Now she knew something wasn't right.

"Let me go first," Barton told her.

For a moment she hesitated, then she remembered how he'd taken care of Scott. She nodded, but stayed right on his heels.

Every scary movie she'd ever watched, every dorm room tale of ghosts came back to haunt her. Sheesh, she felt as if she were in a slasher movie or something. Mason or Mala would come to the door any second and see her cowering behind Barton. They would certainly get a laugh out of that.

No one was coming to the door, though. She inwardly pleaded for someone to appear, but her prayers went unanswered.

This wasn't good at all.

Barton went up the porch steps. When he stopped in front of the door she collided against him.

"Sorry," she mumbled.

"It's okay." He knocked on the door.

Silence.

When he tried the knob it easily turned.

"Wait," she whispered. "What if they're . . . you know . . ." She could feel the flush of heat climbing up her neck to her cheeks. "What if they're making love?"

"We'll give them enough warning that there won't be any embarrassment."

He opened the screen all the way and pushed open the door. That was as far as he went. Carol peered around him and saw the dried red stain on the floor.

"Oh no . . ." She could feel the color draining from her face.

"Mala," Barton called.

Again silence.

"I think we'd better call the sheriff's office," she said as she tried to swallow past the lump in her throat.

Chapter 25

"Bear!" Mason hissed, pulling Mala behind him. She stretched on her toes and looked over his shoulder. In the shadows of the trees she caught the movement of something very large. She squinted.

"Hypotrond," she stated matter-of-factly.

"It looks like a black bear," he said, as if she hadn't spoken. "Just stay close to me and maybe he won't bother us." He tugged her along beside him, putting her between him and his perceived danger.

"It's a Hypotrond. He's probably more scared of us than we are of him. Hypotronds are very passive creatures. They just look mean. And they have a very strong odor so we should probably stay upwind . . ."

"Shh . . ."

She didn't think he was paying attention to her, anyway. She looked toward a thick stand of trees and saw movement again. It could be this bear Mason referred to. The shape was big enough to be a Hypotrond, though.

Tentatively, she raised her hand and waved. The half man, half beast stepped into a patch of light and waved back, before turning and running farther into the woods.

Definitely a Hypotrond.

It would've been nice to visit with him. Not that

she knew their language. It was a rather guttural speech pattern, if she remembered correctly. She'd caught a glimpse of one in an old hologram that depicted some of their history.

"I think we might have scared it off. Damn, I didn't think we had any bears in this area. At least I haven't heard of one roaming the woods in decades."

"Hypotrond."

They scrambled up a rocky mountainside. When Mason got to the top, he turned and reached his hand toward her to help her the rest of the way.

"What were you saying?" he asked when she stood beside him.

"Hypotrond." When he cast a puzzled look in her direction, she went on to explain. "It wasn't a bear. I got a good look when it stepped into the light. It was a Hypotrond—part man, part beast. I have no idea how one came to be on Earth, though. I didn't know Nerakians traveled here before Hypotronds became extinct."

He didn't look at all convinced.

"So why do think it was one of these . . . Hypotronds?"

Ignoring him for the moment, she slowly turned, looking at the view from the mountaintop. Truly magnificent. Gently rolling hills and tall trees. Mason had called them cedar, oaks and pecan. The cedars had a wonderful smell, but the stuff that ran out of them was sticky and hard to remove from her skin. She'd learned not to put her hand into the orange-tinted substance.

She looked back at Mason. "I know it was a Hypotrond because he waved to me."

His eyebrows rose. "Then why didn't you invite him to join us? It seems like an easy way to prove you're not from Earth."

She shook her head. "They're terribly shy creatures. I'm sure after the men on our planet had them enslaved, it has made them leery of people. Not that I can really blame them."

"So what you're saying is . . . Bigfoot actually exists, only it's a Hypotrond from your planet?"

"Except they're extinct now."

"Are you sure you're not a sci-fi writer?"

"A writer?"

"Fictional stories. Other planets. That sort of thing. It would explain a lot."

She shook her head. She'd known he wouldn't believe her. But how could she prove it to him? The Hypotrond was certainly out of the question. It would take much too long to coax one out of the woods, and they were very good at camouflage.

"How much longer before we eat?" she asked. She didn't like having to go so long without sustenance now that she knew about food. She glanced his way. He was quiet . . . pensive. What was he thinking?

Mason wanted to pull her close and never let her go. Keep her safe forever.

Her ideas were fanciful. Who knew, maybe she *was* a writer. The hit on the head, all these crazy stories she kept coming up with. He'd heard the artistic type could get really eccentric. She could be living her fictional story so it would ring true.

His forehead wrinkled. He didn't much think he cared that she might be using him as a character in a book. On the other hand, it was a hell of a lot better than the alternative.

Alien. He shook his head. Nonsense.

"Mason? Are you hungry yet?"

He looked behind him. The bear had apparently moved on, but he still didn't feel safe from an attack.

"Not much longer," he said.

He held her hand as they made their way down

the other side of the rocky slope. The last thing he wanted was for her to fall and injure herself or the baby.

One more day and they should reach civilization—then she would be safe. He doubted they would reach town any sooner.

Unless a search party found them.

Someone would know by now they were missing. Would they come in this direction, though? Even if they had search parties out looking for them, he didn't think they'd come this far north.

He glanced up. The darkening sky didn't bode well for them. They'd have to find cover soon.

Anger flared inside him. Harlan damn well better take cover himself, because as soon as they made it home his ass was grass.

"Where are they?" Carol asked, looking up at Barton.

"I don't know." The sheriff from the next county joined them on the front porch. Carol hadn't been able to go inside. The red stain on the floor turned her stomach every time she looked at it.

"Let's go over your story one more time," he said.

"Do you think it might have changed from ten minutes ago?" Barton asked.

The sheriff's eyes narrowed before he spat a stream of brown tobacco juice off the porch. He wiped the back of his hand across his mouth. "You gettin' smart with me, boy?"

Barton opened his mouth, but before he could say anything Carol stepped in front of him. "This is my friend . . . from England. He doesn't understand how we do things here."

"Yeah, well, we're not in England now and this is the way I do things." He hitched up the side of his pants that his gun and holster were on.

"I would think you would be concerned about the extra set of tire marks," Barton said, then continued. "Because of the recent rains the tires left imprints in the yard. Whoever was here pulled to the back of the house, probably to hide their vehicle.

"If you'll also notice, the tire marks are deeper than Carol's compact or one of the patrol cars. That would suggest it was a bigger vehicle and probably carried more passengers."

"How do you know all this?" There was more than a touch of suspicion in the sheriff's eyes.

"He works in law enforcement," Carol quickly explained before Barton could tell the sheriff he was from another planet, or worse—that he was a robot. They'd lock them both up!

A hint of respect showed in the sheriff's eyes. "That's why you know so much," he said. "Got any ideas who might have done this?" he asked them.

She hadn't really thought about possible suspects. As far as she knew, Mason didn't have any real enemies. At least not someone who would attack him. They lived in a small town and stuff like this didn't happen.

Nothing had really happened out of the ordinary in the last ten years, until the reporters from *The National Gossip* came into town. They'd been here for so blasted long people were starting to ignore them . . .

The reporters! Of course. Carol opened her mouth, but before she could say anything, Barton spoke.

"We don't have any clue as to who would have committed this crime."

Her gaze swung toward him. Why not tell the sheriff the reporters could've had something to do with Mala and Mason's disappearance?

"If you think of something, let me know. Mason's a good sheriff."

"Of course," Barton nodded.

As soon as the sheriff walked away and was far

enough that she wouldn't be overheard, she turned to Barton. "Why didn't you tell the sheriff it might be the reporters? They've been causing Mason lots of problems."

"Because Mala is an alien, and I don't know what information they have about her . . . if any. I think I need to investigate a little before I suggest anything to the good sheriff."

"I'll help."

When Barton quirked an eyebrow in her direction she raised one of her own and planted her hands on her hips. "What? Don't you think I could be of any help? Let me tell you this, just because I was stupid enough to let Scott take advantage of me doesn't mean I haven't come to my senses. They're my friends and I plan to help find them."

"Then let's go." He walked toward her car . . . just like that. Scott would've been telling her how crazy her idea was and that she would only get in the way. But then, Barton wasn't Scott.

I think I'm falling in love.

Ridiculous.

But as the sun began to set, Carol wasn't sure how much help she actually was. They'd followed the older male reporter half the afternoon and gotten nowhere. He'd gone inside Anna's candy store about ten minutes ago.

The sign in the window of Carol's store still read *closed*. She was losing money, but Mason and Mala meant too much to her to worry about losing a day of business.

"Maybe it wasn't the reporters," she said. "Mason does arrest people. I'm sure he has enemies."

"Who?" Barton said from the passenger seat of her little compact.

"I don't know."

"Then this is the only lead we have."

"But it's getting us nowhere."

She watched as the reporter left the candy store and meandered down the sidewalk.

"Don't you think it odd that this reporter is very relaxed?" Barton asked. "It's almost as if he already has his story. And when we passed his van, there was mud caked on the tires."

"Amazing." She turned in her seat, looking at him.

"Not really. Simple deduction, actually. Even I've noticed them rushing about town, and Mala mentioned they were causing havoc everywhere they went. Except for now."

She grinned. "You are a genius."

"Actually, my IQ is much higher than genius level."

He was so different than Scott. Scott had the IQ of a doodlebug. "Do you think he'll lead us to them?"

"Eventually."

She caught the worried look in his eyes and knew they were thinking the same thing. *Would they be in time?*

"He's going to his car." She sat straighter, peering over the steering wheel. "Look how he's glancing around. Oh no, he's looking this way!" She leaned across the seat and planted a kiss on Barton. His arms wrapped around her, pulling her closer.

For a moment she lost herself in the warmth of his touch, the heat of his kiss. Her nipples tightened, pushing against the thin cotton of her shirt. Tingles spread over her body, settling in the juncture of her legs. She moaned, pressing closer.

That's when she realized what the hell she was doing. Damn! Mason and Mala were her friends, and she was practically having sex in the car.

She moved back into her seat, smoothing her hair in place and straightening her clothes.

"Sorry about that," she mumbled, and started the car. "I was afraid he would guess we're trailing him."

"I think that would be sufficient to prove otherwise."

Her cheeks grew warm.

"It made me forget," he continued.

"Are you sure you're not one hundred percent human?"

"Positive."

After she saw the direction the reporter was going, she put her car in reverse and backed out of the space.

"He's headed out of town." She kept her distance so he wouldn't get suspicious. Ten miles later, he turned off the main road. Another two and he turned again, but this time she kept going straight.

"You missed the turn," Barton said.

"There's only one place to go down that road—the Millers' cabin. It's very secluded and deep into the back woods. The Millers are on vacation, not that they use it that often. I came out here with Scott when he hunted and I know another way in."

She kept driving until they topped a small rise, then eased to the side of the road, shifted into *park*, and got out. The gate wasn't much. Just barbed wire strung between two cedar stays, but it kept any cattle from getting out. She'd have to push in the stay and slip the loop of wire over it.

She put her shoulder behind it, pushing the stay closer to the post, but it didn't budge. It reminded her of the time Margaret came into her store and attempted to put on a girdle two sizes too small. After much heaving and grunting she got the girdle up, but lost her balance and pitched forward out of the dressing room, with her dress over her head and displaying a wide expanse of white Lycra and elastic.

At least she'd gotten the girdle on. Carol wasn't having any luck with the stay.

Barton stepped forward and moved her out of the way. With one hand and what looked like no effort at all, he pushed the stay toward the post, slipped the wire ring over the top and opened the gate.

"Have I mentioned you're handy to have around?"

"It's good to be needed."

Yes, it is, and I need you so much, she thought—but didn't voice what was in her head or her heart.

She climbed back into her car and drove through the opening, waiting just on the other side while Barton closed the gate.

"We can get pretty close to the cabin," she said. "Hold on to your seat because it might get bumpy."

"You mean more than it already has?"

She chuckled. It was nice being around someone with a sense of humor.

The drive was slower than when they'd been on the paved road, and this one was even rougher because it wasn't meant for compact cars. Eventually they came to a place where she could park. They'd walk the short distance to a stand of trees. From there they might be able to see if Mala and Mason were being held against their will.

But as soon as they were near the trees, they saw the reporter run out of the house, practically falling down the steps and racing to his car. A few seconds later he peeled out in a cloud of dust.

"Something's wrong," she said as she hurried to the cabin.

Please, don't let me find their bodies tied up and ripped to shreds by some wild animal.

She hurried up the steps, pausing to take a deep breath before pushing the door open.

Chapter 26

Mala hadn't thought she would ever get tired of sightseeing and walking across this great land. She'd been wrong—her feet were killing her. She needed an energy smoothie and a pain reliever smoothie. Then she needed a hologram of tranquility.

Within the next few minutes would be fine.

"Let's rest." Mason tossed the satchel onto the ground and took the blankets from her, spreading them out. He sat down, then patted the blanket beside him.

It didn't take any more encouragement than that for her to crumple beside him, leaning her head against his chest.

"How much farther?" she asked.

"Just a few more miles."

"Miles are very far when you're walking."

"Don't you walk . . . where you're from?"

"It's called Nerak." She jerked her arm upward, pointing at the sky. "It's another friggin' planet, Mason!" She sat up enough that she could glare at him.

His eyes widened. "Where the hell did you hear the word *friggin'*?"

"You said it as we left Harlan's store." She shrugged,

crossing her arms in front of her. "Right now it seemed more than appropriate."

"Okay, don't you walk much on your . . . planet?"

She rolled her eyes. "If you have this much trouble comprehending that I'm not from Earth, what are you going to do when our baby is born with three eyes?"

That certainly got his attention. Maybe a little too much. His face turned a deathly pale. "I . . . uh . . . I mean . . ."

She leaned back against him. "Really, Mason. If Nerakians had three eyes don't you think *I* would have three eyes?" Men! No wonder they fixed the DNA so there would be no males born. She was starting to understand why.

"That's not what I was thinking."

She was tired and she wanted to go back to the ranch. She needed chocolate!

"Your stomach is rumbling," she said.

"Not mine. Maybe yours."

She raised her head. "I can still hear it. Listen."

"Damn, those are four-wheelers. It could be the reporters."

She grabbed the blanket and rolled it up. Being tied to another chair was not on her list of things to do while on Earth. She wasn't sure exactly what a four-wheeler was, but from the sounds it had a motor, and if it had four wheels then it meant the machine could travel faster than they were going.

"We should run," she pointed out.

"It could be help, too. The sheriff's office would have people looking for us."

She frowned. "If you thought they might come looking for us, then why have we been doing all this walking?"

"Just in case they didn't."

That made sense. She lay down on the ground and scooted up to the edge of the rock near Mason. From this vantage point they could see quite a bit of the surrounding area below them.

The noise of the four-wheeler engines grew louder. Her body tensed as she waited for them to come into their line of vision. She and Mason would have to either hide and hope no one spotted them, or stand up and wave and hope they were seen.

She held her breath.

"It's Carol and Barton," Mason said as he jumped to his feet. He grabbed one of the blankets and began to wave it above his head.

Mala stood, waving the other blanket. They were saved! No more walking! She wondered if Carol had any chocolate. It didn't matter. They were saved.

Barton glanced up and saw them. He motioned Carol and they turned the four-wheelers toward the small mountain.

"Are we glad to see you two," Mason said after they stopped the vehicles and turned off the engines.

"You found us." Mala hugged Barton around the neck, then Carol.

"Actually it was Barton. He's a genius when it comes to math. He figured out all the coordinates and where you would be right now if you were walking."

"I was about a mile off. You walked slower than I calculated."

"How did you know where to look?" Mason asked.

"We decided to watch the reporters," Carol told them. "The older one, Perry, led us to the cabin. When he discovered you were gone he high-tailed it out of there like his pants were on fire."

Mala twined her fingers together and looked at her feet. This wasn't going to be easy, but she had to tell Barton where they stood. "They have my craft."

"You didn't secure it?" She heard the disbelief in his voice.

"I thought I was dying. That my lifeblood was draining away." She raised her eyes, then hurried on. "I know that's no excuse, but I was bewildered. I didn't want to fade away without seeing a little bit of Earth, then Mason found me and I . . . well . . ." She drew in a deep breath. "It's no excuse."

Mason stepped forward, wrapping his arms around her. "It's time to quit playing games," he spoke quietly.

Barton raised an eyebrow. "He still doesn't believe you're an alien?"

She shook her head.

"This has got to stop." A tinge of anger colored Mason's words. "You are not . . . not some kind of machine, and neither one of you are from some planet called Nerak. Damn it, Mala, you've got to face reality."

Barton looked at Carol. "Please look away."

Her face lost some of its color. "What are you going to do?" She nervously glanced around.

"Trust me."

She clamped her lips together and nodded, facing the other direction.

Mason stiffened when Barton reached inside one of the saddlebags attached to the four-wheeler and pulled out a knife.

"What are you doing?" Mala asked. Barton had never caused harm to anyone. Well, except maybe Scott, but not very much and he'd deserved it for hurting Carol.

"I'm going to give him proof." He pushed up his

shirtsleeve and sliced across his arm at the same time Mason leapt forward.

"Don't!" Mason yelled, as he grabbed for the knife and took it away. "Mala, get the blanket so we can control . . ."

"What?" Barton asked. "The bleeding?" He raised his arm.

"You didn't cut any wires, did you?" Mala rushed forward.

"No, it's only deep enough so that Mason would believe."

She looked at his arm, folding back the skin. Lights sparkled, but she didn't see any damaged wires. Still, she wanted to be sure. "Move your fingers."

He did and they worked fine.

"You're not real," Mason mumbled, his face turning pasty.

"I assure you I'm quite real," Barton said. "Would you like to touch me?"

Mason took a step back. "You're a machine."

Mala bristled. "He might not bleed, but that doesn't make him any less than you or I." She happened to glance up and saw Barton's smile. She returned it with one of her own.

"Do you have anything in your bag that will hold you together until we can find some adhesive?"

"I believe so."

"I'll do it," Carol said as she turned around. She took one look at his arm and cringed. "That doesn't hurt?"

"No. It doesn't bother you to see that I'm . . . not quite human?"

"You're more human than most people I know."

"But you're not really an alien . . . are you?" Mason asked. "I mean, your family is just really high-tech or something. Right?"

"It's okay if it takes you a little while to digest. I know we're somewhat of a shock." Mala sighed as she went to him and took his face in her hands. "I did try to tell you, though. Several times."

She noticed his face turned a shade whiter—if that were possible.

"And the baby? It's real, too. I wasn't really sure."

Concern rippled down her spine. "You should sit down." She took his hand and led him to the nearest rock. He still looked quite shaken by everything.

"What you've been telling me has been the truth. I was just too damn hardheaded to believe you. What the hell am I going to do now?"

She sat beside him. "Am I still the same person I was a few minutes ago?"

"Except for the fact you're an alien?"

She frowned. He wasn't making this easy. "Except for that."

"Yeah."

"Have we not enjoyed each other?"

He nodded.

"Then I don't see the problem."

He shook his head and laughed, but the sound wasn't happy. "You don't see the problem?" he asked. "Of course there's no problem. You're an alien. And you're going to have my baby." He visibly swallowed. "It *won't* have three eyes, will it?"

Sheesh! She shook her head. Men.

"That should stabilize your wound." Carol dropped the tape into the bag. "At least until we can get back."

"But it doesn't solve our immediate dilemma," Barton said. "Mason, we'll need your help."

Mason seemed to forcibly pull himself back to their current situation and stood.

Barton continued. "If the reporters show Mala's

craft to the world, there could be a crisis we cannot avert."

"What do you need to do?"

"If we can get to the craft, I can activate the invisibility shield until it can be moved to a safe place."

"Then let's get going."

As they rode the four-wheelers back to the pickup Carol had borrowed, Mason couldn't help still feeling slightly dazed by everything. As if she sensed how he was feeling, Mala hugged him a little tighter around the waist.

Of course she would know what he felt . . . she was a . . . What the hell had she called it? A sensitive? Yeah, he thought that was right. Someone who knew what the other person felt just by a touch.

This wasn't happening. It couldn't be. There was no such thing as aliens and robots that looked and acted human.

"It'll be all right," Mala yelled above the roar of the engine.

No, it wouldn't. Nothing was ever going to be all right again. His whole belief system was in shambles.

But Mala was right about one thing—she was still the same as she was yesterday and the day before. Nothing about her had changed.

There was one thing about him that hadn't changed, either. He loved her and he wanted this child. She was the missing piece that he needed to make his life complete, and he wasn't about to lose either one of them to a crisis started by a bunch of idiot reporters and Harlan.

Fear ripped through him. He couldn't lose them, not now. Not while there was breath in his body.

It didn't take them that long to reach the pickup, and only a few more minutes to load the four-wheelers on the flatbed trailer. In no time they were headed back to the ranch.

"When Perry ran out of the cabin, we knew he'd be making a beeline to tell the others," Carol said. "We need to get to them before they can expose the spacecraft." She reached across the seat and squeezed Barton's hand.

Mason was driving, but he caught the gesture. Hell, maybe Barton was exactly what she needed. Scott damn sure hadn't been. And even though he was a machine, Barton seemed a hell of a lot more human.

"But what will we tell everyone?" Carol nibbled her lower lip.

"The truth."

Mala choked. "We can't."

"We'll tell them that Harlan convinced a bunch of reporters from *The National Gossip* that Bigfoot was hiding in the woods, and when nothing panned out he turned on Mala, who is new in town, and claimed she's an alien. They kidnapped us in an effort to prove their idiotic story."

"But what if they believe the reporters rather than us?" Barton asked.

"They won't. We'll be free and clear."

"Except for Mala's spacecraft," Barton said, meeting Mason's gaze in the mirror.

"Yeah, except for finding the craft."

Chapter 27

Convincing the sheriff that the reporters were stretching for a story and that Harlan was out for the easy buck wasn't hard. Mason had known Jack Reynolds for a long time, and the man didn't suffer fools. He didn't believe in aliens from another planet, either. Mason didn't plan to enlighten the man.

"Looks like they're going to be facing some pretty serious charges," Jack said as they stood on Mason's front porch. "How in the hell can anyone believe life exists on other planets, or that some half beast, half man is running around in the woods? Bigfoot, no less!" He guffawed, almost choking on his chaw of tobacco.

"They got them," his deputy said as he leaned his head out of the patrol car's window. "They're bringing them into the sheriff's office now."

"Let's get down there and see what kind of welcome we can give them," Jack said, as he hitched up his pants and lumbered down the steps. "Got any straightjackets?" He chuckled.

"No, but we have a few extra cells and they have bars on them."

"Good enough. We'll see you down there." Jack climbed into the passenger seat and the deputy began backing out.

Mason turned to Mala, Barton and Carol. "As soon as I find out anything I'll meet you at Carol's store."

"Be careful," Mala said.

"Always." He couldn't keep himself from pulling her into his arms even if he'd tried. But he also knew if he kissed her he might not be able to stop, so he settled for a brief brush of his lips across hers. Even that almost did him in.

A loud rumbling startled him. He looked at the sky but there wasn't a dark cloud in sight.

"Oh, no," Mala whispered.

He looked down at her but it was Barton who spoke. "The Elders."

His arm tightened around Mala's shoulder as he drew her in closer to him. "I won't let them take you away."

"And I won't go—no matter what they do."

He glanced down at her. "What exactly will they do if you refuse to go?"

"You don't want to know."

Every sci-fi movie he'd watched on the big screen flashed before his eyes. "They don't . . . uh . . . vaporize people, do they?"

Before she could answer the sky seemed to open, and six golden tubes descended. With a loud *whoosh*, a burst of grayish air shot out from the bottom and the tubes slowed until they came to a stop ten feet in front of them.

Blue howled and jumped off the porch to hide beneath the house.

Each tube opened simultaneously, and females wearing flowing robes stepped from four of them. The other two were empty. Three of the women wore white, but the fourth wore bright orange.

They didn't say anything. They didn't have to. Their presence demanded respect.

Mala slipped from under Mason's arm and reverently bowed her head, as did Barton. Carol looked at him, then bowed hers. Mason decided it might be prudent to follow protocol at this point and bowed his.

"Oh great Elders, I'm humbly grateful to be in your presence," Mala spoke.

"I sincerely doubt you're thrilled to see us, Mala."

Mason jerked his gaze up. She sounded just like . . . well, hell, she sounded sort of like Doc.

"You have disobeyed our laws by traveling to another planet. Space travel is strictly forbidden." The orange-robed Elder spoke. The other three kept their gazes on the ground. Apparently they were only there for support.

They didn't look like Elders, either. They had no wrinkles, but there was something about them that he couldn't quite put his finger on. Maybe it was the wisdom that shone in the orange-robed Elder's eyes.

"And Barton, you were supposed to bring her home."

"Earth is a wondrous planet, Elder. I only wanted to gather information."

"That is no excuse."

The Elder turned slightly and met Mason's gaze head-on. Damned if a moment of panic didn't wash over him. He had no way to defend any of them if it came right down to it. He put a protective hand across Mala's shoulders.

The Elder arched an eyebrow. "Don't worry, human, we haven't zapped anyone in . . . years."

"Yeah, but that's not to say you won't start again," he said under his breath.

"You have a valid point," she said.

Okay, they had better-than-normal hearing. He'd have to remember that. At least he didn't feel quite like his days on Earth could be figured in seconds rather than years. If the Elders were going to vaporize them, they would've already done so. He thought.

"It is time to go." The Elder bowed her head and stepped backward into her tube, apparently expecting Mala and Barton to follow suit without question. Carol sobbed and clung to Barton.

"No!" Mason held on to Mala. "I won't let you take her."

The Elder stepped from her tube. "You have no choice." Her face softened. "She isn't from your world. Mala is a Nerakian. You don't understand the . . . havoc that could be caused if she stayed. The problems she has already created."

"But I do understand what it would do to me if she left."

"I'm sorry. This is the way it must be."

Mala turned to him, tears sliding silently down her face. "I'm so sorry, Mason." She raised her hand and touched his face. "I have no choice. The Elders are all-powerful, and I must respect their decision."

He grabbed her hand and brought it to his lips. "No, you can't go." He kissed her hand, hugging it close to his face.

"It is time," the Elder spoke.

Carol sobbed in earnest now, as Barton tried to comfort her.

"She's going to have my baby," Mason blurted out.

The Elder stilled. "No, she can't! It is forbidden." Her icy gaze swung to Mala. "How could you let this happen?"

Mala shook her head. "I didn't know. I didn't think. The Elders choose who will have a child, but the baby has always been delivered to one of the homes."

"It's so women won't have to suffer the pain of

childbirth. Do you not realize what having a baby entails?"

"I understand some."

"A sickness comes upon you, your stomach grows to horrible proportions. It was written that the feet swelled along with the stomach, disfiguring the female body and causing abnormal cravings."

Mala laid her hand on her stomach. "I want my child."

"What if it is a male child?"

"I still want it."

"What exactly do you have against men?" Mason wanted to know. They were acting like men caused all the problems in the world. Had they never heard of PMS?

The Elder cast a glare that almost made him take a step back, but he held his ground.

"Men cause wars. Without men on our planet we have peace that's lasted for many years. Nerak is perfect."

Her smile was a little too condescending to suit him. Even though Mala squeezed his hand in warning, he opened his mouth and retorted, "Nerak sounds pretty dull if you ask me. I bet you don't have much excitement there."

"It suits us." The Elder's words were frosty.

Mala took a deep breath. "No, it doesn't. I wanted to come to Earth because Nerak is dull. And I will have Mason's baby. It's my child as well." She thrust her chin forward.

He had to admit he liked her spunk. He'd already come to the conclusion that she was full of fire—unlike these Elders, who looked frozen.

"You can't stay. It creates problems!"

"You mean others have stayed on Earth?" Barton asked, catching the Elder's slip.

Mala looked at Mason, her eyes wide and with just a spark of hope.

The white-robed Elders, who until now had kept their eyes reverently downcast, jerked their heads up and stared at their leader.

"It doesn't matter. Mala cannot stay."

"But others have stayed?" Mala pressed.

The Elder looked to her companions but they quickly lowered their heads once again. She was frowning when she looked back at Mala. "Yes, they've stayed, but we never know what kind of changes there will be from Nerak's atmospheric pressures to Earth's."

"It can't do a whole hell of a lot since I've never heard of anything strange happening."

"Oh, haven't you?" the Elder said. "There's a small town south of here you call Marfa, which has flickering lights in the sky. Who do you think causes them?"

"I'll be damned. You mean to tell me there are other Nerakians living in Texas? There must be a whole colony in Alaska."

"We don't acknowledge them anymore."

"But they are here," Mala said, her excitement rising with each word. "That means I can stay."

"No . . . we cannot take another chance. Each Nerakian is different. We don't know what havoc you might cause." She shook her head. "It's out of the question."

"Would you rather I went home carrying a child? And what if it's a male? Since the male population has died out, the Elders have promoted life and done everything to make it perfect. Would you destroy my child?"

"Of course not!"

"Then let me stay. Please, I love him," Mala pleaded.

"I'll take good care of her," Mason promised. Maybe

there was going to be a light at the end of the tunnel after all.

"I can stay to assist in the transition," Barton added. "That way, I can see nothing untoward happens."

"We will confer," the Elder stated majestically.

The Elders put their heads close together. Mason couldn't hear what they were saying. When Mala looked at him with worried eyes, he smiled reassuringly, but he wasn't at all confident about what they would decide, and he knew there wasn't a damn thing he could do if they forced her to go back with them.

He could fight criminals, but he couldn't fight the Elders.

They stood once more in front of their tubes. Mason held his breath. He was certain the others were doing the same.

"You will stay."

"Thank you!" Mala exclaimed.

The Elder held up her hand. "But you must accept the consequences."

Mala deflated before his eyes. He brought her closer to his side, letting her know without words that he would be right there.

"What?" Mala asked.

"You will be erased from our records as if you never existed. No one will speak your name. You will no longer exist on the planet Nerak."

Her words were clear and distinct, ringing across the space and landing hard, from the look on Mala's face.

"Can you accept those conditions?"

Mala looked at Mason. "I love you with all my heart."

Here it comes, he thought to himself. This is where she says she can't give up her country or something. Hell, he couldn't blame her. God, he didn't want to lose her, though.

"I love you with every breath in my body," he told her. "If you stay, I promise to love you forever."

"Forever is a long time," she said.

"Not when I'm with you. It wouldn't be nearly long enough."

She turned back to the Elders and bowed her head, then slowly raised it. "I cannot leave Mason. He is my destiny."

"So be it," the Elder said. "Barton will also stay, but everything that has come from Nerak will return. Your spacecrafts will be sent home and you will have no way to return. Do you understand?"

Mala stood tall. "Yes, Elder."

"Then so be it." They stepped in their tubes, and a few seconds later ascended toward the sky.

"I'm yours now and you are mine," Mala said.

"Forever," he confirmed and hugged her close, his lips brushing across hers. She tasted even sweeter knowing that he'd almost lost her.

Her body trembled when he ended the kiss. "Never ever let me go," she said.

"Never."

She frowned.

"What?" he asked.

"Barton," she began. "How will they get our spacecrafts back?"

"Like I told you before. The ones we used are very antiquated, but they're equipped with a device that can return them to Nerak with just the push of a button by the Elders."

"Then it was a good thing they didn't know when I left Nerak, or I might not have gotten very far."

"True," Barton said, wrapping his arms around Carol.

"Just so they can't push a button and send you back

to Nerak," Carol told Barton, then frowned. "They can't, can they?"

"No. I'll always be here for you as long as you want me."

"Good. I like the sound of that."

Mason's radio crackled and Francine's voice came over a few seconds later.

"Sheriff, we have a situation."

"What now?" Complications. Always something happening.

"Those reporters got away from Clayton and now they seem to have vanished."

He keyed the mike. "Good, maybe they'll stay gone."

"Sheriff?"

"I'll be there in a while." He looked at Mala with apologetic eyes.

"Go." She gave him a gentle nudge toward his car. "It's what you do, who you are."

"I'd rather stay with you."

"You will. For the rest of our lives."

He pulled her into his arms and lowered his mouth. She tasted sweet and hot and seductive as hell. She tasted like Mala. His Mala.

Chapter 28

"I told you we shouldn't hide in the spaceship," Perry blustered. "I can't get the blasted door open."

Harlan pushed against the door right alongside Perry, but it wouldn't budge. "There's gotta be a way out!"

The spaceship rumbled and groaned as it lurched about. What the hell? He whirled around, glaring at Alice and the young reporter.

"You pushed the green button," Harlan yelled at her, grabbing onto the back of the seat when he nearly lost his balance.

"I didn't push anything, you ignoramus," Alice said, turning the full force of her fury on him as she grabbed onto something so she wouldn't lose her balance. "Just figure out how to stop this damn thing! Now!"

"I want my mother," Aaron whined, and huddled in the corner, tucking his head under his arms.

Lot of help he was. "We've all got to push at one time," Harlan said.

The three of them turned their attention back to the door, and shoved with all they had. Harlan grunted and pushed. He didn't know what the hell was going on, but he wanted out.

He glanced over his shoulder to tell the young punk reporter he'd better get off his butt and get over here and help, but the words never left his mouth.

Harlan stopped trying to open the door and leaned toward the glass front. His insides turned upside down as the sky grew dark and the stars grew brighter and closer. He looked to his left and saw Earth, except it was like those pictures the astronauts brought home.

Well, hell, they were in outer space. He gulped. Aliens didn't exist, not really. He'd only wanted to make a few dollars. That's why he'd told the reporters that Bigfoot lived in the hills.

This wasn't happening. "It's not real," he said. "I'm having a bad dream and I'll wake up any second." He looked at the other two. "Right? You're just in this dream with me?"

The other two looked out the window. The color drained from Perry's face as he stared at space. "This isn't any dream."

Aaron began to sob louder.

Alice's eyes narrowed. She planted her hands on her hips. "We can make this work. Think of the story we can get."

"We're in fuckin' outer space, you dumb broad!" If Harlan could open the door and throw her out, he would.

This was just great. He hoped they liked men on this planet they were going to.

Epilogue

"Look, Mason, white rain." Mala pushed back the curtain and stared out the window. It was a wondrous sight.

He came up behind her and wrapped his arms around her waist. Not an easy task, since she was heavy with child and due any day now.

Her child, his child. She could feel the glow as it started from her heart and worked its way outward.

Barton had been right, her stomach had stretched to accommodate this little being that she and Mason had created. Of course now she felt as big as Mason's barn, but she didn't really care.

"It's snow," he said.

"Hmm . . ."

"The stuff falling from the sky is snow. From the weather report we should get a couple of inches. By morning it'll look like a white blanket covering the ground."

"I think I'll like that." She snuggled against him. Her life was so perfect. No, it was so imperfect. Most of the time something was going wrong. Mason would have to work late, but then he would come home and it would be all the more special.

The other day when she was carrying in a bag of groceries, the sack ripped and cans went everywhere, but as she picked them up she realized how lucky she was to have this wonderful food—especially the chocolate.

She no longer had Barton to do everything for her, but she rather liked doing for herself. He and Carol were too happy together anyway. Carol needed him as much as he needed her.

Life was far from perfect, but she wouldn't trade one imperfect day for all her perfect days on Nerak. But she did miss her cousins, Kia especially. Had her friend already wiped Mala out of her memory? She didn't think so. She hoped not.

"You're awfully quiet," Mason whispered close to her ear.

"I was thinking about how lucky I am." She started to turn in his arms when a sharp pain stabbed her abdomen. "Oh, Mason," she gasped.

"What?" He helped her to the sofa where she could sit.

She took two deep breaths and the pain began to subside. "I think it might be time."

He knelt beside her. "Time? Time! The baby. Oh, my God." He jumped to his feet and ran into the other room, but immediately came back, sliding halfway across the hardwood floor before he came to a stop. "I'm going to call the doctor." He hurried back out.

Mala frowned. Mason wasn't acting like himself. He seemed quite anxious. They had both taken the classes that would prepare them for the birth of their child. Had he forgotten everything they'd learned? Strange.

She lumbered to her feet, grabbing the arm of the sofa to steady herself. She would need her overnight bag and a coat.

"What the hell are you doing?" Mason ran to her side and helped her to ease back down on the sofa.

"I was going to get my coat and my bag that I packed for the hospital."

"You sit right there and I'll get it."

"Did you call the doctor?"

"He'll be waiting for us," he called over his shoulder as he rushed from the room. But a few moments later he came in, again sliding halfway across the room before coming to a stop. "Red or blue?" he asked, holding up two bags.

"The blue one." She started to stand, but he pressed her back down.

"No, keep your seat. Damn, I need to start the Jeep or you'll freeze before we get there." He dropped the case and ran out the door.

"Your coat . . ." She didn't think she'd be the one freezing. "Ohhh . . ." She grabbed the armrest as another contraction hit her. Pain was not good. Not good at all. She wanted a hospital and she wanted one now. The doctor said she wouldn't have to hurt. Where was Mason?

As if he'd heard her silent plea, he came barreling inside again.

"Forgot the suitcase." He grabbed it, but paused long enough that he noticed her expression. "Oh, Lord, we're going to have a baby."

"And if you don't want to deliver it you'd better hurry," she said through clenched teeth. She started to stand but he sprinted over and pushed gently on her shoulders.

"Stay there. I promise we'll leave in a few minutes."

He hurried out of the house, taking her bag with him. A few moments later he came back inside, shivering.

"It's freezing out there. The roads will be getting icy if we don't hurry."

She started to stand. He quickly pressed her back down.

"You'll need a coat. We don't want you or the baby catching a cold." He darted from the room.

She shook her head and tried to get comfortable, but her back was hurting, and no matter what position she arranged herself in she was still in pain. Where was Mason?

Ow. It hurt.

"Mason!"

He slid around the corner, his feet not stopping until he slammed into the front door. The coats he held fell to the floor.

"What? Are you okay?"

Her eyes narrowed. "No . . . I . . . am . . . not . . . okay! I'm going to have your baby and I want pain medication!" She started to stand. He rushed over. Her glare would've made the most hardened criminal cringe. "Don't touch me," she said between gritted teeth.

"I was just trying to help."

"My coat, please."

He scooped her coat off the floor and helped her into it, but he didn't say a word. She had a feeling he was afraid to, but she didn't really care at this point. If she didn't get pain medication soon she might commit murder, and she rather liked having Mason around—most of the time.

"Be careful, the steps are getting slippery." He held her arm with one hand and wrapped his other one around her.

"I can't breathe."

He loosened his hold.

When he took the first step off the porch, his feet almost went out from under him. He let go long enough to grab the rail. Once he had his balance, he grinned up at her.

"Ready?"

"Darn, I wanted to have your baby on the steps. Do we have to go?" she said with more than a touch of sarcasm . . . and she didn't care!

He frowned. "You've picked up a lot of bad words since coming to Earth, Ms. McKinley."

"And who do you suppose I learned them from, Mr. McKinley?"

"Can we just go?"

She gripped the rail and let him help her down the rest of the stairs. Just as she reached the passenger side of the Jeep, another contraction hit her. This one was harder than the last.

"Breathe," he told her. "In and out."

"I . . . know . . . how . . . to . . . breathe!"

He opened the door, but rather than waiting for her to get in, he picked her up and placed her in the seat. He was so tender that she had to sniff back the tears. She was still sniffing when he climbed in on his side. The contraction had eased but was replaced by guilt.

"What's wrong?" he asked as he helped her fasten her seatbelt.

"I'm being mean. I don't want to be mean." She hiccupped.

He smiled so tenderly that she started to cry. "Aw, honey, it's okay. Everything will be fine. You'll see."

"It will?"

He nodded and put the Jeep in reverse, slowly backing out. "Trust me on this."

"I trust you on everything." Another contraction started and she grimaced. "But try to hurry."

"I will."

She noticed sweat beaded his brow, and it wasn't

that warm inside the Jeep. She closed her eyes and leaned her head against the back of the seat, willing the pain to go away.

The ride seemed to take forever. Maybe because Mason had to drive slower on the icy road. Once he hit a slick spot and cursed as he steered into the slide and got the Jeep going in the right direction. It was a good thing. She certainly didn't want to have their baby on the side of the road.

As they pulled under the hospital awning, the glass door swished open and Barton and Carol hurried out along with the youngest nurse in history. What was she, thirteen?

"Barton," she whimpered, then looked gratefully at Mason.

"I thought you would want him here."

Her door opened and Barton lifted her out of the Jeep and carried her inside, ignoring the wheelchair the nurse pushed.

"You can't carry her up to the second floor so you might as well put her in the chair," the nurse told him once they were inside.

"You can put me down," Mala told him. "It's okay."

"Are you in much pain?" Barton asked, as he gently set her in the chair.

"A little." A lot. She would be brave, though. She was an earthling now—sort of.

Oh no, another contraction! She held her stomach and gritted her teeth.

"Breathe," Mason told her as the kiddie nurse aimed the chair toward the elevator.

"I know how to breathe. You don't have to remind me."

"He's only trying to help," the cutesy little nurse said.

Die, bitch.

Oh, damn, the pain was terrible. The lights flickered in the elevator. Please don't stop between floors, she silently begged. It was way too crowded for her to have the baby here.

Calm. She had to stay calm. She did the breathing exercises they'd learned in class.

It didn't help.

What the hell good were they if they didn't help?

The pain began to subside as the elevator came to a jarring stop and the door opened. Dr. Lambert and Emma stood waiting on the other side. As she looked from one to the other, tears began to roll down her face.

"Ouch."

Dr. Lambert issued orders as they wheeled her into a room. Everything began to happen quickly after that. But the best thing of all was the medicine they put in her back to stop the pain.

Relief.

She sighed. Mason was ushered into the room. He looked a little hesitant about coming inside until she smiled at him.

"Feeling better?"

She nodded. "The pain is gone. Just like Dr. Lambert said. Listen." She nodded to the fetal heart monitor. "That's our baby's heartbeat."

He pulled a chair close to the bed and sat next to her, taking her hand in his.

"Have I told you how much I love you?" he asked.

"Every day."

"You're not sorry about all this, are you?"

"I'm going to have our child. How could I ever regret that or the fact I love the father so much?"

Dr. Lambert pushed the door open and came into the room. "Just a look to see how the patient is doing." He did a quick exam. "Better get her to the delivery room. She's dilating a little faster than normal for a first baby."

Mala squeezed Mason's hand, and in almost a blur she was wheeled into the cold delivery room. Everything seemed to be happening too fast. Did Dr. Lambert look a little worried? Where was Mason?

Please let our baby be okay, she silently begged.

What if she couldn't have a normal baby? Women on Nerak didn't have babies.

Mason came into the delivery room dressed much like the doctor.

"It will be okay," he told her. "I won't let anything happen to either one of you."

"Even if our baby has three eyes?" Her laugh was wobbly.

"And two heads, and four legs. It'll still be our baby and we'll love it no matter what."

"You're crowning. Okay, Mala, I want you to push now."

She gritted her teeth and pushed.

"That's good. One more really hard push. Just like that. Here it comes."

She squeezed Mason's hands.

"You're doing great, sweetheart."

Then why did he look sort of green?

"It's a boy!" the doctor said. There was the tiniest of cries, then she saw the nurse take a small bundle to the bassinet.

Joy wrapped around her heart and gave a powerful squeeze. A boy. They had a son. She looked at Mason, saw the moisture in his eyes, and knew he was feeling the same thing.

"Wait," Dr. Lambert said. "Something isn't . . ."

Mala's heart skipped a beat.

"Doc?" Mason squeezed her shoulder.

Dr. Lambert laughed. "Now, where were you hiding?" He looked over the sheets. "Give me another good push, Mala. It seems your family has just grown."

"Twins," Mason said, and smiled at her.

"Another son!" The doctor beamed. There was another little cry and the nurse took the baby.

A few minutes later the first infant was placed in her arms, sucking gently on a pacifier. "Our baby."

"He's beautiful." Mason kissed the top of her head, then his new son's.

"Here's the second one," Emma said as she placed him on Mala's other side. "I must say, these are the most beautiful boys that we've ever had born in this hospital. Funniest thing, though, I could've sworn I didn't give either one the pacifier, but when I turned around, each boy had one in his mouth." She shook her head. "I really need a vacation."

Mala looked at Mason and shrugged. He looked nervously from one baby to the other.

Telekinetic. She had a cousin who could move objects with her mind.

How sweet.

Life might prove interesting over the next twenty or so years. She glanced at Mason. Should she tell him? No, there would be plenty of time.

Yes, life was good.

Well, hell.

Can't get enough of Karen Kelley's sexy aliens?
Try the rest of the series!

EARTH GUYS ARE EASY

The truth is way out there . . .

Kia can't imagine why her cousin Mala left planet Nerak—utterly perfect in an ever-so-slightly boring kind of way—to go in search of Earth men. At least, not until she meets a virile, muscular human intent on rescuing her (how quaint!) from a bar brawl. And while at first Kia just wants undercover cop Nick Scericino to help locate her cousin . . . well, it would be a shame to come all this way without finding out whether everything really is bigger in Texas . . .

Nick knows trouble when he sees it. And right now, trouble is sitting at the bar—black-clad, sexy as hell, and about to mess up his sting operation to take down some Russian mobsters. Could she have Mafia connections? Kia's certainly not like any woman he's known—flat out demanding sex, and following through with a sensational romp that leaves his mind blown and world rocked. Other options: a) she's crazy, or b) she's not kidding about being an alien. In which case, he's in even deeper trouble. Because the only thing worse than falling wildly in lust with someone who's not playing with a full holodeck is the thought that she'll soon be leaving for a galaxy far, far away . . .

"**I** don't have anything to eat. We can stop at a Micky D's for breakfast."

From the confused look on her face, he didn't think she even knew what a McDonald's was. His amnesia theory was starting to make a lot more sense. "I just have to get my wallet."

Nick hurried to the bedroom but there was a pop as he reached the place where his door used to be. His head smacked into a hard surface.

His door was back.

Great timing.

He rubbed his forehead.

"She is not an alien. She is not an alien," he mumbled as he opened the door and grabbed his wallet off the dresser.

On the way to the fast-food joint, he covertly observed her every move and noticed how she watched him before repeating what he did. He still hadn't ruled out that she could be from another country.

He parked in front of the fast-food place and they went inside.

"What do you want?" he asked, looking up at the menu.

"I've never had food before."

He glanced around. Good thing everyone was busy

and no one had come over to wait on them yet. "You don't eat . . . where you're from?" he asked, keeping his voice down.

"Food capsules. It provides plenty of nourishment and we don't have to bother with using space to grow anything."

She turned those dark blue eyes on him and his insides began to melt.

"But I'd like to try your food. The soda was quite refreshing."

Hell, he'd give her anything she wanted if she kept looking at him like that. Food, sex . . . state secrets.

He cleared his throat and ordered two pancake breakfasts and two milks, then carried them to a table in the far corner. Keep a low profile, that was the name of the game.

He covertly watched her as she slid into the booth across from him. Man, if she was playing him for a fool and Sam was in on this, he'd kill them both.

She just stared at the white Styrofoam, then pinched off a corner of the lid and put it in her mouth. Before he had a chance to react, she spit it out. "Ugh, your food isn't good."

He quickly glanced around to make sure she hadn't been seen, breathing a sigh of relief. No one was paying them the least bit of attention.

"That's the box," he told her, then opened it and poured syrup over the stack. "Like this." He cut into one, then forked it into his mouth. She followed suit.

Her eyes closed, she moaned. The overhead lights began to flash. A bulb popped.

"Mmm . . . this is good. Oh, yes . . . yes!"

Nick's gaze scanned the room. A busload of geriatrics had just come inside. Their expressions ranged from amusement to reprimanding looks to fear as some noticed the wild light display above their heads.

"This is so wonderful, Nick." She rolled her shoulders, her back arched, her tight nipples clearly outlined through the material of her top. "I've never had anything this good before."

He realized he was holding his breath when the room began to spin. He exhaled, but continued to stare. She was giving him a major hard-on as her tongue came out to slowly lick the syrup off her lips.

She opened her eyes and forked another bite into her mouth. "I think I love your food, Nick." Her words were raspy, like a woman ready to smear syrup all over his body and lick off every drop.

He grabbed a paper napkin and wiped the sweat from his forehead. That's when his attention was drawn to the lights. They were still flickering, but that wasn't all. A wave of bright blues, yellows, and pinks swirled like the aurora borealis.

Damn, the same thing had happened last night when they'd had sex, but he'd dismissed it as a figment of his imagination. She'd been really hot in the sack and it'd been a while for him so he hadn't really thought much about them. Only that his eyes had to be playing tricks. It had been a really fantastic orgasm.

Kia squirmed in her seat as she shoved another bite in her already stuffed mouth. Syrup drizzled down her chin. She swallowed.

"More. I want more . . . thank you."

She looked like a woman in the throes of passion.

THE BAD BOYS GUIDE TO THE GALAXY

Take me to your leader. Come to think of it, just take me.

Planet Nerak was perfect—no disease, no darkness, no hunger—until an expedition to Earth brought back an unwanted guest. Enter one talented Nerakian named Lara, sent on a special fact-finding mission in the vast region called Texas. Fortunately, a warrior (he calls himself a "cop") named Sam Jones has offered to help. Unfortunately, Sam's skill at sex is quite distracting—as are plenty other earthly delights, like the dangerously addictive substance called chocolate. Temptations such as these could seriously compromise Lara's—ahem—research . . .

Crazy, that's what Sam is. What sane man would voluntarily isolate himself in the Texas woods with an alien, not to mention a female one with a superiority complex, legs that won't quit, and a penchant for walking around buck naked? Between bragging about her home planet and levitating, Lara wastes no time getting on Sam's last nerve . . . and even less time getting into his bed. Talk about going where no man has gone before. Of course, when you're from Texas, nothing—not even an entire planet—is going to stop you from getting what you want.

"**W**here's your dress . . ."—he waved a finger around—"thingy . . . robe, whatchamacallit?" He finally pointed toward her.

She raised an eyebrow. He didn't seem to notice the clean floor. Disappointment filled her. She'd hoped for more. Silly, she knew. After all, he was an Earthman, and she shouldn't care what he thought.

"My robe was getting dirty along the hem, so I removed it."

Her gaze traveled slowly over him, noting the bulge below his waist. It was quite large. Odd. She mentally shook her head.

"Your clothes are quite dirty. Once again, I've proven that I'm superior in my way of thinking," she told him.

"You're naked."

She glanced down. "You're very observant," she said, using his earlier words. "Did you know there's a slight breeze outside? It made my nipples tingle and felt quite pleasant. Not that I would be tempted to stay on Earth because of a breeze."

"You . . . you . . . can't . . ."

She frowned. "There's something wrong with your speech. Are you ill? If you'd like, I can retrieve my diagnostic tool and examine you." He was sweating.

Not good. She only hoped she didn't catch what he had.

"You can't go around without clothes," he sputtered. "And I'm not sick."

"Then what are you?"

"Horny!" He marched to the other room, returning in a few minutes with her robe. "You can't go around naked."

"Why not?" She slipped her arms into the robe and belted it.

"It causes a certain reaction inside men."

"What kind of a reaction?"

What an interesting topic. She wanted to know more. Maybe they would be able to have a scientific conversation.

Kia had only talked about battles, and Mala had talked about exploration of other planets, but Sam was actually speaking about something to do with the body. It was a very stimulating discussion.

He ran a hand through his hair. "I'm going to kill Nick," he grumbled. "No one said anything about having to explain the birds and bees."

"And what's so important about these birds and bees?"

He drew in a deep breath. "When a man sees a naked woman, it causes certain reactions inside him."

"Like the bulge in your pants? It wasn't there before."

"Ah, Lord."

"Did my nakedness do that?"

"You're very beautiful."

"But I'm not supposed to think so."

"No, we're not talking about that right now."

She was so confused. Sam wasn't making sense. "Then please explain what we are talking about."

"Sex," he blurted. "When a man sees a beautiful

and very sexy naked woman, it causes him to think about having sex with her."

He looked relieved to finally have said so much. She thought about his words for a moment. A companion unit did not have these reactions unless buttons were pushed, and even then, their response would be generic. This was very unusual. But also exciting that her nakedness would make him want to copulate. She felt quite powerful.

And she was also horny now that she knew what the word meant. She untied her robe and opened it. "Then we will join."

He made a strangled sound and coughed again and jerked her robe closed. "No, it's not done like that. Dammit, I'm not a companion unit to perform whenever you decide you need sex."

"But don't you want sex?"

"There are emotions that need to be involved. I'm not one of those guys who jump on top of a woman, gets his jollies, and then goes his own way."

"You want me on top?" She'd never been on top, but she thought she could manage.

He firmly tied her robe, then raised her chin until her gaze met his.

"When I make love with a woman, I want her to know damn well who she's with, and there won't be anything clinical about it." He lowered his mouth to hers.

He was touching her again. She should remind him that it was forbidden to touch a healer. But there was something about his lips against hers, the way he brushed his tongue over them, then delved inside that made her body ache, made her want to lean in closer, made her want to have sex other than just to relieve herself of stress.

And here's a sneak peek at Karen's newest book,
HOW TO SEDUCE A TEXAN,
out this month from Brava . . .

She skidded to a stop just before she hit the cow that languidly stood in the middle of the road looking unconcerned that it had almost been splattered across her windshield.

Nikki's heart pounded inside her chest and her hands shook. She closed her eyes and took a deep breath. When she opened them again, the black and white cow looked at her with total unconcern. This was so not how she wanted to start her vacation slash investigative reporting.

"I almost wrecked because of you." She glared at the cow. Her cold-eyed, steely glare that she'd perfected over the years. If it had been a person rather than a dumb animal, it would've been frozen to the spot.

The cow opened its mouth and bellowed a low meandering, I-was-here-first moo.

She didn't think the cow cared one little bit that it had almost become hamburger meat. Damned country. She'd take city life and dirty politicians any day.

"Move." She clapped her hands.

The cow didn't get in any hurry as it lumbered to the side of the narrow road and lowered its head. The four-legged beast chomped down on a bunch of grass, then slowly began to chew.

She waved her arms. "Shoo!"

Nothing.

She honked the horn.

Nothing.

The hot sun beat down on her. A bead of sweat slid uncomfortably between her breasts. She judged the narrow road, wondering if she could maneuver around the cow without going into the ditch.

Before she decided to attempt it, another sound drew her attention. She glanced down the dirt road, shielding her eyes from the glare of the sun as a cloud of dust came toward her. The cloud of dust became a man on a horse.

Correction. A cowboy on a horse.

Hi-ho, Silver, the Lone Ranger, she thought sarcastically.

But the closer he got, the more her sarcasm faded. The Lone Ranger had nothing on this cowboy. Broad shoulders, black hat pulled low on his forehead . . .

Black hat. Bad guys wore black hats. Right? Things were looking up.

At least until he brought the horse to a grinding halt and dust swirled around her—again. She coughed and waved her hands in front of her face.

"Bessie, how the hell do you keep getting out?" he asked.

His slow southern drawl drizzled over her like warmed honey, and she knew from experience warmed honey drizzling over her naked body could be very good. Sticky, but oh so sexy.

Did he look as good as he sounded?

She shaded her eyes again at the same time he pushed his hat higher on his forehead with one finger. Cal Braxton's tanned face stared down at her. His cool, deep green eyes only made her body grow warmer with each passing second.

So this was the infamous playboy/star football player. The man who had a pretty woman on his arm almost every night of the week—at least until Cynthia Cole had come into his life.

"I almost hit your cow," she told him as she slipped off one of her high heels and rubbed the insole with her other foot. It didn't stop the tingle of pleasure that was running up and down her legs. He could park his boots by her bed any day.

"Sorry about that. Bessie thinks the grass is greener on the other side of the fence,."

He pulled a rolled up rope off the saddle horn and swatted the end of it against Bessie's rump. The cow gave him a disgruntled look before ambling down the road.

His gaze returned to her . . . roaming over her . . . seducing her. "Are you lost?"

"On vacation."

He easily controlled the prancing horse beneath him. "Staying nearby?"

"At The Crystal Creek Dude Ranch."

His grin was slow. So, he did have all his teeth, and they were pearly white. She ran her tongue over her dry lips.

"My brother owns it," he said. "I'm helping him out. It looks like we might be seeing a lot of each other. Name's Cal—Cal Braxton."

His thumb idly stroked the rope. For a moment, she was mesmerized as she watched the hypnotic movement.

"You know, you shouldn't drive with the top down in this heat," he said.

She almost laughed. It wasn't the heat from the sun that had momentarily stolen her wits. Cal was good. Ah, yes, he knew all the moves that made a woman yearn for him to caress her naked skin. And he made those moves very well.